TO OLUHOSA,

THANKS !~

signature

The Coward

Tim F. Miller

Copyright © 2017 Tim F. Miller

This is a work of fiction. Any names, characters, businesses, places and events are either the products of the author's imagination or used in a fictitious manner. Any resemblance to actual persons, living or dead, or actual events is purely coincidental. Some of the language and actions used in this story are not condoned by the author but are used purely for entertainment and character development purposes.

All rights reserved.

ISBN: 1548159875
ISBN-13: 978-1548159870

DEDICATION

To my wonderful wife, Kirstin, and beautiful children, Ashley, Caroline and Jack.

ACKNOWLEDGMENTS

Without a doubt, this book was a labor of love and insight. Spawn from a nightmare so vivid that I could remember intimate details. For some reason, I decided to write them down. Next thing you know, a novel was born. I am not a writer, per say, but a storyteller. I hope this book is both thought-provoking and entertaining. I am truly grateful to all those who read the early drafts of this book and sent helpful suggestions: Kirstin Miller, Mark Miller, Jonathan Miller, Ashley Twichell, Rick Neal, Mark Stewart, Jan Daniel, Brandon Whitaker, Bill Lightle, Rick Sanderson, Stephen Bain, Lynn Delage and Barbara Sims. Thanks to Vizual Designs and graphic designers Michael and Kellan Davis for the book cover. Special thanks to my parents, Tom and Mary Anne, whose unconditional love made my life possible. The primary force and spirit present in my life has and always will be Jesus Christ—in whom all things are possible.

.

"A coward is much more exposed to quarrels than a man of spirit."

-Thomas Jefferson

<u>Chapter 1</u>

There was a cool breeze drifting across Lake Shillito. The morning dew had just covered the grass as the sun peeked above the tree-line. Jack threw a wool blanket off his naked body. He was always a little self-conscious about being naked. Lying on a soft comforter, he was relaxed, serene and at the same time distressed. Clothed he was perfectly at ease in nature. Naked was much different. Although he was toned and ripped and had the physique of an Adonis, being outside, exposed as he was, made him feel vulnerable. His head felt groggy but that was to be expected after what he drank last night. He looked down at his chest and ran his hand across his abdomen. Jack worked hard on his body and was proud of it.

He was in his third year at the University of Kentucky and believed that to be successful in life you needed to develop your mind for the future and your body for the present. It also made life easier on campus. Jack was handsome and that had opened many doors, not just in the business world, but on a lively college campus. Like most young men who took pride in sexual conquests, Jack enjoyed the chase. Spotting a beautiful, twenty-something at a campus bar and then swooping in with his charm, wit and winning smile— the prey was ensnared. *Speaking of which, where was the prey from last night* Jack wondered? He leaned up on his elbows and began scanning the wooded perimeter. Looking down to his right, he smiled at the sight of two rolled out condoms. *Oh yeah*, Jack thought, *it was a good night.*

He heard the rustling of leaves and cracking of branches coming just beyond a pair of picnic tables and outdoor grill. He could see a tall, blonde figure wrapped in a UK blanket walking towards him. She, too, was wearing nothing as she lay down next to him.

"Where did you go?" Jack asked.

"Had to take care of some morning business." Pausing briefly, she added, "You know, Mother Nature called."

She locked her legs around Jack and began nibbling on his neck. It was apparent that Mother Nature was making a different call as Jack could feel another part of his body wake up.

"Well, looks like someone's ready to get the morning started the way they ended last night. Hope you brought enough protection, Jack." the blonde said tauntingly with a giggle.

"Oh, don't worry. I'm always prepared."

"I bet you are."

Jack couldn't believe how great life had become. He was lying on his back with a hot member of the varsity volleyball team straddling him as their third round of making love had commenced. The fall semester started Thursday morning and he couldn't think of a better way for it to begin. *What a great day this is going to be*, Jack smiled.

__Chapter 2__

"A man that flies from his fear may find that he has only taken a short cut to meet it."

−J R R Tolkien

Jack tied his running shoes tightly and adjusted the iPod band around his right arm then carefully twisted the wrap-around ear buds into place. A brief leg stretch against the front steps of his apartment complex and he bounded out onto Maxwell Street to begin his five-mile trek. His pace was lively at about 6 minutes per mile. Running through the park off Clay Avenue, he noticed a used condom in the grass. A huge smile spread across his face as he knew it wasn't his though he used several like it last night.

Thoughts of the previous night began streaming into Jack's brain. Last night's affair was being played in Jack's visual high definition memory. Her smooth, soft butt and long, athletic tanned legs wrapped around his waist. Then, of course, her small but perky breasts left a powerful imprint in his mind. Jack's pace picked up a bit remembering how exciting it was the first time you saw a girl's breasts in a make-out session.. He tried to remember things about the girl besides her killer body. *I think she played volleyball at UK and…she loved Pina Coladas and…her name? Wow, what was her name? Was it Tami…no Terri…it was some sort name that ended in an "i"…I think.* Anyway, he remembered meeting her at Three Goggles last night and then driving to the lake off campus at Shillito Park, a notorious "Lover's Lane". Replaying the whole event helped Jack keep a good pace and get through some of the tough inclines. Eminem's "Lose Yourself" started pounding its climatic beat in Jack's ear buds as he accelerated up a hill.

Just as he was trying to remember details about "Terri/ Tami", his memory was jarred by the erotic image of a beautiful, long-haired red-head from the dance floor at Three Goggles. He saw her long legs in a tight-fitting mini skirt with an even smaller top that just held in her bronze, sun-kissed breasts. Her alluring, green eyes staring at him pushed Jack's pace. Again, his memory flashed back to last night as the tall beauty strolled up to the dance floor alone with Usher's "Scream" blaring out of the DJ's speakers. Jack loved this song and enjoyed dancing at night clubs. He had learned early in high school that girls loved to dance and really loved guys that could. He had good moves and an athletic, limber body that allowed him to move freely to the beat. He also had confidence in his dance grooves, unlike his stiff, uncoordinated posse, Rick and Tater.

Jack hit a downhill slope and allowed his legs to absorb the increased speed. Knowing he was approaching an easy part of the run, he allowed his mind to wander again to last night's action. It was a Wednesday night just before for the start of the fall semester and Jack and his buddies were eager to see some action. They usually started drinking beers at their place on Maxwell Street around 8 o'clock to get a healthy "buzz" and save money on drinks at the bar.

They arrived at Three Goggles, a popular three-story bar in the heart of UK's campus, around 10 o'clock. The entrance was crowded with eager students ready to get the new semester started with a bang. Jack knew exactly where he wanted to go. Looking back at his roommates, he nodded for them to follow him up two flights of stairs located in back left corner of the bar. His roommates made an audible groan and grudgingly followed him as he bounded up the stairs two steps at a time.

Reaching the third floor, Jack quickly surveyed the large open dance floor with flashing lights and a DJ's nest built on the far right front corner. *Wow, the floor is packed tonight*, Jack quickly surmised. There were a number of tall bar tables sprinkled around the dance floor. He spotted an empty table near and prodded his two roommates to snatch it. Rick and Tater weren't thrilled about being near a dance floor. They operated best near the bar where their charm and wit worked better than their hips and feet.

Once seated, the trio ordered a pitcher of Budweiser and quickly scoped the room and floor for hot prospects. Usher's song hit the air as Tater and Rick sighed. They knew they were about to lose their boy early tonight. Jack felt energized by the powerful beat and was instantly taken in by a stunning redhead that just walked onto the dance floor alone. She turned and stared directly at him. Her dress seemed painted on as she ran her hands through her long hair and then down the side of her smooth, slim body. She motioned her finger for Jack to come out. Stunned, Jack casually looked around to make sure she wasn't signaling someone else.

Then Tater blurted out, "Oh shit, look at that hot babe on the floor. Damn, I think she wants me to come out there".

"Are you sure she's looking at you? Looks like she's looking at me." Jack insisted.

"Damn man, you think all the babes are looking at you!"

"All right, go out there. Dance with her." Jack said with a knowing laugh.

"I should. She obviously wants me… Hell you know I can't dance to this kind of music. It needs to slow down so I can work my magic up close."

Rick started laughing then added "Whatever! There's only one way to find out. One of you needs to…."

Jack stood up and moved quickly to join the enticing redhead on the dance floor. It didn't take long to realize who she was signaling as Jack's body moved up on her and to the beat of the music.

The pair looked as if they had danced together all their lives. They moved in a slinky, erotic beat. Her hands aggressively moved up and down his body while her hungry eyes hypnotically locked onto his. She grabbed his lower back and slammed it into her body. With their bodies sealed, she latched her lips onto his neck and began working her magic with her tongue. *Oh God, she's a freak*, Jack thought, *an incredibly hot freak!*

Suddenly her hand ran down his chest and lower abs and firmly grabbed his butt. Jack smiled at the playful gesture and looked down at his desirous partner and noticed no change in her serious expression. She looked as if she were playing a part in a cheap music video but Jack didn't mind. She was beautiful and moved like a professional dancer whose sole purpose was to enflame her partner and all Jack could think of was how well she did her job.

As the music slowed, she pulled Jack closer running her hands from his hips up over his broad shoulders and then back down again before brushing her hand across his growing male member. It didn't take long to get the appropriate response from Jack's body. He was getting light-headed with the swirl of lights, moving bodies, heat and the powerful, pulsating beat of Usher's "Scream".

The gorgeous siren continued the scintillating dance for what seemed an eternity. They were so close Jack could smell her sweet mixture of perfume and body spray. Letting his head drift up to the ceiling, Jack relaxed his body and mind. He closed his eyes for a few seconds to take in the mad rush of excitement. He could feel his dance partner release her hold on him near the end of the song. As he looked down to lock onto her gorgeous green eyes, he lost her. She was gone.

Just as suddenly as she had burst into his life, she was gone. The dance floor had dimmed for a slow song. Jack's eyes desperately searched the floor, the bar and nearby tables. Nothing. The place was crowded with long-haired women. He ran down the stairs to the second floor and still came up empty. It seemed as if she had simply vanished. Jack returned to his table hoping she would come by later. If she wanted him, she knew where he was. *Jack Miller doesn't have to chase women. They come to him* he concluded. Tonight, would be the exception.

Shaking his head out of last night's excursion, Jack pushed the pace on his jog. Looking down at his stopwatch, he realized his daydreaming had cost him a few precious minutes. *Damn she was hot!* Jack continued to torment himself with more flashbacks of the beautiful redhead with stunning emerald green eyes. *"Terri/Tami" was a nice and sweet girl but that redhead from Three Goggles was at another level of hotness* Jack sighed. Her eyes, hair, alluring body stuck in Jack's brain. The boldness of her moves on the dance floor and daring, aggressive hands and tongue simply electrified him like no other woman. Jack had encountered a healthy share of women since he started at UK three years ago but none of them stirred him like her.

Jack accelerated his pace as LMFAO's "Sexy and I Know It" blasted through his ear buds. As he approached the Seaton Center, he hit his kick and sprinted across the multitude of ball fields adjacent to UK's student recreation center. Jack always finished a five-mile run with a hard kick because the burn was essential and "runner's high" euphoric. Slowing down near the entrance, he saw his buddies waiting on him. Slightly out of breath and sweating everywhere, Jack grabbed a towel slung over Tater's neck.

"Damn it Miller! That's my work-out towel" Tater barked and then snatched it back. Jack grabbed Tater's shirt and wiped the sweat off his forehead.

"Oh great! Now you've ruined my shirt. Can you hear me? Damn it, take off those ear buds!" He jerked them out with the music screaming: *I'm sexy and I know it!*

"Ah, I should have known you'd be listening to something like that. Miller, you're a narcissist."

"Uh-oh, someone's learned a new word and classes don't start till tonight." Jack smiled and then gave Tater a playful smack on the butt. "Come on big boy, let's get in there and pump some iron."

"You've ruined my shirt, you know. Now, I'm going to have take it off!"

"Oh yeah, you hate that. Just an excuse to show off" Rick teased.

"Hey, it's not my fault that I'm built like a Mack truck with huge pecs and guns."

"And a small dick!" Rick added as he and Jack busted out laughing. All Tater could do was mutter "Fuck you. Fuck you both."

The three amigos entered the student recreation center like they owned it. A quick student ID check at the front desk and Jack and Rick were in the cavernous weight room stocked with the latest fitness equipment. Tater was briefly held up at the desk by an obnoxious fraternity senior who took his job a bit too seriously. He refused to let

Tater enter without a shirt on.

It clearly stated on the rules sign above the check-in desk: "NO SHIRT, NO ENTRANCE". Jack and Rick jeered Tater relentlessly to "follow the rules" and just put his shirt on. Tater was in no mood to be toyed with and wanted to "bust up" on the student desk clerk but that approach had never worked in the past. In fact, he lost his student rec center privileges for six months for a similar approach to another clerk who insisted he was supposed to wipe down the machines and bench after he used it. Tater loved lifting weights and showing off his upper body to the co-eds in the student rec center. Reluctantly, he put on his t-shirt with Jack's sweat on and endured the teasing from his buddies.

The Seaton Center's weight room was a beautiful, state of the art facility packed with dudes and "dudettes". The ladies mostly occupied the stationary bikes and elliptical machines. Jack and his posse were "old school" and liked to work out with the free weights. No sissy nautilus machines for these guys. Only real weights pushed by brute force to develop their tanned taut bodies.

The boys worked like a highly efficient assembly line, loading weights onto bars and positioning dumbbells near the weight bench for easy transition from one exercise to another. Jack always warmed up with a 30-pound dumbbell for single arm curls and then moved to a 50-pound dumbbell for bicep up/downs.

"Jack, where the Hell did you disappear to last night? I didn't see you come home?"

"What, Jack didn't come home last night? I hope he didn't make another Seaton Center shuffle!" Rick teased.

"Shut the fuck up, Rick!"

"What the hell are you talking about? What's the Seaton Center shuffle?" Tater asked.

"Nothing. Just something Dick made up. Right, Dick?"

Now laughing even harder Rick added "That's Rick and you know very well what the Seaton Center shuffle is and I didn't make it up."

"Alright, alright tell me what happened to my boy."

Rick couldn't stop laughing and then looked over at Jack for permission to tell the story. Jack just lowered his head staring at the mirror working the 50-pound dumbbell in silence.

"Come on Jack. You guys know everything about me and tease the shit out of me. Surely the great Jack Miller can fuck up once in a while." Again, Jack said nothing just pushing and pulling the dumbbell: first with his right arm and then with his left. It was apparent that Rick's secret story bothered him.

"Oh come on, you big baby. It's not that bad. It's funnier than anything else. It's not like you have a small pecker like Tater!"

"Fuck you Rick! At least Jack and I aren't afraid of taking our shirts off. We've got a chest. What the hell is that caved in thing under your shirt?"

"Hey, don't mess with Rick. In high school, he was the shit. Prom King senior year. Stud baseball and football player for three years. You might not know it today, but our boy here had it going at Jessamine Co. High" Jack added, hoping to get Rick onto another subject.

"No shit! Really?"

"Yep…he even outmaneuvered me on the Prom queen?"

"What do you mean?"

Jack looked over at Rick who just nodded his head and looked away.

"Our boy here took Heather Mills to our Senior Prom, even though he knew I liked her and was going to ask her."

"Come on Jack that's shit and you know it. She didn't like you like that. I told you I was going to ask and you said it was cool."

"I know…just busting your balls."

"There's fucking no way Rick hustled you out of girl?"

"What the hell is that supposed to mean!" Rick asserted with growing anger.

Things started getting serious and the atmosphere was overheated with raging testosterone. Tater jumped up off the bench and got up in Rick's face. That was never good as a punch was usually thrown when Tater pushed up on somebody. Jack quickly jumped over the bench to separate his buddies.

"Calm down, you two! Geez, you guys are about to square off over some stupid insults that neither of you mean. Damn it guys. I tell you what, tell your stupid story. I don't care. Just back down you two. Hell Tater…its not even about you… go ahead Rick. Tell your little story."

The anger disappeared as quickly as it had risen in Rick. He loved telling stories especially ones with damaging secrets.

"Okay, you remember last spring when Jack and I played in the intramural league championship game?"

"Yeah, I remember. You guys wouldn't let me play."

"You don't know how to play. You just push, shove and get into fights. Our team was thrown out the league two years ago because you punched some dude in the balls."

"I told you. I didn't punch him. It was simply a hand check, besides the dude blocked my shot. It was payback. Basketball would be a better game if you added some football and rugby rules" Tater asserted.

"Whatever. Anyway, Jack was having a great night, as usual. Draining three's and driving to the hole. But he was getting hit hard and often."

"Who were you playing, the football team?"

"Yes, exactly. The team was mostly varsity football players and they were HUGE, but a bit slow. Jack was beating his man off the dribble easily until Jabari Robinson came into the game."

"The 'shut-down' cornerback who just signed with the Pittsburgh Steelers?"

"That's the one. He pushed up on Jack and they started going at it. The play got real physical. Do you remember Jeff Adams?" Tater nodded. "He got elbowed in the mouth by one of the big-ass linemen and had to leave the game with a missing tooth and eighteen stitches. He was our only big man. The piece-of-shit student referees were too afraid to call fouls on them. So, they got away with murder. Well you know how mad Jack gets on the court when dudes are fouling him, especially on his shot…"

"Damn right I do. It's the only time I see him get mad. I love it. What happened next?"

"Well the game got tight. We were down by two. Jack took the ball down the court and drove Robinson off a high pick. Robinson plowed over the pick and knocked Jack to the ground but not before Jack made a 'tear-drop shot' in the lane."

"Dude was all over me and the 'dickless' refs called nothing." Jack added.

"Anyway, Jack jumps up and starts jawing it up with Robinson down the court. The dudes were trash talking each other all night. But now the games near the end and we're tied. There's a loose ball under the basket after an ugly shot by one of the defensive tackles, Corey Hart. Jack can't grab it but screens Robinson off from getting it as well. Robinson is pissed as it goes out on his team. He shoves Jack out of bounds in frustration but once again, the refs do nothing. Robinson gets up in Jack's face and says, 'after the game, I'm going to kick your ass!'"

"Holy shit! Robinson threatened you?"

Jack stared off in silence changing the weights from the bench bar that Tater had been lifting. Tater was too enthralled in the story to notice that Jack had moved him off the weight bench.

"Damn, you were threatened by an NFL player."

"He wasn't in the NFL last spring. He was just a prick on the basketball court." Rick added.

"Well what happened next?"

"Jack was rattled. I'd never seen that look on his face before. No one knew what had happened or what was said, but Jack was different. With just twenty seconds left in the game and tied, Jack dribbled down the court and passed me the ball. I was so shocked that he passed it, that I mishandled it. One of their guys picked it up and scored on the other end of the court just before the horn sounded. They won and were jumping up and down."

"So. What's the big deal? Those guys usually win every year. Jack still played a good game. Nothing to be ashamed of. Is that it? Did anything else happen?"

Rick looked down at Jack who was pushing 215 pounds off his chest for the fifth time. After cradling the bar back on the bench, Jack silently nodded for him to continue the story.

"Well, after the game, Jack split. I mean we couldn't find him anywhere. The football players seemed to cut off their celebration early, picking up their trophy and t-shirts and then ran out of the building."

"What happened Jack?"

"Hell, I got outta there quick because Robinson said he was gonna kick my ass. I couldn't fight him. He's huge and fast. Plus, his boys would have been there. I would have gotten killed."

"Where did you go?"

"I sprinted out of the door and ran to the one place on campus that those guys knew nothing about…the library." Tater and Rick broke up in laughter and helped him off the bench.

"That's not the end of the story" Rick added.

"Holy shit…there's more?"

"Well two days later, Jack and I had just finished our Poly Sci. class and ran over to McDonald's on Limestone. Jack, why don't you tell him what happened next?"

"Alright, I had just sat down to eat a good Big Mac when I looked up and saw Jabari Robinson walking in with some of the football players. I panicked, looking quickly for a way out. Rick went to the bathroom, as usual, to wash his hands. I couldn't just get up and run. That would have drawn their attention. There weren't that many people in there. So, I grabbed a newspaper from the table next to me, lowered my head and pretended to be reading it."

"Did it work?"

"I thought so at first, but then I felt a strong hand grab my shoulder from behind. I turned and looked up. It was Jabari Robinson with this 'eat shit' look on his face. I thought a punch was coming but instead his face brightened and a huge smiled emerged. He stuck out his hand and said 'Where'd you go after the game? You forgot to shake hands.' Man, I was shitting my pants but felt a huge relief. He just wanted to say, 'nice game' and 'no hard feelings'. He also told me they talk like that all the time in football games because it rattles some dudes. I just nodded. He also said I was one of the toughest dudes he had ever guarded."

"Yeah, that's my boy! Hell, what's wrong with that story?"

"Nothing, except Jack was scared shitless."

"So what? Who wouldn't be? Damn the dude's a huge football player in the NFL. It'd be an honor to get your ass kicked by him. Think about it. You could tell your grandkids that you got in a fight with Jabari Robinson."

Tater had a way of cracking everyone up. He could take a tragedy or scary moment and make it funny. That's why the guys loved him. He had a ferocious temper when mad but rarely turned it on his boys. He was a short, compact man built like a pit bull on steroids. Like a dog he was extremely friendly and loyal to his friends and had their back.

After the laughing subsided and the boys refocused on their exercise regimens, Jack couldn't shake the embarrassment of the "Seaton Center Shuffle". It wasn't the teasing that bothered him. He was raised under incessant taunting and badgering from his two brothers. Survival in the Miller family depended on the ability to absorb a barrage of barbs from your brothers and even an occasional zinger from their mother. No, Jack was bothered by the ribbing from Rick.

What nagged at him was the real fear he felt at the end of the game. Talking trash was part of the game and he certainly contributed his fair share but the thought that he could face a physical encounter after the game against an adversary so imposing really scared him. *Damn it…that guy really scared me. Why? He wasn't that much bigger than me. I should have stood my ground* Jack sighed heavily as he pulled a seventy-five-pound curl bar back towards his chest. *Alright, it happened, let it pass. The guys don't seem too bothered by it maybe I should just let it go…but damn, why did I freeze up?*

Chapter 3

"Cowardice rightly understood begins with selfishness and ends with shame."

−Jose Rizal, ***Noli Me Tangere (Touch Me Not)***

Jack and Rick had known each other since 7th grade. They played all three sports together up until their sophomore year. Rick got cut from the basketball team and focused instead on football. Jack made the varsity basketball team and dropped football. In the spring, they played on the varsity baseball team. They learned how to drive a car, double-date and drink Maker's Mark at the tender age of sixteen. They were as close as brothers.

After graduation, they set out for the University of Kentucky just twenty minutes north of their home in Nicholasville. Together, with two other high school friends, they rented a broken down old house on Clay Avenue. That first year on campus was a learning experience as their friends struggled to pay their end of the rent and after just one semester they were kicked out of the house.

Fortunately, that semester they took a racquetball class where they met Tater. He seemed like a bull in a china shop on the court. The guys loved how funny he was, especially his self-deprecating humor. They started hanging out, going to parties and bars. They bonded over beers, bongs, babes and boobies. Before long they vowed to go into law together after they graduated. What area of law? They didn't know. It just sounded good and it was a plan.

They decided to get a place together on campus because campus life was great. You sleep later in the morning and don't have to worry about parking because you can really walk anywhere. They tried to coordinate their class schedules around their lifestyles. No morning classes before eleven and no evening classes or labs past seven. They took the minimum hours required to be full time students as they were not in a hurry to graduate. The freedoms and liberties of college life had to be greater than the "real world" of clocked hours and responsibility.

One of the first truths they learned early about college life was that their professors didn't always live by the "real world" maxim of being at work on time and facing penalties for late assignments. Responsibility and accountability were preached in high school as students were lectured that in the "real world" you would be punished for tardiness. Those "real world" maxims didn't always exist in the world of academia. The boys had heard nightmare stories about tough professors that held firm to attendance policies and stiff penalties for late work but so far into their third year, they had yet to experience it.

In fact, in several classes roll was never taken and many of their professors were very forgiving of late work. This laxity made college life even more enjoyable. They made sure to schedule just two classes a day. The rest of the day was theirs. Many students used that time to study, work odd jobs or join clubs and fraternities. The three amigos were no different. They worked part-time at a local grocery store as stock boys or "code one" employees. It paid enough to meet their weekly expenses of food and alcohol. Most of their "free" time was spent playing sports such as basketball and softball. They had joined several local teams that were very competitive and it fulfilled their competitive nature. After class, they would often go to the ball fields outside of the Seaton Center to hit several buckets of softballs and every other day they would hit the weight room. It was Thursday, so the boys were in the weight room.

"Dude you still didn't answer my question. Where'd you go last night?" Tater inquired after reclaiming the weight bench from Jack and adding four more 45 pound plates to the bar.

"Do you remember anything about last?" Jack chuckled.

"Of course…well sorta. We were drinking a pitcher of Natty-Lites and firing on those girls at the bar."

"It was Budweiser and is that all you remember? Those girls came over to our table and were really only interested in talking to you."

"Bull shit. You're messing with me now."

"Yes, he's messing with you. Dude you were so shit-faced that when the girls came over you started grabbing them. As always, your approach is a bit too strong," Rick added.

"Bull shit. I don't remember that."

"No kidding. Dude, at one point you downed an entire pitcher by yourself trying to show off for the ladies. Of course, most of the beer ended up on your shirt, the table and Jennifer's blouse."

"Who's Jennifer?"

"The girl who dared you to do it and then threw her drink in your face!" Rick said laughing again.

"I don't remember that. Seriously Miller, did I do any of that?"

"Yeah, I afraid it's all true. After she hit you with her drink, you slammed the pitcher, stood up on the table and ordered another, daring the bartender to 'bring that shit on'. It was hilarious. I'm really surprised they didn't throw you out again. The crowd loved it and started chanting your name. The manager, Bob, told you to sit down and behave or he'd call the cops. Anyway, the tall blonde, Teri, wanted to go someplace a little quieter. We went to Lake Shillito for the night."

"Oh yeah!! Sounds like someone scored last night. By the way, her name was Tami," Rick stated matter of factly.

"Really? She looked like a Teri?"

The trio spent the next hour in complete silence. Lifting weights was a serious endeavor. Tater insisted they focus on the workout. This was one field where he was an authority. Jack and Rick marveled at the number of reps Tater could with 225 pounds on the bench. He easily pushed it up twenty times. In fact, that's where his bench workout started. Often for Jack and Rick that's where theirs ended. Today they worked predominately on their upper body. Tomorrow would be legs. Tater finished his work out with a 350-pound bench with Jack and Rick on either side of the bar to provide a spot.

After the workout, they decided to walk over to the quad where most of the classrooms were located across Euclid Avenue up the hill to Patterson Tower and the Classroom building (White Hall). They wanted to scout out the trek of this Fall's classes.

"Jack, did you sign up for that Psych. class?" Tater asked.

"Yep."

"Why are you taking a Psych class?" Rick asked pointedly.

"I'll tell you why. Those Psych classes have the hottest chicks, man. They're just looking to land a hot intellectual type, like me and Jack."

"Intellectual? Seriously Jack, why?"

"Okay, Tater's right about the hot chicks. Last year, I sat in on a class with a girl I was dating, Sara, and the room was packed with hotties. Besides, taking this class helps me avoid taking any of the math requirements."

"Hey, did you get the 6 o'clock section that starts tonight?"

"Yeppers. I think the class is meeting in the White Hall building. Better make sure. I don't want to miss any part of the first class. That's when you scope out which girls are compatible…you know as a study partner."

Chapter 4

"A coward is incapable of exhibiting love; it is the prerogative of the brave."

—Mohandas Gandhi

Fall in Kentucky was beautiful. The air was as crisp as the leaves turned a bright mixture of red, orange and yellow. The trees in front of their apartment complex had covered the entire yard with leaves. It really needed to be raked but that was the responsibility of Sid the owner of the building. Their apartment was one of four that had once been a magnificent home off Maxwell Street. It was converted into apartments to maximize renting to college students. The walk to the main campus was extremely short, just a few blocks away. The boys shortened the walk by cutting through the yard of a sorority house, Beta Gamma Beta, across the street.

Initially, the sorority house was seen as an asset to renting Sid's apartment but that was offset by an extremely annoying ritual that the Greek girls did each morning for a week at the start of the year. Like clockwork, every morning at six, there would be a crowd of girls lined up in front of their building chanting some slogan and then singing to the top of their lungs. It really got in the way of some great morning sleep.

Plowing through the leaves, Jack and Tater crossed the street heading to class a few blocks away. The main campus quad wasn't usually as crowded at six but because this was the opening day of classes many underclassmen were scampering around looking for their classroom buildings. The boys ran up the stairs of White Hall looking for room 121. It wasn't hard to find. There was a crowd at the entrance. Jack and Tater worked their way into the auditorium. Standing at the top, they surveyed the room looking for the best place to sit nearest the hottest co-eds.

Unbelievably, Jack spotted Heather Mills, the same Heather that went to prom with his best friend Rick. Jack had a crush on her in high school and it had nearly broken his friendship to Rick. He hadn't seen her since high school even though he knew she was at UK. The hurt of losing her to his best friend was something he had gotten over in college. In fact, he had forgotten all about her until just now.

She looked up at him with a huge smile on her face and waved for him to come over. *Damn she still looks good* Jack thought as he started down the auditorium and stepped toward her. Tater grabbed his arm tightly and pulled him back up.

"What the hell, Tater?"

"Dude, look over in the corner near the front," Tater was pointing at a red-head with long flowing wavy hair. She had just settled into her seat and was pulling a notebook out of her pink book bag. Jack froze with his mouth open. Tater pushed it shut.

"Isn't that the hottie from Three Goggles last night?"

"Yeah…" Jack replied in utter disbelief. There she was in the flesh. He had been thinking about her all day wondering if she was real or some fantasy from one of Tater's crazy drink concoctions.

"Come on let's grab those two seats next to her before someone else snags them." Tater insisted.

The two bounded down the side steps nearest the far wall. Jack made a smooth cut across Tater and elbowed past him to enter the row first. He slowed down as he approached the red-head who had her back turned.

"Hope you don't mind if I sit here." Jack pointed to the empty seat beside her. But the red- head was still shuffling through her book bag seemingly ignoring him. Jack was still standing waiting for an answer. The red-head sensed that someone was near her. Slightly annoyed she looked up and instantly changed expressions.

"Oh no. I mean, I don't mind."

"Thanks. I didn't get a chance to introduce myself last night. You left in kind of a hurry. My name is Jack."

"Hi Jack. I'm Candace Echols."

"Whoa, sounds like a terrorist!" Tater cracked. He loved using that corny line every time Jack introduced himself to a girl. He thought it was a cute, clever line that women appreciated, though Jack told him otherwise. Jack spun around and gave Tater the 'shut-up' look and then turned back to the red-head.

"Ignore him. He's still reeling from last night. It was his first beer."

"Oh, its okay. I'm really embarrassed about last night…I sorta lost my head."

"Oh, no need to be embarrassed, I thought…"

"Hi Candace. My name is Tyler and you must be from Tennessee" Jack lowered his head because he knew what's coming next. "Cause yer the only ten I see!" Tater finished with a chuckle.

"Yeah, nobody cares" Jack interrupted turning his back to Tater and blocking his view of Candace.

The classroom was filled to capacity in eager anticipation of the course's professor, Dr. Jan Daniel, a dynamic speaker and published author of several articles in the field of psychology. She had won numerous awards as well as praise from both the student body and faculty as an outstanding educator. Though she mostly taught upper level psychology courses, she enjoyed taking on an introductory level course as well. She had a passion for teaching and loved to engage an audience of young fertile minds by challenging their orthodoxies and opening their brains to new concepts. Splashed across the large rectangular dry erase board was a simple phrase: **THE BRAVE VS. THE COWARD**.

"Who can tell me some differences between these two people?" Dr. Daniel inquired walking in front of her desk with an authoritative voice that got everyone's attention.

Several hands flew in the air as Dr. Daniel repeated the question while planting her butt up on the desk before selecting a tall goofy kid overly eager to answer.

"The brave are heroes that save and protect lives whereas the coward does nothing," Goofy stated with smug satisfaction.

"Okay, that's good. What else?"

Jack saw more hands go up but was more interested in Candace. She seemed receptive to his attention so he scribbled a few sarcastic observations about the present academic environment that caused her to laugh quietly while playfully slapping his hand.

"Cowards are pitiful fools" and "Cowards are gutless weaklings" were a few phrases Jack heard among the multitude of answers given to describe a coward. The class was lively with glowing descriptions of courageous acts while equally damning of cowardice.

"Okay, you guys did a fantastic job describing and listing traits of bravery and cowardice. Let's focus a bit on the cowardice. Now tell me what causes cowardice? In other words, how does one become a coward?" Dr. Daniel asked in an attempt to create some critical thinking.

The question piqued Jack's interest for a second but he was easily distracted again as Candace wrote down her wry assessment about the classroom's studious occupants.

"Some of these guys seem to know so much. Maybe they should be teaching?" Candace scribbled.

"Trust me, they don't know shit! They're just trying to impress the cute girls in class?" Jack wrote back on her psychology notes page.

"Who are the cute girls in here?"

"The blonde in the 3rd row near the wall. The other blonde near the aisle on the 8th row."

"So, you like blondes?"

"Among others."

"What others?"

"There was a smoking hot redhead at Three Goggles last night."

"Oh, really? Did you like her?"

"Hard to say."

"Why?"

"She ran away just when things were getting interesting?"

"Wow, these kids seem to know their psychology stuff. Look how eager they want Dr. Daniel to pick them."

Jack flashed an approving smile. He could tell Candace was a bit uncomfortable talking about last night and her performance at Three Goggles. So, he dropped it and started doodling on Candace's notebook. Candace responded by drawing a small flower on his hand. Jack didn't mind. *My God, she is beautiful* he thought as he tried not to stare too often at her.

Tater got up several times in class and moved around. Jack knew exactly what Tater was up to and was glad to be rid of him. Tater's overt "hunting" and "scouting" missions in class always annoyed him. The success rate of those excursions rarely netted anything other than alienation.

Over the next thirty minutes, the classroom was filled with a din of student voices discussing and debating the merits of bravery as well as the causes of cowardice. Jack heard a statement called out from the auditorium that drew his attention: Cowards are selfish, immature and incapable of love. *Wow, I'd never heard that before. What a weird comment* Jack mused. The room grew quiet as Dr. Daniel's eyes lit up with excitement.

"Bingo, young man! Bingo! Now class I want you to write down that statement that our young friend dressed in an odd color combination, just made. Then, I want you to explain what it means. Have it written out and prepared to discuss at our next class on Tuesday."

Jack scratched out the statement on his paper and then stared at it for a moment. *Cowards are selfish, immature and incapable of love. Does that even make sense? What does love have to do with cowardice or even your maturity? What an absurd statement but Dr. Daniel seems to agree. Why?* Temporarily lost in thought, Jack noticed Candace putting her books away preparing to leave. Looking around, he also saw that the auditorium was mostly empty except for the few students who had cornered the professor down in the front asking about the dates on the syllabus.

Jack didn't want this moment with Candace to end and at the same time he didn't want to come across as too eager. Fortunately, Candace eased his dilemma by suggesting they get coffee at "Cup O Joe" a small diner near the edge of campus. It was a bit of a walk but Jack didn't care. He would be with the most beautiful girl on campus.

As they ascended the stairwell of the auditorium and emptied into the main lobby, Candace slid her hand into Jack's. He was on cloud nine but felt the need to make a quick bathroom stop before the long walk. He was in a real dilemma as he was afraid that if he went to the bathroom, he would lose her again. But Candace assured him that she was going nowhere and that she would wait for him.

Jack quickly took care of "number one" and then washed his hands praying she'd still be outside the bathroom in the lobby. When he stepped out he saw many students shuffling around but no red- head. Frantically he scanned the crowd but no sign of her. He couldn't believe he'd lost her again. What was even more shocking; he couldn't believe how much he missed her. He barely knew her yet he was completely absorbed in her. Still searching, Jack felt two warm, soft hands cover his eyes from behind.

"Did you miss me?" Candace said playfully.

The sweet sound of her voice allowed Jack's tensed body to relax from the brief worry of their separation.

"Well, I couldn't find you and I thought... wait, what's so funny?"

"The look on your face! You looked as if you had lost something very valuable" Candace continued to laugh. Her laugh was quite appealing. Not a giggle nor a snort, but a vivacious tease where her face would light up a room with those sparkling green eyes and ultra-white perfect teeth. Her playful energy charmed everyone she came into contact with. She just had an aura of happiness about her. Again, she latched onto Jack's hand and lovingly looked into his eyes.

"Don't worry Jack. You haven't lost me… not yet…"

Candace popped open the doors and sprinted down the steps laughing and occasionally looking back at Jack.

"Come on Jack! You love to run!" she shouted back. Jack instantly chased her through the quad and seemingly all over campus. She was quick but Jack wanted to play and see where she was going. She disappeared behind an old classroom building on the east end of campus. Jack followed but had trouble seeing as it was quickly getting dark.

Suddenly he felt a small body jump on him. He knew it was Candace by her lovely scent and long hair that fell across his face. He wrestled her to the ground and pinned her. Even in the dark he could make out the beautiful soft features of her tanned cheeks, perfectly pointed nose and round supple red lips. She laid there on a bed of colored leaves that blended nicely with her hair. She looked up at him longingly and said, "Now what?"

Jack leaned down slowly, slightly turning his head to kiss those soft lips. He could feel her hand grab the back of his head and run her fingers through his hair. The kiss lasted about two minutes but seemed like an eternity. Jack slid off of her to cup her face in his hands. Again, they kissed with even more passion. Jack instinctively ran his hands across her breasts. They were ample and firm. He worked his hand down her side and then inside her tight fitting, cashmere sweater. Candace stopped his advance with a firm grip of his wrist.

"Let's get that coffee. I'm thirsty."

"Okay, but I was rather enjoying this."

"I know you were." Candace shot back with a smile and a wink.

Jack pulled her up and helped get the leaves out of her hair. She locked hands again with Jack and led him back to Euclid Avenue heading east to the diner.

Two blocks away from Cup O Joe, Candace saw a dark figure crossing the street toward them. She released Jack's hand and ran to hug the figure. He was a sharp dressed black student who introduced himself as Geoffrey. It didn't take long for Jack to feel at ease around him. Geoffrey seemed extremely friendly and effeminate. Quite frankly, he wasn't a threat to Jack. Candace invited him to join them for coffee. Usually the third party intrusion would have bothered Jack and he would let the third party know that he didn't appreciate the "cock-blocking". However, Jack sensed something different about this guy and didn't mind his presence at all.

"So, Candace, you got yourself a boyfriend?" Geoffrey playfully inquired.

"Oh yes. Jack is a pre-law major and we're engaged to be married! Right Jack?"

"Oh yeah." Jack stated flatly opening the door to the diner. As Geoffrey followed Candace in, Jack nodded to him no. Geoffrey quietly laughed as if to say, *'typical silliness from Candace'.*

The group sat in the diner for a little more than an hour covering all sorts of topics from politics, sports and fashion---Jack was mostly silent on that last one.

"You know Jack, our girl Candace has been stalking you for several weeks," Geoffrey stated with a playful smile.

"I have not," Candace retorted with equal playfulness and in mocked offense added, "Its been closer to three weeks."

"Really?" Jack replied with shock and a bit of embarrassment.

"Yeah, she said she noticed you running near the Seaton Center without a shirt on and that she followed you in to watch you lift weights."

"Geoffrey, stop." Candace warned feeling a real blush warm her cheeks.

"Well, its true!"

Jack didn't know exactly how to respond so he just turned to Candace smiling and waiting for her response.

"Okay, its true but it's not as weird as Geoffrey is making it sound. I'm not a stalker or anything. Besides, I thought guys liked being pursued. I mean, modern literature tells us that men are the hunters and enjoy the pursuit of the prey. But what if the prey was tired of being pursued by ugly, horrible hunters and wanted to do some hunting of her own? What's wrong with that?"

"Nothing. I love it. Its very modern and new. A fresh approach to the twenty-first century dating scene."

"Look honey, there aint nothing new about a girl setting her sights on a man and using all her assets to draw his attention." Geoffrey added with a huge laugh that caused Candace to blush again and look down at her coffee.

"Well, I say there's nothing wrong with using your God-given talents to get what you want out of this life." Jack inserted looking lovingly at Candace and then added, "Especially when those talents are so beautifully adorned in long red tresses and soft supple skin."

Candace looked up from her coffee and stared longingly into Jack's eyes. She just knew in her heart there was more to Jack than just a beautiful exterior. He had a kindness that she was unaccustomed to, especially from her background. Most of the guys she had known were after one thing and one thing only. That could be the case with Jack, as well, but she sensed something different about him. There was an indescribable quality about him that seemed to draw her. It was an ease to his expressions and the way he carried himself with confidence but not arrogance that made her feel safe.

"Okay, its getting a bit awkward in here. Maybe I should step out and give you kids some space." Geoffrey scoffed noticing that he was being ignored.

"No, it's okay. I'm ready to leave. What about you Jack? Are you ready?"

"Sure. Where to?"

"Oh, I don't know let's just walk and talk."

"Sounds good to me."

Wow, she was scoping me out! That's really cool. The thought surprised Jack even though his roommates teased him all the time about being a "pretty boy". Jack still had those old lingering doubts from high school when he hadn't fully developed both physically and emotionally. He had been rather thin and unaccustomed to the attention of beautiful girls. A late bloomer physically, he was still vulnerable as the shy, thin kid with zero confidence in high school and still couldn't believe someone like Candace existed on campus and more incredibly, had sought him out.

Jack paid for everyone's coffee and they exited out into the cold, dark night. Candace snuck her arm up under Jack's and laced her fingers into his. She enjoyed the comfort and security of his arm. She led him down the street moving away from the campus. After a few moments, she asked him to walk her home as she didn't live too far from the diner. Jack was more than eager to take her home. Geoffrey followed but seemed lost in conversation on his cell phone and fell further and further behind.

Again, Jack didn't mind. He loved the idea of some one-on-one time with Candace. She started chit-chatting again about school and what she hopes to accomplish this year. She was technically a freshman though 22 years old. After high school, she had to go to work to help support her mother and sister. Her father was presently in a federal prison in Manchester, Kentucky.

"I hope that doesn't freak you out. He's not a bad guy. He just got mixed up with a bad crowd trying to make more money for our family."

"Oh no, it's alright. I guess…a man trying to provide for his family." Jack said reassuringly trying to find the right words because he could see how the subject affected her. "People make mistakes and I guess, you know, he's paying for it."

"He is. He's a beautiful person full of life and spirit. You know, people were just drawn to him like a magnet. The problem was too often it was the wrong sort of people and my Dad had trouble telling people no. He's a 'people-pleaser.'"

"Well he sounds like a nice man. Do you mind me asking what he's in for?"

"Oh no. It was drugs. Something to do with moving drugs from Florida to Kentucky in violation of interstate commerce laws. That's why he's in a federal prison in Manchester. He didn't do drugs or sell them. He just transported them. I'm not trying to minimize what he did but I don't want you to think he was some druggie or hardened felon that killed people."

"Oh yeah. Sure. Well, its no reflection of you guys. You know the rest of the family. When parents make mistakes, its not a reflection of the children or even their responsibility to clean up the mess left behind. Besides you're here at school studying to be a pediatrics' nurse to help others. It's an honorable profession."

Candace smiled and gripped his hand tighter. She was relieved that he seemed so caring and understanding about her difficult home life. Yet she had many more dark secrets and was worried about revealing too much too soon. After all it was just their first unofficial date.

"So, what's Jack's story?" Candace added playfully swinging their arms.

"Oh, it's kinda boring"

"I seriously doubt that. Let me guess" she teased as they stopped and she sized him up with her eyes. "You're part a big family that lives in the suburbs. Right?"

Jack lowered his head and smiled.

"And you have some brothers and sisters."

"Just two idiot brothers."

"Ha, I bet they're as pretty as you"

"Ha…I don't think anyone would call the Miller boys pretty."

"Well, you are!"

Jack looked up and found himself lost in her eyes again. All he could think about was their next kiss. The scintillating silence was broken as Candace lowered her head in embarrassment and then she recovered, "Anyway…I bet you have a beautiful mother and father that spend a lot time with you guys. Your mother stayed at home to raise you and your father makes a ton of money as a banker. Am I close?" she added gazing hopefully into his eyes.

"Well, partly. My mother did stay at home when we were small but eventually went to work as a bank teller when we got into high school. My father is a Baptist minister who doesn't make much. In fact, they still live in the church parsonage. We never really had much money but never felt like we were poor either. I guess in our neighborhood everyone was pretty much the same. As we got older and went over to other kids' homes we sorta wished we had a lot of the things they had, but what could you do about it. My dad's a good man who makes an honest, respectable living without much money. I mean we wished he made more but…"

"I know…its okay. Hey, look at me. I understand" Candace lovingly cupped his face and kissed him gently on the lips.

Jack hated talking about his background. He never really felt poor until he started middle school and many of his new friends lived in huge, swanky neighborhoods. They owned lots of fancy toys that only big money could afford. He loved his parents but often resented their meager existence.

Even in college, he scrimped and saved every cent he could to create the impression that his parents had money. Fortunately, his best friend, Rick, couldn't care less about money, though his parents were loaded, and enjoyed his company. It was rare that their friendship had developed given their differences in background and continued into college. They had planned on going into business together. Jack loved the idea of making a ton of money and emerging from his humble origins.

He couldn't believe he had revealed the truth about his background to Candace. Usually when the subject came up with a pretty girl, he just lied and invented a fantasy family loaded with money. The girls seemed to buy it and even if they didn't Jack didn't care as long as he got what he wanted from the brief relationship. He wasn't looking for anything but a good time with a few laughs. He understood that many of the campus co-eds were there in search of a husband and that was fine with him as part of the social game. He would go along with the illusion of a relationship to get what he wanted which was usually obtained quickly.

Once bagged and bedded, Jack moved on to different game. But Candace was different. She was a potential game-changer and Jack sensed it. It took him off guard and he opened up as never before. He felt he could tell her anything and not have to pose or play a game.

"Jack…I'm sorry I pried."

"No, it's okay. Its funny…I never really told anyone about the truth about my family. It's not like there's anything wrong with them. They're great, loving people. Its really just me…I guess I always sorta resented that they didn't have a bigger house or couldn't afford a lot of things. But that's not their fault."

"Of course, it's not. They gave you the best gift of all…their love and time. I wish I had more time with my father" Candace professed squeezing his hand and leading down the road.

Deep in thought and conversation, Jack was unaware of his surroundings. They had been walking for about twenty minutes eastward towards the "Zone".

The Zone was a poorer area of Lexington just off UK's campus. It was littered with low rent apartment complexes and was reputed to be a drug haven with a number of violent gangs fighting turf wars. Recently the gang activity had subsided as it was believed one gang, led by a drug lord, had seized control of the area. Cops didn't seem to mind as violent crimes such as assaults and murders were way down.

As far as crimes in the Zone, drugs of all descriptions, proscriptions and lifestyles were sold rather openly. Law enforcement mostly looked the other way because so many of Lexington's finest citizens had take-out orders from the pharmacy. As long as violent crimes were down, this "victimless" crime was harmless. Jack knew a few kids on campus that supplied many frat parties with drugs from the Zone. No matter, the area gave Jack the creeps. Too many street lights were out giving little illumination. He could feel himself shake with nervousness and hoped Candace hadn't seen it.

"Do you live around here?"

"Yes...I 'm sorry. I know it's bad but it's really all I can afford right now."

"No, no...it's alright. I'm just worried about your safety."

"Oh, I'm alright. Look there's a thousand things I need to tell you. I want to tell you..."

Jack was lost in her eyes. Every word she spoke, every breath she took, he absorbed it. He couldn't believe how much he wanted her or how soon he seemed to have fallen for her. All he cared about was holding and protecting her in this moment. Looking up at him she seemed small, though she wasn't. She was about 5'10 with those gorgeous long, athletic legs. But next to Jack's 6'2 frame and under these conditions she appeared tiny and helpless. Jack wrapped his arms around her.

Looking back towards UK's campus he could see Geoffrey leaning against the only light post that appeared to be working. He was still on the phone. The silence of the embrace was broken by Candace's phone. She checked the number and then answered. Jack could only pick up bits and pieces of the conversation as Candace turned her back and began walking deeper into the Zone. Jack trailed behind but wanted to give Candace her space and privacy. The conversation escalated in volume and Candace's mood swung dramatically. Gone was the happy, carefree spirit that had entranced Jack for the past three hours. Candace turned serious, if not a bit frightened. She hung up.

"I need to go home now? Can you walk with me?"

"Sure, where do live?"

"Near…" she mumbled as her voice trailed off. She picked up the pace of her walk and moved into a jog.

Jack followed her deeper into a seedy world he had never seen or experienced. The streets were filled with dark figures milling about from one spot to another. Chasing behind her, Jack looked into the faces of some of the dark figures. They had a scary, lost look in their eyes. Many of them asked for money and why he was running. The voices got louder and louder as more people started to emerge from the shadowed streets. Candace seemed oblivious to what was going on behind her. She sprinted across a field behind a run-down gas station that hadn't pumped gas since the Reagan years.

He remembered Tater talking about going in the Zone once and how he vowed he would never go in there again. He had rolled in there with some rich fraternity boys looking to score a few hits. Tater warned that these drug runs, initially marijuana, were a "gateway" into a seedy, dangerous criminal world that he wanted no part of. The frat boys seemed oblivious to the apparent danger of their surroundings, but Tater convinced them to leave after a dispute arose on a price increase. It wasn't worth it, he warned them, and later warned Rick and Jack to stay away from that area.

Now Jack had willingly run in following a beautiful girl he hardly knew. It was crazy but he had really fallen for this girl. He called out for her to slow down but it didn't seem to faze her. *She probably didn't hear me.* He watched her run across another street and then scaled a rusty, rickety stairwell with a wrap-around enclosure that ran straight up. When Jack got to the stairwell, he could see Candace about twenty-five feet above on the last rung. He quickly ran up the old stairwell reaching the top just in time to catch sight of Candace sprinting across an open field that led to a nasty, two story apartment complex that was probably built in the Seventies during an urban renewal project that got some local politicians re-elected.

It looked as if the city had forgotten all about it once everyone had received their "pat on the backs" for a job well done. Like most government projects, this one failed because there was no follow up, enforcement of rigorous building codes or even verification of the applicant's backgrounds. Seemingly anyone and everyone of all sketchy backgrounds moved in while law-abiding residents moved out. Jack was looking at the end result of an urban renewal project gone woefully wrong.

Candace banged on the door of apartment 121. It opened with a large black man taking up the entire entrance. He was wearing a couple of gold chains and a "wife beater" t-shirt that bulged out with his ample gut. He had on big gray, baggy sweat pants and house slippers. *My God, he must be about 6'8 and weigh well over three hundred pounds* Jack thought while scanning the area.

The huge man was not in a good mood and grabbed Candace by the back of the head shoving her roughly through the door. Once the door shut, Jack had to make a quick decision. Should he follow Candace into the dangerous unknown or wait? It was a tough agonizing decision. *Candace is obviously in trouble…a lot of trouble. Shouldn't I help her? YES…but how? That dude is huge. There's no way I could take him…maybe if I had a weapon like a pipe or something.* Jack searched the area for any kind of weapon that could be of use taking down a grizzly bear. Jack found nothing but instead discovered a clump of hedges near a long fence to hide behind and waited frozen in fear and indecision.

Chapter 5

"In self-defense and in the defense of the innocent, cowardice is the only sin."

—Dean Koontz

Candace was suddenly thrown right back into the world she thought she had left behind. With one shove from behind the head by Big Jr, she knew she was back and might never leave again. All her worst fears and trepidations come rushing back in that single moment she re-entered apartment 121. She was pushed into a hall closet and told to be still. The Boss would be down to see her shortly. Candace began sobbing quietly because she knew this routine all too well. She had seen the Boss do it to other girls, junkies, rivals, drug mules and anyone else who he believed owed him or turned against him. Candace's sorrow intensified as she could only think of one person, Julia, her two year old daughter being held somewhere in this two story apartment.

Standing in the small dark closet Candace pondered how she got into this mess and this evil seductive world of the Zone. She remembered how she enjoyed a normal life in Lexington attending Henry Clay High School and playing basketball her freshman year before joining the cheerleading squad to meet more boys and become more popular. Her senior year, tragedy struck the family as her father was arrested for trafficking cocaine out of Miami. He was sentenced to ten years at the Federal Corrections Institution in Manchester. Shortly thereafter her mother's health declined rapidly and Candace had to go to work. She started out as a waitress in several nice restaurants but a friend convinced her to try dancing in a strip club at the tender age of nineteen. There she met the Boss, Marcus X, who introduced her to the fast world of drugs with a little hooking on the side. Soon Candace was a junkie living in apartment 121 turning a few tricks to pay the rent.

In the darkness of the closet, her thoughts turned to her beautiful Julia. At once believed to be a curse, an inconvenience— nature's proof that mankind's clumsy attempts to control or manipulate her were foolish. The procreative forces of nature can no more be tamed by man than gravity or the tides of the ocean. Nature found a way through the series of man-made obstacles as one of her "tricks" got her pregnant. She saw it as a blessing from God but Marcus X saw it as an inconvenience and wanted it aborted. He gave her $500 to clean up her "mistake" sending her off to a clinic escorted by Big Jr.

Sitting in the front lobby of a Planned Parenthood clinic alone, Candace had time to ponder the biggest decision of her life. She knew aborting the child was the quickest and easiest way out of her mess but she couldn't shake the thought of a living being growing inside her. *I wonder why an abortion clinic is called "Planned Parenthood". No one in here has talked to me about keeping the baby…keeping the baby.* She imagined what the child would look like; the soft features of its hair, fingers, toes and skin. She sensed it was a girl and instantly sought to protect her like a delicate flower blowing in the wind, wholly dependent on her for protection from the storm. These waves of maternal emotions enveloped her as she clearly saw this child was not a curse but indeed a blessing. She envisioned a new life, a fresh start, an escape from the hellish environment of the Zone.

The long wait in the front lobby had produced a life-changing decision that would save two lives. She called an old friend from high school to pick her up as she would run away to her grandmother's house in Versailles and start life anew for her baby.

She had turned her life around and escaped her past finishing her GED and was accepted to UK. Or so she thought until twenty minutes ago when the past reached her through her cell phone with news that Marcus X had her daughter. *He must have nabbed her from my roommate Mikayla. Damn, I knew I shouldn't have left Julia. I can't believe I moved back to the Zone, but I was desperate to find a cheap place on campus. The commute was just too long from Versailles and I couldn't bring Julia on campus to class. God, why did I reach out to Mikayla? Just because we were once close is no reason to leave your most precious possession with someone still living in the Zone. Oh God…I should've known! Julia…. I'm so sorry! I'm so sorry!* Candace quietly sobbed.

The closet door opened abruptly as Big Jr. grabbed her by the arm and yanked her out onto the floor. When she looked up through the billowing clouds of smoke emanating from the numerous "business suites" for entertainment, she saw Marcus X standing over her with his distinctive goatee and long black leather coat. He had an air of "master of the manor" in apartment 121, a darkened den of iniquity that reeked of swirling wisps of marijuana, opium and crack cocaine. Scattered about the reconstructed two-story apartment was an odd assortment of druggies, hookers and handlers that Marcus X presided over. His authority was unchallenged and his command absolute. He held the chilling power of life and death over all the occupants which kept them in fearful check.

He made sure his "employees" were dependent on him for everything to insure their loyalty as drugs were a quick and easy lure to hook them. Few had escaped his compound for more than a couple of days as they usually struggled to go clean. Invariably they begged to return to the addictive lifestyle and authoritarian rule of the master, Marcus X.

Each occupant served an important function and filled a need in the drug lord's multi-million-dollar operation though few were indispensable. Those who proved unreliable or undesirable were "disposed" of quickly and discreetly in various construction sites or landfills as few had families concerned about their well-being which was a large factor in the selection process to membership in apartment 121.

Though not as tall as his loyal bodyguard, Big Jr, Marcus X held a commanding presence in a six foot two-inch frame cloaked in mostly muscle mass of two hundred and forty pounds. His imposing size usually did all the talking as Marcus X was a man of few words who knew how to check his emotions. Rarely did he give in to fits of rage but some people just got under his skin and unfortunately, Candace was one of them.

"Well, look what the cat dragged in? If it aint my favorite Candy." Marcus sneered.

"My name's not Candy anymore. Where's my baby, asshole? What have you done to my beautiful little girl?" Candace cried out with increasing anger.

"Who are you calling asshole, bitch! Who the fuck do you think you're talking to?" Marcus threw a back-handed slap to her face that opened up her lip. "Don't come in here making demands like you own the place. Just because you're dressed like a lady, all prim and proper, doesn't mean you are. We both know what you are. You're just one of my ho's that owes me money."

"I don't owe you anything! You used and abused me for over a year. I got pregnant thanks to your pimping ways and left to get clean. I've made a new life for myself. Just give me my daughter back and leave me alone!" Wiping the blood from her lips, Candace realized how dangerous her situation was and tried to soften her approach. "Please, I'm begging you Marcus…please give me back my daughter. There's no reason for you to hold on to her. She's not yours. You didn't even want her. Why are you holding her?"

"I don't know Candy. Maybe it has something to do with the way you left. You just ran out on me. No 'farewell' or 'goodbye' dear Marcus. Thanks for saving my pretty little ass and giving me a good paying job!" Marcus added getting control over his emotions. "You left me high and dry with a wealthy client that figured to pay four figures for your pretty little ass. I figure you owe me big time for that client plus time lost being away so long. It aint that easy leaving this lucrative lifestyle, Candy and you're looking really nice. In fact, I can make some real money with you escorting some bigger paying clients."

"Fuck you! I'm never doing that again. Where's my daughter?"

"Look, we aint getting nowhere here. If you want to see your daughter, you're going to have to turn a few tricks to make up for the lost time. I figure you owe me about twenty-five thousand dollars."

Fighting back tears Candace again wiped her bleeding lip. Slowly she stood trying to figure out her next more. *Right now, the most important thing is to get to Julia* she reasoned. *I need to calm down and try talking rationally to him. He never responded well to outbursts of emotion, especially screaming. I can't bark at him. Just telling him what he wants to hear so you can get to Julia* Candace reasoned looking down at the floor and then back at Marcus.

"Alright, I really have no choice, do I?"

"Nope." Marcus answered flatly.

"I'll do a few escorts to pay the $25,000 but that's it. No more. I'm free of you and this shit! Now please let get my daughter."

"You can see her but you aint getting her. In fact, you'll move back into your old room until that debt is paid."

"Fine. Where is she?"

"I just told you…in your old room."

Candace gathered her composure and walked over the dead beats lining the halls hooked on some sort of drugs. She could hear music and sexual activity coming out of several rooms along the hallway. Peering in, she could see several groups going through the motions of some kind of sex with little to no clothes on. Walking through the kitchen she quickly darted up the stairs desperate to hold her daughter and find a way out of this hell hole.

<u>Chapter 6</u>

"To know what is right and not to do it is the worst cowardice."

−Confucius

Jack was worried. This was taking too long. *My God what is she doing? What is happening in there? Why am I even here?* These thoughts were plaguing Jack as he sat idly by behind the bushes in a notorious gangland. Scanning the landscape for any signs of trouble, Jack could hear the old iron stairwell rattling like someone was climbing up. Looking over, he saw Geoffrey surface walking confidently across the yard. Jack was stunned to see someone like Geoffrey in the Zone. He just didn't fit the part.

Geoffrey rapped a coded knock on the door and was greeted by another big black man but nowhere near as big as the first dude that snatched Candace. This guy was wearing a huge black leather coat and looked like Denzel Washington. He gave Geoffrey a big hug and welcomed him in slamming the door. That puzzled Jack even more but he was still frozen in fear and unable to figure out what to do next. He still held out hope that Candace would walk out and they could finish the night together.

∽ ∽ ∽ ∽ ∽ ∽ ∽ ∽

As Candace reached the door handle of her old room, she felt a wave of fear crawl over her body. The door seemed jammed. She pushed harder and finally the door gave way. Candace called out to her daughter several times but there was no response. Her hands fumbled across the wall searching for the light switch. Flipping it on she saw an empty room with a few mattresses on the floor and a small blanket wadded up in the far corner. Looking closer at the blanket she could see a small foot poking out. Her heart sank as she ran across the room and scooped up the blanket. There was her sweet angel, Julia, lying dead in her arms. Julia's face seemed bruised and battered with claw marks around her neck. Candace released a blood-curdling scream that only a parent's pain can make. The marks around Julia's neck had to have come from the long, curled nails of Marcus X.

She gently laid Julia down on a mattress and retrieved a chef's knife she had hidden in the closet a few years ago. She ran down the stairs two steps at a time to kill Marcus.

Just as she hit bottom stair her face was hammered by the meaty fist of Big Jr., Marcus X's trusted body guard. Dazed, Candace tried to get up but Big Jr's size 19 foot slammed down on her neck and held her firmly to the floor. Marcus entered the kitchen.

"What the hell was all that screaming?"

"I don't know but she came running down the stairs with this knife. I think she was intending to use it." Big Jr grinned.

Leaning down to the floor to make eye contact with Candace, Marcus asked "Were you trying to kill someone, Candy?" Big Jr. removed his foot and pulled her up.

"Well, Candy?"

Still dazed and hurting Candace mumbled "You killed my Julia."

"I killed your Julia? What she talking about?" Marcus asked as Big Jr shrugged his huge grizzly bear shoulders.

"Look bitch, no one comes into my house waving a knife at me!" Marcus slammed several punches to her once perfect face as she slumped over. He then grabbed her hidden weapon and thrust into her heart killing her instantly.

"Clean this shit up and dump her body in the usual place. What's this shit about her daughter being dead?"

"Apparently someone in this den of iniquity must have lost their mind and killed little Julia" Geoffrey stated returning from the upstairs bedroom.

"Damn…" Marcus said shaking his head ruefully.

"Hey, what did you do with the white dude she was with?"

Geoffrey asked.

"What white dude?" Marcus shouted.

"Man, she came up here with some little prick. A college boy."

"Fuck, nobody like that came up here. Ask around the house and complex. Dude like that would be easy to spot around here!"

"He's gotta be around here somewhere. I saw him climb the stairwell out back."

"Fuck! Fuck! Big Jr get some of the boys. We gotta hunt down a little white boy who's obviously lost."

The boys Marcus X was referring to were high school "recruits" Big Jr. snared. They were low performing students from poor, often single parent homes trapped in a dead-end environment. Many of these young guns dreamed of the fast life with wads of cash, drugs and women. Big Jr filled their heads with this fantasy, but the reality of apartment 121 was far different.

Lying around semi-conscience most days in a drug-induced haze helped coat their meager existence. However, Big Jr wouldn't allow the new recruits this luxury. He kept them mostly clean because he needed them to street hustle and push the product. He also needed fast runners to catch the rabbits. Once caught, Big Jr. would do the rest. Right now he was hunting a white rabbit and ordered his quarry into action.

❧ ❧ ❧ ❧ ❧ ❧ ❧ ❧

Jack heard the terrifying scream of a woman in agony and sensed it was Candace. Again, he was frozen in fear and resentment that he seemed unable or willing to do anything. *What's wrong with me? I should go in a get her out. It's obvious this beautiful girl is in trouble. She asked me to go with her. Did she know something could go wrong? Did she sense danger? If so why did she go so willingly? No one dragged her in. She left the safety of campus to come here. Why?* These thoughts kept running through his mind.

The outdoor light suddenly flashed on and the front door opened with several young toughs carrying bats spilling into the open yard. The huge black yeti re-appeared in the entrance with a flashlight as the air was filled with voices screaming something about "white meat". *Oh shit...they're looking for me.* He also saw another large figure in the doorway dressed in a long black leather coat barking orders. *He must be the boss. Damn, he looks just like Denzel Washington! Oh my God, he's got blood all over his hand and a long knife.*

Jack could see that they were about a hundred yards away walking toward the old iron stairwell and looking through bushes on the opposite end of the apartment complex. Looking back to his right, he saw the parking lot of another rundown apartment complex enclosed by an eight foot high fence. Beyond the parking lot, Jack could barely make out what appeared to be a steep slope that emptied out on the street. He knew this was really his only option.

He needed a distraction to give him time to scale the fence. He felt the ground and found a large rock. It seemed corny but again he had no choice. He hurled the rock across the yard near the old iron stairwell. Somehow the distractive sound work as Big Jr. led his posse towards the sound. Jack hit the fence high and landed his foot on the supporting cross bar allowing him to launch off and over the fence with little effort.

He could feel the adrenalin pumping through his body as he landed safely on the other side. But the clinking sound of the chain link fence drew Big Jr's flashlight revealing a dude in a blue hoodie scrambling on the other side of the fence. Jack could hear a booming voice ordering the quarry to the fence. Looking down at the steep hill that disappeared somewhere in the dark, Jack could feel the panic of real fear. This was a hill that should be cautiously walked down in daylight but hearing the quarry hitting the fence, Jack knew he had no choice. His powerful legs absorbed much of the rocky, uneven slope in stride but midway down his foot step into a hole causing him to lose his balance. He tumbled down the last half of the hill hard, hitting his head abruptly on the pavement. Dazed but conscience, Jack scrambled back to his feet. He could hear the big voice ordering his boys down the hill.

Big Jr knew he was in no shape to descend that hill in the day time much less in the middle of the night. This was a job for his young toughs. He ordered them down but the loudest of the three, Wheels, said "No! I mean, hell no!" Big Jr shoved him down the hill with the others watching in awe before quickly agreeing to descend. They could hear Wheels screaming and complaining as they cautiously watched their footing. Big Jr screamed for them to hurry because the white rabbit was on foot again and running.

Jack felt his left ankle throb and knew he had twisted it maybe even sprained it. But he had no time for pain. He would have to block it out. Jack had to get out of the Zone and back onto his home turf, the campus. Pushing through the pain he sprinted across several yards into in the dark. He instantly came to a stop running into an unseen low chain-link fence. The useless four foot enclosure held a huge Doberman pincher that was roused from its sleep and began barking. Real fear returned to Jack as the Doberman came within a foot of mauling his face but was restrained by a large chain posted in the ground near its house. The loud barking alerted the black posse who started running in his direction. Again, Jack scrambled to his feet and ran towards the lamplights of freedom on the outskirts of the Zone.

As he neared the lights of the town, Jack knew he needed to get back on campus near a large crowd to blend and hopefully lose his posse. The best place was near Three Goggles. It was always lively and active with students just about every night. He knew this would be a long run but he was in shape, used to covering long distances and knew where he was going. That gave him a slight edge over his pursuers who he could sense was still near.

Jack zigzagged through the campus quad running in and around several dorms and classroom buildings. Several times during the run he thought about ducking in one and hiding. However, he knew the chances of any of them being open were slim and he couldn't chance slowing down. No, he surmised, his safety was in the open and in a big crowd. He pulled his hoodie over his head hoping to confuse his quarry. Running into the bright lights of the campus bar scene was a relief, especially seeing how packed it was. Many of the college kids were standing around drinking and socializing. Jack slowed to a quick walking pace and began mingling through the crowd.

Looking back, he could see several black kids running into the crowd. *Damn... how the Hell did they stay with me?* Frustrated Jack lowered his head bobbing and weaving his way towards Three Goggles.

Several students that he had taken classes with before recognized him and tried to stop him to talk. He simply begged off and kept walking. He felt a burning sensation in his lungs as he exhaled a burst of air. He hadn't realized how tired he was or how fast he had been running. He had to stop to catch his breath and rub his aching ankle. He found a bench near a crowd of students and plopped down. Resting and rubbing his ankle, Jack tried to think of his next move. Suddenly a hand grabbed his shoulder. He looked up and it was Tami/Teri. *Damn what was her name?*

"Hey stranger, you're just the man I was looking for. Don't you answer your cell?

"Oh, hi. No...I don't have my phone on me. I was..."

"Hey Jack!" the voice was too familiar and way too loud. Looking up to his left he could see Tater leaning out the 2nd floor window of Three Goggles. "Jack, wait there buddy I'm coming down!"

Looking back towards his pursuers he could see that Tater's scream had turned them back onto his scent. Jack got back on his feet and ran towards Three Goggles trying to get in but the entrance was too crowded. He quickly darted to the side of the building as he knew a there was an outdoor patio. As he turned the corner he could see several large figures approaching the side ally of Three Goggles from another street about 75 yards away. Jack was frozen in indecision. *Now what? I'm trapped.*

Suddenly Jack felt a powerful blow to his lower back that threw him forward onto the pavement behind a row of garbage cans. The shove had nearly knocked the breath out of him. Looking up he could see Tater wearing a blue UK hoodie running down the alley laughing. He was obviously drunk and thought this was a game of "beer tag", a rough game he learned from some rugby players. Jack tried to get up but was horrified by the sight of three dark figures running past him and catching up to Tater. They quickly seized the slower runner with a flying tackle. Two of the figures held baseball bats and began pummeling him. It was a grizzly scene. Tater never had a chance as the first blow was to the head knocking him senseless. They relentlessly hit the mangled, lifeless body for what seemed like several minutes. Jack was terrified and horrified at witnessing his best friend's death. And again, he was paralyzed in fear. That fear amplified as Big Jr and Geoffrey strolled back into the alley past Jack's row of trash cans. Jack curled down lower to avoid any detection.

Geoffrey grabbed the flashlight from Big Jr. beaming it onto the bruised and battered victim's face. He frowned and grew angry.

"You dumb fucks killed the wrong dude!"

"Are you sure…look again and try to imagine his face less puffy and cut up? This is the dude we were chasing…I mean a white dude in a blue hoodie running towards this building. Can't be too many of those guys around!" Big Jr fumed.

"Yeah I'm sure! Their faces are much different and Jack Miller's a lot taller…around 6'2 or 6'3 with auburn, reddish hair. This dude's tiny and thick with thinning brown hair. Fuck man! Look around you! We're surrounded by white dudes wearing blue sweatshirts, jackets and hoodies. We're on UK's campus! He knew that and ran you here to blend in and confuse you."

"Damn man…. the problem is that all white dudes look alike." Big Jr sneered.

"Well we'll never find him tonight. He's lost in the crowd and is probably heading home. Don't worry. I know his name and can get his class schedule. Let's get outta here before someone sees the body" Geoffrey concluded.

"Hey boys…pick up that body and dump it over there behind those trash cans. We gotta get outta here. We sorta stand out in this snow-covered town." Big Jr ordered.

Jack lay silently on the ground behind the cans suppressing his anguish. He could hear them walk past him as his heartbeat pounded against his chest. He closed his eyes and waited for the worst. He felt the huge dead weight land on his back. Turning his head slightly up, he was looking into Tater's lifeless eyes. *Oh dear God...Tater...I'm so sorry. What I have I done?* Between quiet sobs and sniffs he could hear the black boys mumble something about stupid white people and how heavy that body was. Slowly Jack pulled the body off of him and limped out of the back alley away from his quarry. He knew they had lost his scent but for how long?

<u>Chapter 7</u>

"Long before morning I knew that what I was seeking to discover was a thing I'd always known. That all courage was a form of constancy. That it is always himself that the coward abandoned first. After this all other betrayals come easily."

—Cormac McCarthy, ***All the Pretty Horses***

Sunlight streamed into the spacious oblong apartment on Maxwell Street. Its usual arrival preceded the neighborhood woodpecker that started attacking a pine tree every morning around six o'clock. This Friday morning was no different. Jack could feel the bright single beam on his eyes. It peeked through a crack in the blinds on Tater's side of the room.

But a crack and a few missing slats in the blinds was the least of the problems on Tater's side of the room. He had clothes, dumbbells, shoes, magazines, tennis balls and an assortment of protein powder canisters strewn all over the floor. You would hardly know that a beautiful red-stained pine wood floor was beneath Tater's possessions. Rick and Jack's side of the bedroom was meticulously neat with every item stored in its proper place. Jack had a large entertainment center on the side wall where their Bose stereo system rested. Rick had secured 4 speakers around the top walls surrounding the bedroom giving them the maximum music experience.

Their apartment was comprised of three rooms plus a kitchen and only one bathroom which usually posed a problem for the guys especially in the morning. Posters adorned the walls in the bedroom ranging from sports, rock groups to Maxim pin-up girls. The hottest poster belonged to Tater— Danica Patrick was draped across a stock car in just a string bikini. Not shockingly, it faced Tater so that she was the last image he saw at night and the first one in the morning.

Annoyingly, the sole sun beam woke Jack from his deep sleep. Opening his eyes, he quickly looked to his right to see if Rick was in bed. He wasn't but his bed was made. Of course, it was. Rick was the only one who made his bed every day.

Looking at the blue soft glow digital clock that read 10:38 am, Jack sighed with relief. *Rick has already left for their Poly Sci 311 class in Wofford Hall. He always allows about 25 minutes to get to class, though I can get there in ten* Jack reasoned. Leaning up on his elbows, he anxiously looked over for Tater. Not there. Jack could feel his heart pumping a little quicker as memories of last night came flooding in. *No! That was a bad dream. None of that happened. Tater's missing but that could be for a number of reasons. Often, he stayed out late, drunk and passed out wherever he landed. Once we found him two blocks away in some neighbor's back yard sleeping on their deck. It was funny and embarrassing.*

Jack got up and went to the bathroom. He noticed Rick's toothbrush was wet but not Tater's. Again, not unusual as Tater was not the most hygienic person on the planet. There was no time for a regular shower so Jack had an "Irish shower" by wetting his hair back, applying deodorant and spraying on cologne.

Throwing on a pair of jeans with a long-sleeved polo over a white t-shirt, Jack grabbed his book bag and headed out the door. Before leaving the apartment building, he did a quick search of the bottom floor hoping to find Tater curled up against the stairwell. He knocked on the neighbor's door across the hallway, again hoping Tater was pulled into their place. There was no response but Jack really didn't expect one. The occupants were Korean and rarely spoke to them. Slinging his book bag across his left shoulder, Jack exited the building.

He started to run across Maxwell Street but felt a throbbing pain in his left ankle. *What the hell!* Memories of his fall down a massive hill landing badly on his ankle in the Zone sent a chill through his body. *No that's not how that happened. I must've injured it jogging yesterday. Remember that ankle has always bothered you since your tore ligaments during the District tournament your junior year in high school. Come on Miller, keep it together. Okay, jogging to class isn't going to happen. I guess I'll be a little late. No big deal. Rick's taking good notes.*

The walk to the main campus was always one of the best experiences in the world of academia. Throughout their primary to secondary education, most students in public schools are housed in penitentiary-style buildings with little to no view of the outside world.

During class changes, they're rustled like cattle from one room to another with just a meager recess period outside. But in college, students roamed all over open spaces lined with trees and kept immaculately by the physical plant. Jack loved the crisp cool air of autumn as he began the long incline into the main campus across from Memorial Coliseum. The sun had disappeared giving way to low gray clouds as the wind blew colder. Nearing Stoll Field, Jack now wished he had put a jacket on.

Memories of events from last night crashed his brain again. *What a beautiful face and long red hair she had. The sizzling dance at Three Goggle; the flirting in class; run through campus and sensual kiss on the grass.* Jack smiled but was soon hit with the painful memories of watching Candace flung into a run-down apartment and hearing a horrible scream. Watching Tater get beaten to death and then his lifeless eyes staring at you! Pleading with you! Begging you to do something! *Stop! Stop! None of that happened…but if none of that happened, why am I remembering so much in such vivid detail? No one remembers dreams good or bad in this kind of detail. Okay stop it!! Damn these memories are haunting me. Alright, let's get focused. We're coming up on Wofford Hall. I have a Poly Sci. class on political ideologies with Professor James Shuttlesworth. He's supposed to be really hard but entertaining… 'that's what she said'…ha, ha. Okay that's more like the old you. Tater always loved those jokes…okay stop thinking about Tater right now. He's okay. Probably banging some ugly broad this morning that he picked up last night. He'll try to convince us that she was hot…ha, ha.*

Jack picked up his pace passing the old library, M.I. King building, on the left. His ankle was still sore but the long walk had loosened it up a bit. He hit the Wofford Hall stairs two at a time and pulled the huge door open. He knew his room was 320 on the third floor. *This climb will definitely loosen up the old ankle.*

Reaching the top floor, Jack froze in his tracks. Standing in front of one of the rooms down the hall was Geoffrey and three thugs from the Zone. Jack watched as two of the darker thugs were slapping at each other's hands apparently playing some "hit you last" game. Jack's eyes looked up at Geoffrey who was staring directly at him. *Holy shit!* Jack quickly stumbled back down the stairs trying to land safely on each step but panic had taken hold of his body and seemed to be pushing him to go faster. Only the hand rail saved him from crashing down the stair well. He could hear Geoffrey calling out to him, trying to get him to stop. He yelled that they just wanted to talk. Jack wasn't buying that garbage. The last time he saw Geoffrey he remembered what they did to Tater.

Nearing the last steps Jack leaped to the floor landing hard on the ankle and again injuring it. He had no time to think about a bad ankle. Popping through the big entrance doors, Jack again attacked the outside stairs two at a time. *Damn it, there's a lot of stairs on this campus!* He turned right and hobbled down a sidewalk leading to the Chem-Phys building. He briefly thought about running into the Chem-Phys building but he didn't know it as well and could get ensnared. Instead, Jack sprinted between the President's residence and the Chem-Phys building and then crisscrossed Rose Street's traffic perfectly like the old "Frogger" video game.

His posse struggled to get across as efficiently. Running between the Hilary J. Boone Center and the Mining Resource Building, Jack could see the finish line, The W.T. Young Library. But that was still about five hundred yards away and he could hear his Zone pursuers catching up. Jack kicked it into full gear as his adrenalin glands coated the pain of the injured ankle. He knew exactly where he was going and there would be no daytime zigzagging. The W.T Young Library was a magnificent five story brick building with huge gothic windows in the front. Jack knew if he could make it into the library he could lose these thugs in a maze of books, shelves, desks and students.

Grabbing the massive heavy handle of the entrance door, Jack slowed his pace through the second set of double doors into a five-story atrium. Sprinting past the round security desk and up a wide-open stairwell, he knew he had to get to the third floor. He could hear Security Guard Bob James warning him to slow down. He hoped old Bob would notice his pursuers and call the cops. But he couldn't count on that. Using the Core 2 stairwell, Jack hit the steps two at a time racing to the top. He shuffled quickly through the East Stacks, a series of book shelves, and then ran into a familiar face from the past sitting in a student carrel.

ન્ડ ન્ડ ન્ડ ન્ડ ન્ડ ન્ડ ન્ડ ન્ડ

Outside of the library, Geoffrey shouted out to the quarry to stop. He knew that three young black kids running into a college library would draw unhealthy attention. The tallest pursuer, C.J., relayed Geoffrey's orders to the others. The four gathered in front of the library's four-arched entrance to catch their breath and talk to Big Jr. on the phone.

"Damn that white boy is fast!" Jumpy cried.

"Yeah, I'd had my hands on him if he hadn't run across that street at the right time. I almost got hit by two cars. Damn, people don't stop for anything on that road." Wheels complained.

"Alright, Big Jr wants you guys to walk in the library with your phones on. Sweep the floors but stay together or you'll get lost. This boy obviously knows this place pretty well and is hiding. You guys need to thoroughly and quietly scan the floors. Leave no place unturned or unsearched. He's likely hiding in a room or desk. Don't draw attention to yourselves and act like you've been in a library before." Geoffrey barked.

"I've been in a library before." Wheels snapped.

"Not like this one. It's loaded with shelves, reading rooms and lots of students on five different floors. It will be tough to find our boy in a sea of white kids. He was smart to run in here." C.J. remarked.

"Nonetheless, he's in there and we have to find him." Geoffrey added. "Big Jr. and I will be waiting at the entrance in case he tries to back track. There's only one way in and out of this building."

∽ ∽ ∽ ∽ ∽ ∽ ∽ ∽

Jack couldn't believe he had run into Heather Mills, yet again. She was sitting in the first carrel in the 319 reading room with a ton of books spread out across the desk. Jack moved her book bag and sat next to her nervously looking around.

"Well hi, Jack. What's wrong? Why are you out of breath and looking around?"

"Can't really explain right now." Jack said between gasps "I may need you."

"Need me for what?" Heather inquired softly.

Jack shot out of his chair and zigzagged through the East stacks looking out into the atrium. He could see his pursuers walking together with book bags up the stairwell. *I bet those bags don't have books in them and they don't know where the hell they're going.* His eyes follow them towards the Core 2 stairwell. For some crazy reason, they skipped the second floor and entered the third floor. *Oh crap they're coming right toward me.* Jack sprinted back to Heather's carrel jumping under her legs and crouching under her desk. He grabbed her book bag to shield him.

Heather was stunned but not upset. She thought it was another campus prank that Jack and his friends were constantly playing on each other. She actually enjoyed the sudden attention she was getting from him. She could feel Jack squirming under her legs trying to get settled.

"What are you doing?"

"Shhh! Lower your voice. Some crazy black dudes are chasing me. I need you to cover me."

"Who's chasing you...wait why are they chasing you?"

"Heather, that's a real long story and I promise to tell you some day but right now, I really need you to cover me...and stop talking. Just keep your head down and pretend you are studying."

Heather could sense this was no practical joke and that Jack seemed really scared. She quietly obeyed and moved the chair next to her further into the desk covering Jack's legs. She placed some of her books in the chair to provide further cover.

Jack's eyes were scanning the reading room's entrance floor. He saw several sets of worn tennis shoes shuffle in. He could hear one voice tell the others to split up and look through the rooms meeting him back by the East Stacks entrance. Once again, Jack could feel his heart pounding through his chest quicker and quicker. It was just a matter of time before they looked under Heather's desk. *Then what? What's my next move? I can't let them hurt Heather or try to do anything to her. I'll have to try to sprint again hoping to get to the security desk on the first floor. Bob will help. He's always been helpful to me in the past. Oh, but that was different. Letting you in to study past hours isn't the same as stopping killers. Oh shit, I'm in trouble…"*

Jack spotted a pair of shoes stop behind Heather. They paused for an eternity. Heather turned and looked at the stranger with annoyance. He shuffled on into the East Stacks to meet with the others. Heather pushed her chair back and ducked her head into the East Stacks moving gingerly through the seven foot high book shelves. She returned after what seemed about twenty minutes. It was actually five as she slid herself back into the desk.

"All clear. They ran up to the fourth floor."

"Oh God… thanks Heather. I owe you big time!"

"I'm going to hold you that."

Scrambling out of the desk and through the East Stacks, Jack returned to the stairwell heading down to the first floor. He thought he had lost his pursuers and was going to exit the library when he spotted Geoffrey and a huge black dude standing next to him at the outside entrance. *Damn, it's the same big dude from the Zone, apartment 121. Oh crap, they've blocked my exit. Now what?* Jack knew he had to get out of the building quickly as it was only a matter of time before the Zone gang spotted him. He looked up at the atrium skyline and locked eyes with the tallest Zone chaser. He motioned the others to follow him. Jack again sprinted up the open stairwell in the atrium to the Core 2 stairwell.

He remembered there were emergency exit doors. It was sure to set off alarms but that would help create a distraction and maybe buy him time to get out of the building. Reaching the second floor landing in Core 2, Jack read "Emergency Exit Only. Alarm Will Sound After 15 Second Delay." Jack quickly popped the door handle and darted back down another stairwell that had a small nook. The wait seemed forever as he felt the throbbing pain from his ankle more acutely. He could hear feet from above scrambling down stairs. The air was filled with an extremely loud siren as the door popped open. Students lifted their heads up and many started heading for the emergency exits thinking this was a fire alarm. Soon the Core stairwells were full of confused students that boxed in the Zone boys.

Jack bolted out the emergency door onto a patio deck with metallic rounded railing. He could see he was on the Columbia Avenue side of the library. He scaled down the side of the building onto the ground and sprinted across the parking lot with his head down. Weaving through parked cars, Jack squatted down and looked back at the library. Students were filing out in all directions covering the entrance. He could see Geoffrey and the big dude bobbing and weaving through the crowd trying to find the right white guy. Jack smiled knowing he had just gotten out of a huge mess.

The squatting position reminded Jack of how much his ankle hurt. He knew he couldn't run back across campus and about four blocks to his apartment on Maxwell Street. He noticed he was near Sorority Row and the Pi Beta Phi house. He had dated a sorority girl, Kelly Greenwell, from that house. *Oh God, I hope she's there. She can give me a lift to my apartment.*

Cautiously, Jack crossed Columbia Avenue. He could now hear police cars arriving on the scene. *Perfect, that'll scare away those black thugs. Nothing like the presence of cops to get people running.* Jack knew the entrance of the sorority house had a coded key pad so he waited for someone to enter or leave. Within a few seconds he recognized a familiar face exit the house. He quickly scrambled over to the door and caught it before it slammed shut. The girl laughed at him and told him Kelly was on the second floor in room 207. Jack thanked her and hobbled up yet another stairwell.

Kelly Greenwell was a cute, perky sorority sister bent on landing a rich husband. She had met Jack at a pledge party and they dated a few times. She was smitten but apparently Jack was not. She hadn't seen him over the summer but was excited to see him now standing at her door.

"Jack! Oh my God, what brings you here?"

"I really need you to drive me to my apartment. My ankle is busted pretty bad and I can't make the long walk."

"Okay…are you okay? What happened to your ankle?"

"It's a really long story and I'll tell you all about it. I promise but we need to hurry."

Kelly grabbed her keys off a desk and threw a long heavy coat on. Jack followed her down the stairs and out the back to the private parking lot. He loaded his throbbing ankle into Kelly's Volvo as she shifted the car into second gear pulling out onto Columbia Avenue.

"Wow, there's a lot people hanging outside the library. Oh man, there are cops everywhere. Are you responsible for any of this?"

Jack nodded yes.

"Are you running from the police?" as she slammed on the brakes at the Rose Street intersection.

"No. It's nothing like that. I'm running from some bad dudes. I had to trip the library alarm to get away… I swear Kelly…I'm not in trouble with the police, but I really need to get to my place now."

Kelly was trying to make sense of all this. There was pandemonium over at the library, cop cars wailing, lights swirling and Jack, a boy she wanted to pursue her, sitting in her car pleading for help.

Looking back into Jack's eyes, she nodded okay, shifted the car into first gear and turned right onto Rose Street. Jack instructed her to circle around to the back of his apartment where his car was parked. As they approached his apartment complex he told Kelly to pull over to the side curb.

He could see two dark figures milling around the complex parking lot. Jack could feel his chest pounding again with the fear that these guys were from the Zone and had him cornered again. After a few painful minutes the two figures lit up a cigarette and walked away down Maxwell Street. Jack could feel relief course through his veins. He reached for the door handle but felt a hand firmly grab his left arm.

Kelly was glaring at him with concern.

"Jack, I don't know what's going on. I'm sure you'll tell me when you're ready. But I just want you to know that you were right to seek me out for help. I'm here for you now and always will be."

"Okay…thanks a lot. Again, I owe you big time. But don't worry. This isn't a big deal. Again, thanks." Jack said flatly trying to get out of the car without being rude.

Jack liked Kelly but she was too eager about starting a serious relationship. He had no intention to be in any kind of relationship in college at least until last night. Thoughts of Candace were flooding his memory. *I can't think of her right now. I'm in huge trouble. Thinking about her will distract me.*

Jack waved goodbye to Kelly and fired up his compact car. His mind was racing trying to figure out his next move. He knew he couldn't stay in Lexington or anywhere near the campus. Apparently, Geoffrey knew his class schedule and maybe where he lived on campus. There was really only one place he could go— home.

He turned his car off Rose Street right onto Euclid Avenue. He knew he would be safe at his parent's house in Nicholasville. He was born and raised in the sleepy rural suburbs south of Lexington. There was no way the Zone would know of it and follow him. He could go home for a few days and figure out his next move. Turning left onto Nicholasville Road gave Jack a sense of relief. He was on a familiar path leading him to the comforts of his surroundings.

<u>Chapter 8</u>

"Home is the place where, when you have to be there, they have to take you in."

−Robert Frost

Nicholasville was a growing, bustling town just 15 miles south of Lexington. The 1980's housing explosion doubled a community of about 12,000 into a residential haven from Lexington's high taxes. A bypass was built to relieve downtown traffic and the main artery into Lexington, Nicholasville Road, was widened to four lanes. Suburbs rapidly spread over rural areas and more businesses re-located to Nicholasville to accommodate the growing needs of its residents. No longer were a few fast food restaurants the only source of dining options. Large sit-down restaurant chains were built along the widened highway and a movie theater opened across from Brannan Road. Nestled in Jessamine County, Nicholasville offered cheap land with quick and easy access to Lexington.

As Jack drove through downtown Nicholasville, he was comforted by the many familiar sites— the courthouse, Hemphill's Pharmacy and the large Baptist church off Main Street that his father pastored. The old church was built in the antebellum and served as a field hospital during the Civil War. Many of its members seemed to be relics of the War Between the States.

Turning right onto Chestnut Road, he could see nothing had changed with his dad's church. Instinctively turning left onto First Street and right again on Broadway, Jack saw the dirt path through some neighbor's yards used by his brothers as a short cut was now paved. Wheeling the car onto Third Street and then turning right onto Greenwood Drive brought a smile to Jack's face. He noticed there were three cars parked at his parent's place. *Oh good, Luke's home. It'll be good to see him.*

The Miller's home was a source of pride to the boys. It was a small two story brick house with a basketball goal attached to the roof of the garage. The front yard was small filled with a large maple tree but the back yard was larger and home to thousands of football games, Olympic events and anything else the eldest brother, Joseph could think of. Though the house belonged to the church as the parsonage, but the boys saw it as their personal playground. The Miller's had filled the home with happy memories for more than twenty years.

Slowly hobbling up the steps of the front porch, Jack opened the door to a familiar smell emanating from the kitchen. His mother, Melinda, was humming a church hymn while stirring a pan of chicken noodle soup. Jack darted through the front hallway to the kitchen and hugged his mother from behind. Startled, Melinda turned to see which of her three sons was hugging her. She instinctively knew it couldn't be Joseph, the eldest, because he was attending the Southern Baptist Theological Seminary School in Louisville. It certainly couldn't be her middle child, Jack, as he rarely visited from college in Lexington. She figured it had to be her youngest, Luke, who was presently living in the basement while attending the Lexington Community College. Melinda's eyes widen in shock to discover that Jack was not only hugging her but had tears in his eyes.

"Well stranger, what brings you to this neck of the woods?" Melinda asked in her "down-home" country expressions that used to bother him in high school but now was welcomed.

"Just missed you and your cooking?"

"Jack... what's wrong?" she added as her tone and expression quickly turned serious. "Are you in trouble... why aren't you in school?"

"Whoa....no mom, I'm not in trouble. I've already had my morning classes and its Friday. I thought I would crash here for the weekend and save some money."

"Honey, its 12:15 and you're already done with your classes? I don't know about college these days. In my day, classes were still going until about 4:00 o'clock."

"Yeah, in your day they had to start later because the horses were temperamental and had trouble making it up all those hills. Not to mention the professors had to fire up the wood stoves and kerosene lamps!" Jack added with a laugh.

"Watch it buster… seriously, you look stressed and your eyes are red. You aren't doing drugs, are you? You aren't high? Is that the right expression?"

"Oh, my God! You are adorable, mom. No, I'm not high and yes that is the right expression. Your little angels don't do drugs. The good reverend made sure to fill our hearts, minds and lungs with the gospel, not weed, crack or blow."

"Weed…blow…crack? I don't understand half the stuff you kids bring home. All I know is that I didn't raise my boys to do the Devil's deeds. Your father and I did the best we could to instill good moral values from the Bible."

"Mom, you and pops did a great job! Except for Luke. He's always been the black sheep. You know, the troubled child."

"What?"

"Oh, come on mom, don't tell me you're blind to Luke's drug operations out of the basement?" Jack teased knowing that Luke had just emerged from the basement stairwell.

"What am I doing in the basement?" Luke inquired with a huge smile.

"Oh, hey Luke…I didn't know you were here," Jack added with a mock expression.

"Whatever!" Luke laughed and then hugged his big brother with the one arm "bro-hug" and pat on the back.

"Seriously mom, my eyes are red because of my allergies. It seems like every time I come down here, my allergies act up. Also, my asthma really kicks in during these changes in season. You know, falling leaves and temperatures," Jack tried to be convincing because he knew his mother was a worrier and the truth would crush her. His mother was the most precious person in his life and he would never do anything to hurt or disappoint her.

64

"Well, I don't how any of us live down here. These crazy, seasonal changes. One minute, its 95 degrees in the shade and the next it's below freezing," Melinda then added one of her favorite expressions, "If you're not happy with the weather, just wait, it'll change soon enough!" Jack and Luke mouthed the last part of that saying as they had heard her say a thousand times. "Well, sit down; I'm just finishing Luke's soup. What can I fix ya?"

"Oh…I'll have a grilled cheese sandwich…if it's not too much trouble?"

"And what if it is?"

"Then I'll have it anyway."

Jack sat in his old chair at the family table. It was amazing how familiar that seat was. He had sat in that chair next to that table for eighteen years.

The family table had been a venerable piece of furniture in the Miller household. Many important events had occurred at this station such as political, religious and educational dialogue always led by their father, the minister. He had taught the boys to be bright, independent thinkers and to defend their beliefs. Melinda mostly wanted them to behave and watch their manners. It was always difficult for the Miller boys to sit still especially around each other.

Joseph constantly antagonized and pushed his younger siblings to fight. Jack and Luke were eager to accommodate. It was near impossible for the boys to sit still long enough to eat and listen to their father's sagacious advice about a current event. The boys were constantly finding new and better ways to fight each other at the table without making any contact. Usually looks were the best assault method.

Now, however, sitting across the table from Luke, Jack felt nothing but admiration for his little brother. The same kid he once loathed, he now felt was a true friend and ally. His mother had always beseeched the boys to get along as one day; they would be all they had. That never made sense to them as children but now as young adults they understood.

Jack and Luke had stopped fighting at the end of middle school and started becoming friends in high school. Looking at Luke, Jack thought he had filled out his 6'2 frame nicely. In fact, all the Miller boys had grown tall and developed their athletic bodies. As children, they were woefully thin. Many in the church thought the boys looked underfed. Melinda despaired that she fed them; they just ran around too much to fill in. This hyperactivity led to very competitive games with the neighborhood kids. In all sports, the Miller boys were a team. No matter if it were baseball, football or basketball, it was the Millers against the neighborhood kids usually from Weil Lane.

Due to the one year age difference, Jack and Luke were sibling rivals. They constantly fought over everything from baseball cards, comic books, GI Joes to whichever sport was in season. Joseph, being the oldest, was the unchallenged leader of the pack and he enjoyed pitting his younger siblings against each other. Jack grew up fighting and beating Luke in everything but Luke was gaining— making the rivalry even more intense. The rivals were so intent on fighting and besting each other that they rarely teamed up against Joseph, their antagonist.

Both craved the attention and approval of their older brother and, more importantly, their father. This competitive atmosphere made them good athletes with a strong desire to win at everything. As they matured in high school, they saw each other less as rivals and more as teammates and friends.

They also began to move in different directions and hang out with their own friends. Though they once lived in the same house and shared a fun childhood with great memories, they were different. Jack had quietly admired Luke's spunk and tenacity. He never seemed to be afraid to fight or defend himself, no matter how difficult the odds were against him. Jack was somewhat timid and cautious. He looked for ways to avoid trouble if he could, whereas Luke seemed to seek it.

After lunch and the usual catching up chit-chat, Luke invited Jack to play some afternoon golf at Dearbourne Country Club. Jack thought it was the perfect cure for his present situation. He desperately needed some normalcy in his life and a diversion from his dire predicament.

Melinda heard her boys making plans and it warmed her heart. All her life as a mother she had pleaded with the boys to get along and now that day had arrived. Her boys were friends and her life mission had been accomplished. Several hymns began playing in her mind as she resumed humming and cleaning up after the boys.

Dearbourne Country Club was a small private course tucked neatly between the city limits of Nicholasville and the rural farms of Jessamine County. The Millers had been members for over twenty years when Matthew moved his young family from Owenton, Kentucky to be pastor at Nicholasville Baptist Church. The club had a large family pool, pair of tennis courts to accent the beautiful well-kept 18-hole golf course.

Jack and Luke began their round with the usual warm-up on the driving range. Luke pulled out his pitching wedge and easily arched a high ball that landed just behind the 100 yard marker. After several more swings with his short irons, Luke began launching 300 yard drives with his oversized driver. The flight of his ball was straight and true. Jack watched in envy as his own ball had a 30 yard slicing loop that helplessly bounded in the rough. No matter what Jack tried, he could never really master his swing as Luke had. The brothers were once competitive in golf scores until Luke found his stroke his junior year in high school and left his family behind. It was tough for Jack to concede anything to his younger brother but the "proof was in the pudding". Luke was simply a better golfer.

As the boys walked over to the first tee box, Jack thought about telling Luke what had happened. After all, he was Jack's brother and certainly a sympathetic ear. *Luke is a scrappy fellow and a good guy to have on your side in a fight or dispute. No doubt. But, he's a reactionary. He flies off the handle and runs head long into trouble with little or no thought of consequence. If he knew what was going on in Lexington, he'd probably want to confront the Zone thugs and get us both killed. No...can't get Luke involved. He would try to resolve this on his own and in his own way. Best not to say anything.*

Luke shoved the tee into the ground, stood erect and with a graceful, easy swing drove his tee shot 300 yards down the middle of the fairway. Jack lined up his feet and hips to the left to allow for his wide fading drive. True to form, Jack hit a soaring high slice that cleared the tree line and raced across the rough into the fairway some forty yards short of Luke's ball.

"You know if you just straighten that out, you'll be up there with the big boys!" Luke teased.

"Hey, I got something you can straighten out! Besides it's no fun hitting the ball straight down the middle with an easy shot to the green. That's boring golf. My way is more challenging…scrambling through the woods and rough for pars and bogeys adds to the golfing experience."

"Ha, ha…whatever. Hey, I had a dream about you last night."

"Wow, that sounds creepy."

"Ha…no, it's nothing like that. It was about something that happened when we were kids at the Fayette Mall. Do you remember when we were about 10 and 11 years old, we were walking in the Mall past Allsports and a group of older black kids were walking straight toward us? They looked like some thugs. They came right at us and pushed me into Allsports. I was scared and they told me I wasn't going anywhere. Man, I thought they were going to kill me. Thankfully the store manager came over and ran them off. Do you remember that? You said, you never saw me get grabbed and walked down to Sears?"

"Yeah, I remember. I didn't realize you were gone until I found dad in Sears. You came up a few minutes later about to cry. I just figured, you wandered off to another store. Yeah, I never knew you were missing." That was a lie and Jack knew it. He was frozen with fear and too terrified to confront the thugs who grabbed his brother.

Jack had always rationalized his inaction to a reasonable fear of bigger, older, tougher thugs and that there was really nothing he could have done to protect Luke. Instead, they would have both been in peril. *But you should have TRIED to help your little brother. After all, hadn't your father preached that message enough when you were growing up…defend and protect each other!* Jack had failed this test early in life by simply walking away and doing nothing just as he had failed Candace and Tater last night. He watched in horror Tater's brutal assault and heard the terrifying screams of Candace. *Oh God, Tater's dead! Tater's dead! Candace liked me…trusted me and I let her down. I should have gone in with her. Maybe with me, she would have been safe from those punks. Who am I kidding, she would have been no safer with me than without and we would have both been dead.* Jack's head dropped with that cold splash of reality and remorse over the death of his friends.

"Hey Jack, what's the matter? You okay… your phone's ringing."

"Oh… yeah", answering his phone, "Hello? Rick, slow down. I can't understand what you're saying."

"Dude, Tater's dead!" Rick screamed into his cell, "Tater's dead! They found his body dumped behind some garbage cans outside of Three Goggles. He had been severely beaten. Cops are crawling all over campus talking to everyone, especially his friends. They're asking about you?"

"Me? Why?"

"Cause you're his friend and roommate! You don't seem too shocked by all of this?"

Jack strapped on his golf bag and moved closer to the woods away from Luke and lowered his voice.

"That's because I saw it. I saw Tater get killed. He came running out of Three Goggles, practically tackling me. He shoved me against the alley trash cans. He thought we were playing 'beer tag'. I hurt my ankle and was rubbing it when this gang of black guys from the Zone jumped him and beat him to death with baseball bats."

"What? Why? Why would anyone want to hurt Tater?"

"I don't know."

"Where are you?"

"Nicholasville."

"Why? It seems like you're not telling me everything. Do you know more than you're telling me?"

"No. I'm down here to clear my head."

"Well, you gotta come back up here and tell the police."

"There's no way I'm coming back to Lexington right now!"

"Why?"

"I'll tell ya later. You're going to have to trust me…I'll tell you what. Call the cops and have them come to my parent's home. I'll talk to them there, but not in Lexington."

"Okay, I call them now. What time do you want them there?"

"About seven…after supper. No squad cars and plain clothes officers. I don't want to scare my mom or cause any messy attention to my father. You know how gossipy Nicholasville is and the pastor of a big church in town doesn't need any scandals at the parsonage."

"Okay. I'll get back with you and let you know what the cops tell me."

The golf outing was ruined. Jack could think of nothing but what happened last night, his escape this morning and now he had to confront the cops. How much should he tell them? He wanted desperately to tell them everything and bust those thugs from the Zone that killed two beautiful lives. But there was a constant, nagging memory of a conversation he had with Tater not long ago about the Zone.

Tater not only warned him about shady figures in the Zone but of a drug lord…*Malcolm X…no Marcus X. This dude, Marcus X, was running all kinds of criminal activities such as drugs, prostitution and gambling near campus. It was known by everyone, including the cops, but no one did anything to stop it because violent crimes were down in the Zone and certain "officials" were "tolerant" because pockets were being filled. I bet that was Marcus X at the apartment complex with blood on his hands and that long knife. The same Marcus X who has cops on his payroll. The same Marcus X who may have those dirty cops helping him find the witness to the deaths last night. Shit, I gotta get a hold of Rick and cancel this meeting tonight.* Jack hit re-dial on his cell, Rick answered.

70

"Rick, did you get a hold of the cops?"

"Yeah, I was just about to call you. They said it was cool and that they would be at your parents around seven and no squad cars. They're sending two detectives. Uh, their names are…hold on, I wrote them down. Oh yeah, here they are: Detective Bob Burris and Detective Jeff Stephens. I actually talked to Detective Burris. He seemed cool. Just wanted to ask you a few questions and promised anonymity. He also promised it wouldn't take long. I told him you were pretty shaken up and worried about possible retribution. He said he would take care of everything and not to worry." *Hell, that's easy for him to say. He's carrying a gun and licensed to kill. Most hoods don't mess with cops because pay back is hell. At least that's what they say in the movies!*

"Okay, Rick. Thanks man. Thanks for everything."

"Hey man, it's going to be alright. Tell the cops everything so they can nail the bastards that killed Tater." *Yeah, I certainly owe it to Tater and Candace to nail these bastards. Maybe I'm just being paranoid. Maybe these cops are legit and will help. God, I hope so!*

❧ ❧ ❧ ❧ ❧ ❧ ❧ ❧

Jack knew he had to come clean to his family and tell them most of the story. After all, there was going to an unmarked squad car arriving tonight at the Miller's. Melinda had cooked Jack's favorite dinner, pork chops and scalloped potatoes in honor of his weekend surprise visit. Melinda would use any trick up her culinary sleeve to get her boys to come home occasionally.

Everyone sat in the usual places around the table with Joseph's seat empty. Matthew blessed the food in prayer and everyone quickly dug in to the sumptuous meal. After a few minutes of casual small talk, Matthew asked pointed questions about the true nature of the visit. Jack sensed that his father knew something wasn't right. He proceeded to tell the family the abridged version of what had happened to Tater at Three Goggles. Without getting into too many details, he simply stated that he witnessed the murder and was too traumatized to think or act. In this same paralyzed state, he went back to his apartment and fell asleep.

When he woke up, he hoped the whole ordeal had just been a bad dream so he went to class. He omitted the morning escape from the Zone thugs because his mother was already ashen with worry. She really couldn't handle any more of the truth and it really wasn't necessary that she know any more.

Melinda kept muttering "Oh dear God" over and over while Matthew kept a steady eye on his troubled son. After he finished the shortened version of last night's events, his father peppered him with pointed questions. Mostly in the nature of "why didn't you report this to the police." Matthew couldn't understand Jack's reluctance even if traumatized; he should have notified the cops. From a cop's perspective, his father continued, it looked as if you were running or hiding from something; as if you knew more and might somehow be involved.

Matthew reasoned that leaving the scene of a crime without reporting it might even be a crime. He wasn't sure. The pastor had always been a tough inquisitor for the boys to face. He was an honest man who pushed his boys to be truthful, moral and just. There was something about Jack's story that seemed to be missing, his father thought. The Southern Baptist minister couldn't put his finger on it but was intrigued and glad that the police was coming to talk.

The grandfather clock in the front parlor rang seven times as Jack nervously pulled back the curtain looking at the driveway. A large white unmarked Crown Victoria pulled in front of their house. The driver was a large, beefy man who upon exiting saw the car lift up several inches. Reaching back into the car he pulled out a dress jacket that seemed too small to cover his torso. It stretched tightly across his back as he pulled it to his large chest and just slipped the coat button into the slit.

Detective Bob Burris was a burly twenty-five year veteran of the Lexington police force whose small narrow set eyes worked perfectly with his abilities to get the truth out of frightened suspects. His crew cut was the last vestige of his ten years as a Marine. He was followed up the walkway by a slender younger man wearing sunglasses as the sun was descending. Detective Jeff Stephens resented his place in the partnership with Burris but what could he do. He was a junior partner with no military background or respect for those senior to him and Burris was easily annoyed by his presence. Det. Stephens enjoyed smacking and popping his gum mostly to annoy his partner. With each popping sound of gum, Burris would glare at Stephens the way a grizzly bear looks at intruders to their territory. Stephens was simply waiting out Burris' retirement which was quickly approaching with each smack and pop of his gum.

Watching the pair walk up to the front door, Jack thought they looked like a modern day Laurel and Hardy duo. Normally this sight would have amused him but he was in big trouble and needed to know if he could trust these two. Melinda greeted the officers at the door who held out their badges for a long perusal. The very sight of these men in her house put Melinda on edge.

Everyone scattered to grab an available seat in the small front parlor of the parsonage. Jack sat with his mother on the couch while Luke found the piano bench and the pastor took his place in the recliner. That left the small loveseat for the dynamic duo. Watching Detective Burris plop down on the love seat after his small partner would have been funny under any other circumstance. The very vision of those two diametrically opposed body types sharing a seat forced Jack to suppress a laugh and instinctively look over at Luke who was also smirking.

No matter what the occasion, the Miller boys could generally find humor and often in the most inappropriate places and times. Funeral homes were never safe from Miller humor as they were often shuffled off with their father to perform several services a year for church members. The graver the event the more difficult it was for the boys to suppress themselves.

Again, Jack covered his face as Detective Burris elbowed Stephens to get up. After a few anxious seconds, the small detective squirmed out of the love seat and stood next to the fireplace trying to rest his elbow on the mantel. Jack's eyes fell on Luke as both found Stephens' attempt to get comfortable humorous.

Once liberated from his partner, Detective Burris quickly got down to business and asked Jack "Why are we here?" The question itself seemed to throw Jack off a bit. He lowered his head trying to figure out how much he should tell these guys. *Don't tell them anymore than what you told your parents. I'm not sure they can be trusted. Tater warned me that there were cops on the take from the Zone and I'm not sure one of them isn't in my house. Alright keep it basic. No need to lie, just don't tell them everything, especially about going into the Zone.*

After a few seconds, Jack rehashed the same story he had just told the family. Detective Burris responded with the same line of questions that Jack had just answered under the glare of his father. Why hadn't he called the police? Did he know the victim? Did he recognize any of the assailants? Could he recall them again in a line-up? Then Detective Stephens' horned in with some personal questions that made Jack uncomfortable, especially in the presence of his parents.

"You ever done any drugs?"

"No. Well...unless you count some alcohol. I've had a few beers." Jack stated nervously trying to avoid eye contact with his parents. The revelation had his mother's mouth open with shock.

"No. I mean street drugs like pot or crack cocaine?"

"Wait. What is this? Why are you asking my son questions like that? He's done nothing wrong. He witnessed a brutal assault on a friend and you're treating him like a criminal." Melinda stated with rising agitation.

"I'm sorry ma'am, but I need to establish if the witness may have had any prior contact with the assailants that could have caused this. Did Tater, I mean Tyler, have any dealings with any criminal figures such as drug dealers?"

Jack was hesitant to narc on his buddy but it seemed the best way to explain why these thugs were running around on campus. He told them that Tater had indeed purchased some pot on occasion in the Zone but had never brought it to their house on Maxwell Street, which was true. It was for a frat party but that wasn't important and Jack wasn't relenting more than he had to.

The two detectives looked at each other and nodded. Burris pulled himself out of the love seat and informed the Millers that they knew Tater had a misdemeanor pot possession and that this was probably a simple drug deal gone badly. Since Jack couldn't identify the assailants or explain why Tater was running or tell them much more than three black dudes in a dark alley with baseball bats, there wasn't much they could do. Burris handed Jack his card with his cell number written on the back and told him to call him if he remembered anything else.

There was a strange vibe in the room as the detectives left as quickly as they had arrived and everyone felt it, except Melinda. She was so relieved that the interview was over. However, Matthew slowly rubbed his chin and stated aloud what his sons were thinking; this interview seemed too quick and casual for a murder. It was as if the "dynamic duo" had already decided what had happened and was simply going through the motions of police protocol. Surely there would be a more thorough investigation and a better attempt at discovering the truth of this tragic event. A young man was murdered and the police didn't seem to be too concerned about working hard at investigating.

These thoughts were nagging Matthew. He also wondered how much of the truth his own son had revealed. Jack's story had too many holes and left too many questions unanswered. But Matthew didn't want to press his son too hard. After all, he had gone through an awful ordeal and came home for comfort, support and possibly protection. Matthew was determined to give him all of the above and more if necessary.

In a state of bewilderment, Jack walked outside to the back porch to try and gather his thoughts as well as shake the paranoia that encompassed him. He couldn't stop thinking about Tater's warning about dirty cops working in the Zone. How much trust could he place in the police especially the two he just met? The older detective seemed honest and sincere but the younger, thinner officer was distant and cold. Too eager to impress but not really concerned about the victim just the background of the witnesses.

Rick called shortly after the cops left to say that many of the students interviewed thought the police were too brief and overly concerned about their drug use and possible criminal activity. It was as if they were trying to silence or intimidate witnesses from pursuing the truth of the murder. At least that was the kids' impressions, Rick allowed.

Again, this information fed Jack's gut instinct that he couldn't trust the police and in fact may need to stay clear of them. Luke slid open the back door to break up Jack's anguish.

"Hey, you still thinking about Tater?"

"Yeah… I just feel like a coward. I didn't do anything to help him. I just sat there like a rock…a fucking scared rock!"

"Whoa… what could you have done? You said there was about four or five big dudes with bats pounding on him. If you had tried to help you'd probably be dead."

"Maybe. I might have been able to scare them off or something. You know, if I started screaming to get a crowd to come around. Anything but what I did would have been better. I was scared. It's just that simple and now Tater is dead because of it."

"Yeah and you could also be dead."

"I know. I think about that as well. I try to rationalize and justify my inaction…I want to…I don't know. Maybe I think too much."

"Well this nothing wrong with thinking. More people should try it. Look, I'm not going try to get in your head or judge you. Just let me know if I can help in anyway. Oh, by the way, there's a field party at Sean Shearer's farm after the football game tonight. It might help get your mind off some this stuff. There'll be some of our friends there from our class. You remember the start of the football season parties at the Shearer's"

Oh yeah, Jack remembered those parties from his days in high school. They were usually rowdy affairs with a mixture of past and present high school kids doing drugs, alcohol and each other. Jack was a sophomore when he attended his first "Shearer's Field" party. Eagerly trying to fit in with the cool crowd, Jack ignored his father's teachings and embraced the fast life of young adulthood. He tried just about everything offered at the party in hopes of looking cool and getting some action with the girls. He wanted desperately to be accepted by the older crowd, especially his brother Joseph.

Joseph was a fine athlete and leader amongst his peers. He had been voted "Mr. Jessamine County" his senior year and Jack idolized him. But Joseph wasn't a party animal and resisted peer pressure. He was secure in his own skin and unafraid of what others thought. In fact most of his peers admired his strength of character and ability to resist the fast life. Jack knew he didn't have that kind of courage. Joseph's faith and conviction were pillars built with material Jack seemed to lack. So, he pursued his own path which led to popularity in his class.

Jack had a great time at these parties and loved telling exaggerated stories about what he did and who he did to his buddies. They fed off his energy and enthusiasm which fueled him to want to do more but he lived in a "glass house" at the parsonage ruled by a firm father determined to "trim his sails". These parties were fun in high school but Jack had avoided them since he began college. He didn't want to be one of those losers that tried to hang on to the high school life while living a depressed existence in Nicholasville.

Once out of high school, he wasn't going to return like many of the previous losers trying to impress new girls and bully young dudes. It was a pathetic thought, the idea of a twenty-two year old "clinger" trying to hook up with fresh, high school "meat". None of that seemed appealing to Jack until Luke mentioned that Bobby Joe Bradley would probably be there.

Bobby Joe's name hit Jack like Edison's "Eureka!" moment with the incandescent light bulb. *Bobby Joe! Yes, he's just the guy that could help me get out of this mess!* Bobby Joe Bradley was a large, hulking figure that cut a 6'7 frame. In high school, he was thin weighing about 195 pounds his senior year, but Luke said he had ballooned up to about 250 and was built like a pro wrestler. Luke marveled at how "ripped" he looked and how he had mellowed since high school.

Jack had nothing but fond memories of Bobby Joe. He was like another big brother after Joseph had left for college. He was a year between Jack and Joseph in school. Their friendship developed through Joseph on the varsity basketball team. Like most underclassmen, Bobby Joe looked up to Joseph as the team leader both on and off the court though they parted on the "off court" activities.

Bobby Joe admired Joseph's discipline and skill on the basketball court but enjoyed the sweet nectar of Jack Daniel's and how it loosened his inhibitions. During Joseph's junior year they began to grow apart as Bobby Joe discovered his fondness for alcohol and field parties. They were compatible on the court but were drifting in different directions. When Joseph graduated, Bobby Joe was the undisputed leader of the team but not the same kind of role model. His fast ways landed him in out of school detentions often until basketball season began. There was no way he would miss any part of basketball season. So, he curbed his temper and weekend activities to stay eligible on the court.

Jack had known Bobby Joe through Joseph but only on the periphery. His first real encounter occurred during try-outs his sophomore year. Jessamine County hadn't converted to the middle school model yet so freshmen resided in the junior high. Freshmen rarely played up on the high school teams so Jack's sophomore year he tried out for the varsity. He was nervous being at the high school and trying to make his brother's team as a sophomore. He knew he was a good player and would make the junior varsity but he wanted to play with his brother for his last year. He had a great freshman year leading the team in scoring and to a 15-2 record. But that confidence would be tested at the next level.

He had played against many of the upper classmen before in pick-up games and fared well. He reminded himself often that he belonged on this court and could play at this level. This steely confidence and determination got him in trouble quickly with the varsity players who had heard in the locker room, Jack's boast that he would make the varsity. Bobby Joe was one of those upperclassmen determined to make sure that didn't happen.

During lay-up drills, Jack showed off his leaping ability by putting his hand over the rim and dropping the ball through the net. It wasn't a dunk but real close for a sophomore. Everyone knew it was just a matter of time before Jack was throwing down dunks. The varsity head coach, Jay Stevens, was not amused or thrilled by Jack's "showboating" ways. Coach Stevens barked at the young sophomore "Hey Hollywood, try using the backboard!" Instantly the name stuck with Jack who loved it but knew that the coach didn't mean it as a compliment.

Earlier before try-outs began, Jack had attached some adhesive stars to his high-top sneakers and wore a wrist band on his left arm. Coach Stevens was old school and had no tolerance for "showboating" on his team. During the first varsity scrimmage, Coach Stevens wanted to see how "Hollywood" would handle tough upper classmen competition. He really wanted to see Jack get the cocky arrogance knocked out of him.

Jack dribbled down court, ran off a high screen and nailed a jump shot leaving his shooting hand in the air. Bobby Joe didn't like the gesture and knocked him to the floor running back down the court. Jack let it go but was elbowed in the neck trying to rebound an offensive shot. Bobby Joe was sending a strong message that this would not be tolerated. Running back down the court Jack took a violent elbow to the nose trying to get through a screen Bobby Joe had set. Jack instantly shoved Bobby Joe and swung wildly at his head. Bobby Joe ducked the punch, grabbed Jack by the neck and pinned up against the padded back wall. Joseph ran over to stop Bobby Joe but Coach Stevens restrained him and told him that his little brother needed to learn a tough lesson about varsity basketball. Joseph reluctantly agreed. Jack was cussing mad, screaming at Bobby Joe to let him go. In that moment Bobby Joe tightened his grip and quietly announced that this was "big boy ball, junior. You better get used to the rough play." Jack was kept off the varsity but played well on the junior varsity. He made the varsity the following year but at a high cost. The event would be known in the high school annals his junior year as the "Michael Westbrook affair".

Michael Westbrook was a tough, hard-nosed black kid a year older than Jack. He had been kicked off the varsity the year before for breaking a kid's nose in a game against rival Woodford County. It was a brutal assault as Michael shoved the kid against the wall and proceeded to go all "Mike Tyson" on him. No one knew what caused the fight.

Michael never said but was kicked off the team.

The following year, he promised Coach Stevens he had changed and wanted to be on the team for his senior year. The only obstacle to that goal was a young, hot shot junior with a silky smooth jump shot and a forty inch vertical set to replace him. Jack was excited about making the team. In fact, he was projected to start as the point guard. Michael got cut. The morning after try-outs, many of the players were shooting ball in the gym when Michael ran up to Jack and shoved him against the wall. Jack thought Michael was playing until he looked into his eyes and saw intense anger and hatred.

"What are you doing?" Jack stated in shock.

"I'm going to kick your ass!"

"Wait...why?"

"I saw you flip off my mother last night when you dropped Derrick off from try-outs!"

"What!? I did not. I would never do that!"

The first period bell rang but many kids had formed the "fight circle" hoping to see Michael in action. However, the assistant principal, Mr. O'Connor, quickly broke through the circle and yelled at everyone to get to class. As a former wrestling coach with a huge voice to match his gut, no one challenged his authority and scampered off to class. Michael whispered to Jack, "This aint over!"

Throughout the morning, Jack was paralyzed with fear over the highly anticipated fight. During class changes students followed him around hoping for a good view of the assault. Many kids even gave him updates about what Michael was saying in other classes and his whereabouts. Jack had been in thousands of fights with his brothers and many scrapes with the neighborhood kids but nothing like what was building up in school. The latest update informed Jack that Michael intended to beat him up at lunch.

All during fourth period, Jack prayed and tried to think of what to do. He knew he had not done anything like what Michael was telling everyone and, like many kids, thought the whole affair was over being cut from the basketball team. As right as that sounded, it didn't change the fact that Michael was going to kill him.

Though Jack was about five inches taller, Michael was mean and had beaten the stuffing out of many kids. He was fast and fought with a raging fury. Jack was neither mad nor experienced in real fights at school. On the court Jack played aggressively with a tough fearlessness and didn't mind the occasional fight. But now he was scared. He hadn't done anything wrong and Michael was lying to cover what was really eating at him— he had been cut from the team and blamed Jack. Though most of the students were on Jack's side, none of them wanted to intervene. Most kids were simply afraid of Michael.

Jack had to figure a way out of this huge mess. He thought about getting checked-out of school before lunch but knew how bad that would look amongst his peers. It would be better to get beaten up than to be a coward and run away from a fight. No, Jack had to go to lunch and hope for a miracle. That miracle arrived in the lunch room in a 6'7 frame. Bobby Joe plopped down next to Jack on the far end of the lunch room. He usually ate at the Grill next door reserved for seniors but today was different.

"What's up, Hollywood?"

"Ah, not much. What are you doin here?"

"Just looking out for my point guard. I hear Westbrook's after you?" Jack quietly nodded with his head down. Bobby Joe continued wrapping his right arm around Jack, "Don't worry, man! Michael's not goin touch you. I'll see to that. You're my boy!"

"Ah man...thanks, I can't tell you how much I appreciate that. He wants to fight me but I didn't do anything. He thinks I flipped off his mom or something. Total bullcrap."

"I know. He's really just pissed that you're on the team. He thinks he's better than you, but everyone with any idea about b-ball, knows you're way better. Man, we've got a chance to get to the regionals this year and Michael's not goin hurt my point guard. Dude, you're my boy!"

"Thanks, man. I just don't want to get in trouble with a fight. It's not that I'm afraid. I just don't want to get in trouble at school….and…you know, possibly get kicked off the team or suspended for a few games."

"Look, Hollywood no one thinks you're afraid….at least not any of the ball players. We've seen you in action. Hell, you even tried to fight me!" Bobby Joe added laughing.

"Yeah, I know. Damn you pissed me off. Anyway, thanks man for having my back!"

Michael Westbrook stormed into the lunch room like a man determined to kill someone. He was flanked by about a dozen of his friends and posse. A large crowd quickly formed behind him and swirled towards Jack's table. Michael grabbed Jack's shoulder saying, "Let's go talk outside!" Bobby Joe instinctively slapped Michael's hand away and then stood up. The sight of Bobby Joe towering over Michael was devastating to Westbrook's cause. You could see much of the fight in Michael drain away as did his posse.

"You aint goin anywhere with Jack and don't ever touch him again or I'll beat your ass!"

Michael stared long and hard at Bobby Joe. It probably lasted about 10 seconds but seemed like an eternity. You could see that Michael was trying to assess his chances in a fight with Bobby Joe. He knew the size difference was something he could overcome, but he also knew Bobby Joe was a fighter and wasn't afraid. Michael intimidated most kids at the school because he put out a "tough man" vibe that had been in a few fights but so had Bobby Joe.

In fact, he saw Bobby Joe split a kid's nose open and then proceed to pound the kid's head on the floor. No doubt Bobby Joe was just as ferocious as he was. Ultimately, Michael determined that the size was a too great an obstacle to overcome and he didn't want to get his ass kicked in school. So, he back peddled a bit telling Jack "This shit aint over!"

"Hell yeah, it's over! Don't forget what I told! You touch Miller, you're dead!"

Michael turned his back and walked off, occasionally looking back like he would return. But it was part of his bluff. He was trying desperately trying to save face. He had been stared down by a much bigger dude and realistically no one blamed him. But most thought Michael would get Jack one day because he said he would and few doubted him. Jack felt a huge sense of relief and satisfaction. He had survived the "Michael Westbrook affair" and now had a body guard on the varsity.

The protection and genuine affection of Bobby Joe caught him off guard. He really didn't expect a guy he swung at last year to stand up for him. But now they were teammates and needed each other to successfully achieve their goals of getting to the regionals. The team played well all year and made it to the regionals before losing a heartbreaker in overtime to a talented Lexington Catholic team.

Bobby Joe and Jack became good friends who partied hard together bonding over the usual adolescent activities of drinking, smoking and womanizing. They lost touch with each other the following year when Bobby Joe received a basketball scholarship at St. Catharine's Junior College. Jack had heard that Bobby Joe didn't last long at St. Catharine's due to a fight with the head coach. He was subsequently kicked off the team and lost his scholarship. It was rumored that he was running around with a rough crowd and doing hard drugs. Jack never saw or heard from him after his own graduation or even when he started attending UK. As far as Jack was concerned, his high school days were over and rarely ventured into Jessamine County. Only his mom's cooking or the occasionally laundry run brought him home. Now he was in serious trouble and needed help again.

Luke's mention of Bobby Joe's name was a godsend. Reminiscing about his playing days with Bobby Joe brought a smile to Jack's face and planted a seed in his head. *Man, Bobby Joe would be the perfect guy to help me. He's huge and afraid of nothing.* Turning back to Luke, Jack asked "What time are planning on going to Shearer's farm?"

"Oh, probably about ten or ten-thirty. Are you coming? Do you need to borrow some clothes?"

"Yeah, I think I'll see what's happening. You think Bobby Joe will be there tonight?"

"You never know. He's been there a few times that I've been there and every time he asks about you."

"Really?"

"Yeah…I know what you're thinking. You think…"

"You don't know shit! By the way, is that a legit offer on your clothes?"

"Yeah..."

Jack didn't like what Luke was digging at although he was right. Luke was no dummy and knew Jack well. He sensed Jack's apprehension and probably figured he would turn to Bobby Joe. Jack didn't like that his little brother suspected he was afraid and needed help. But he was surprised that Luke offered him clothes. What a difference a few years make. Grabbing each other's clothes was usually what started many fights at the Miller house. *I guess a few years away from each other have made us less competitive and more mature* Jack thought.

The boys headed downstairs to the basement to rest and relax for a few hours before the big field party. Flipping through the channels, Jack landed on one of his favorite Clint Eastwood western's *High Plains Drifter.* Laying on the couch and resting for the first time all day, Jack's body felt dead and heavy though his mind was racing trying to make sense of the past thirty hours.

He had witnessed the disappearance and probable murder of Candace and the horrific beating of his best friend, Tater. He seemed to be running all over Lexington the past two days and though it felt good to lay down, his mind was pushing his thoughts to a singular truth that he wanted to suppress: he ran from every dangerous occurrence. *Why? What the hell is wrong with me? Why didn't I act or try to do something?*

Jack could hear one of the more memorable quotes from the movie when Clint Eastwood's character said, "It's what people know about themselves inside that makes them afraid." That statement haunted him because it rang true. On the outside, he looked like a great athlete built to be a hero. *Damn it, I'm strong. There's no way I'm a coward. Cowards are nerdy types with thick glasses, pocket protectors and a fascination with mathematical equations.* Jack had built up his physique and starred in many athletic contests. On the basketball court, he was admired not just for his hoops' skills but his fearless, daring play. He stood up to and challenged many bigger and stronger players on the court. In fact, he was praised in the local newspapers as "gutsy" and "courageous" for playing through pain and injuries. But again, that was a controlled environment. There were always adults or officials who would step in to intervene if things got out of control. On the streets of the real world, he faced many challenges and failed miserably.

He was raised in a culture that worshipped and idolized heroes. Good guys who faced difficult obstacles, scary situations but in the end, they always overcame and acted courageously. The ordinary guy doing extraordinary things was a common theme in many western movies. Even the Bible paid homage to courageous acts such as Stephen, the first Christian martyr, who refused to denounce his faith and was stoned to death. Likewise, the early disciples and Paul were brutally murdered for their moral fortitude.

Jack was raised a Christian in a Baptist home. He feared God's judgment. *Would God deny me heaven for cowardice? Was this life just a test and you had to prove yourself worthy of heaven?* These difficult questions kept Jack's brain occupied and eyes wide open. *Am I a coward? Am I a yellow, spineless, gutless... worthless human being?* Tears formed in his eyes and he could feel his heart beat rapidly, increased with each indicting question. To be viewed as a coward by society was one of the worst things that could happen to a man. Women were not expected to be brave or strong. If they cried or ran from a dangerous situation, it was considered understandable. After all society taught boys to be rough with each other but gentle to girls. Boys were raised under the notion that women were the weaker sex and needed a man's protection. *Damn it, didn't Candace ask you to walk with her to the Zone and didn't you freeze with fear when you heard her scream? Didn't you run away from her when she needed you the most? Didn't you watch Tater get beaten to death while you cowered behind a row of trash cans? Oh God... I'm a coward!"* Jack concluded with tears running down his face.

After a few minutes of self-pity, Jack wondered if a man could change his stripes or in this case, his color? Could he steel his nerves and become the man society respected and revered? Could he redeem himself? As these questions lingered, Jack hoped he would be given a chance at redemption. That chance would occur later that night.

The hum of the television playing a western usually enjoyed by the boys was broken by the creaking sound of the stairs. Matthew entered the somber room seeking more answers and trying to comfort an ailing son.

"Hey dad."

"Hey Jack, listen...I know there's more to this story than you're telling. I'm not going to press you to tell more. I just want you to know that I'm here for you anytime and more importantly the Lord is with you."

Luke immediately turned his back to the conversation and seemed more interested in the western. Jack noticed the move and sensed an uneasy tension between his father and brother. *I wonder what that's all about? Oh well, I can't deal with that right now.*

"Dad, I don't...I don't know about God." Jack said hesitantly hoping not to offend the minister.

"What do you mean?"

"I just...I just don't know if I believe in God anymore. I'm sorry Dad. I've just seen and experienced some things since I've been away at college that its hard sometimes to fathom the concept of an omnipresent being."

Luke's head tilted slightly toward the conversation with a renewed interest in a similar scene that had played a few weeks ago.

"That's okay son. Its perfectly natural for a young person going off to college to experience things and ways of living that might challenge their own beliefs, morals and values. God created humans in His own image and granted them special gifts above all of his other creations. The ability to think and reason is among his greatest gifts to mankind. As an intelligent being with a keen curiosity, its natural to question all orthodoxies, especially those you can't see, hear or touch. The seemingly invisible hand and presence of our Creator baffles and mystifies the intellectual man. He can't wrap his mind around God, explain God, can't prove God, so he concludes that God doesn't exist. But just because the intellectual says it, doesn't mean it's true. Man doesn't know everything nor will he ever. Be careful son, of those who think they know all the answers. They are the intellectual lazy because they've stopped thinking, they've lost the curiosity. They've only concluded which ends further thought. Their curiosity is resolved in a rigid dogma and adherence of scientific proof. God's presence is everywhere, yet the intellectual is blind to it. He lacks the curiosity to seek Him and the faith to find Him."

"Dad, I guess. I mean, that sounds reasonable but I guess it would help if I saw some proof occasionally."

"Son, it's the weak of faith that constantly needs proof of God's existence. Look around you, at life. The beauty of the Earth and its multitude of creatures. You honestly think this incredible planet was a mere accident of a series of cosmic collisions that resulted in a life force with no master plan or blueprint. Just haphazardly, beings and species grew and evolved over time functioning chaotically until one species rose up bringing order to the world. Now that story requires more leaps of faith and is abundantly deficit in intellectual reasoning. Most Christians see the intelligence of evolution but we credit our Creator as the engineer and master craftsman. He is the master of our world and like an earthly father, concerned for all His creations. The intellectual has turned away from God and sought to do things his way. This is a dark, cold path. For those who strike a path away from God are truly empty and void of real love."

The reverend noticed he had lost his audience as Jack lowered his head in deference and simply nodded his head obediently. Jack had never challenged his father's authority or his beliefs and he had no intention of doing so now, especially in his house.

"Look, I'm sorry. I didn't mean to preach. Other than your questions about God, what else is bothering you? Are you afraid or worried about what you saw last night?"

There was a long silence as Jack again didn't know just what to say or how much he should divulge about what really happened and what kind of danger he was in. He lowered his head staring blankly at the television. He could feel his father hovering over him. Luke decided it was time to intervene.

"He's afraid he's a coward."

"What? Is that true son?"

"Well what would you call it when you witness your friend getting beaten to death and you just cower in the corner hoping you're not next?"

"I call it a human reaction to a very frightening event. Do you honestly think your intervention would have resulted in anything other than your own death?"

"No." Jack replied with head still lowered.

"I can only imagine how much pain you must be in over the death of your good friend, Tater, but you can't beat yourself up about this."

"I know dad...its just..." Jack could feel the emotion of the past 24 hours welling up inside like hot lava in a volcano just waiting to explode in an emotional breakdown. But he had been raised to suppress those emotions and waited for it to pass. "Dad...my Psych. Professor said something like 'Cowards are selfish, immature and incapable of love.' Do you think that's true?"

"It sounds reasonable...but I'm not sure how it applies here. Do you think you are incapable of love? I mean, sure all kids are immature and selfish to some extent but over time and through proper guidance they learn to see the value of others and develop true feelings of love.

Jack, you're a good person with a kind heart and soul. I should know. I've watched you your whole life. You and your brothers have developed into fine young men. It hasn't always been easy and some of you still struggle with the ways of your parents and your upbringing, not unlike those who fight God and resist Him from time to time," the reverend pointedly glared at Luke over that last statement. "But like your parents, He will never give up on you. Seek His guidance and you'll feel His presence."

"Okay dad…thanks. I'll pray about it but right now I'd like to rest a while."

"Sure thing son. I'll leave you guys alone." The reverend said solemnly and left the room.

Jack sat quietly trying to absorb everything his father had said but still struggled to reconcile that dilemma of cowardice and the inability to love. *I get that part about immaturity and selfishness. Lord knows those two apply to me, but does that necessarily make me a coward. Hell, if maturity and selfishness were the ingredients of cowardice wouldn't everyone under thirty be yellow? The love thing. I'm not incapable of love, am I? I love my parents and brothers but I have never really loved another outside of my family. I wonder if that's part of it.* These thoughts rattled around in Jack's head for a few minutes before he laid back down again. He could feel his body getting heavy as he drifted to sleep.

Jack's confusion was understandable when viewed as an adolescent who was incapable of love beyond one's self. The ability to cherish another is the result of growth and maturity. To sense the needs of others and seek to protect them even at the expense of your own liberty and life is an emotional and cognitive development stage few reach in early adulthood. Jack found himself in a transitional phase of emotional development and could only move forward through the recognition that he was still in the adolescent stage. Once he saw himself as a child living in an adult body and world, only then would he succeed in transitioning to maturity and adulthood.

For twenty-two years, Jack has really only cared about one person—himself. He wanted others to see him as he saw himself; a strong, intelligent and successful leader.

All his life he was consumed with building the image of a hero with a shiny exterior. However, the golden statute he spent his entire life crafting was gilded and void of solid interior material such as character and values. Though he had been raised in the church and was well versed in the Bible, it really held no meaning for him. It was a good book filled with great stories but the meaning of those stories was lost on him. The precepts and moral values of the Bible and the teachings of his father and the guidance from his mother seemed more like societal rules than core beliefs that you fought to defend. These were foreign ideas to a child who saw heroes of the Bible as those easily recognized by their physicality not their emotional and spiritually developed core.

As a child, he mouthed the words of prayer without understanding the need for spiritual development. One cannot be a truly spiritual person without the development of this sensitivity to the needs of others. That's why the statement: Cowards are selfish, immature and incapable of love; would confound him. Until he faced his own shortcomings in the capacity to love others above himself, he would never know courage.

<u>Chapter 9</u>

"Hatred is the coward's revenge for being intimidated."

—George Bernard Shaw

Luke gently tugged at Jack's shoulder a few times before he saw his eyes open. He couldn't believe how quickly and deeply Jack had fallen asleep.

"Hey man, it's eleven o'clock. You ready to go? Still feel up to going to Shearer's?"

"Yeah…yeah. I'm ready." Jack rubbed his eyes hoping Luke hadn't noticed any tears or redness in his eyes. The last thing he wanted was his little brother thinking he was timid or afraid. Jack's whole life as big brother to Luke was based on the perception of strength and courage.

As children, they had fought often and always with Jack winning. Even when Joseph intervened and held Jack down, he found the strength to get at Luke. There was no way he would allow Luke to ever think he could beat him in fights, sports, games or anything. The competition between the two was great mostly because the age difference was so close at just one year. Throughout their childhood, Jack watched with grudging admiration how Luke seemed fearless, especially in neighborhood fights. Even though he was usually smaller and younger than his opponent, it didn't seem to matter. Luke had an inner strength of courage to attack those he felt had wronged him. Often the older brothers had joined in the fight to save their little brother, but Luke didn't seem to want their assistance. He reminded them that it was his fight and that didn't need their help. Jack wondered again, *where does Luke's courage come from? Why don't I seem to have it?*

Jack grabbed his car keys as he and Luke left from the basement back door to avoid their parents. They knew there would be an argument with them over the late night activities especially after what had transpired the previous night. Getting behind the wheel of his car, Jack prayed that Bobby Joe would be at the field party.

The drive to Sean Shearer's farm took about fifteen minutes from the Miller house in Nicholasville. The farm lay just on the outskirts of town about eight miles due west toward Woodford County. Sean Shearer had been a local legendary football player about twenty years ago at Jessamine County High School. During his reign in school, his parents held bonfires out on the back fifty of a two hundred acre farm. It was a quasi-school event that was just for the students. No parents, faculty or administration were allowed. It was organized and run by the senior class with the cooperation of Sean's parents, David and Martha, who parked at the entrance to the field and checked for alcohol or any other drugs. They were determined to have a good clean party especially since David was a deacon at First Baptist Church of Nicholasville. School pride and spirit filled the air with the roar of the fire, cheers, chants and the fight song. Sean's parents patrolled the field just outside the clearing perimeter with their lights on as a reminder of their presence. The party began just as it got dark and lasted until midnight when David flashed his headlights and ran a hose to put out the bonfire. All who attended thought it was the best way to kick off the football season and passed the tradition and torch on to each new senior class for the next ten years.

The trek to Shearer's field became a tradition and rite of passage. Many kids looked forward to high school just so they could attend this storied event. The Shearer's enjoyed playing host to such a prestigious affair as each year the party got bigger and the tales about what happened got crazier. However, tragedy struck when Sean was killed by a drunk driver. Devastated by the death of their son, the Shearer's tried to continue the annual affair but their heart wasn't in it and they stopped hosting the event. That year David died from a stroke and Martha shut herself off from the world. The tradition was too important to die out and each year the students returned both past and present with the party becoming more raucous without any supervision.

On the drive to Shearer's field, Luke assured Jack that the older guys usually didn't mingle with the high school kids and that it was more like an informal reunion. Jack turned onto the old familiar road and could see the night sky lit up beyond a tree line behind the Shearer farmhouse. Driving slowly on a worn dirt path marked by tire tracks that weaved through the woods and opened up to a clearing near a well-stocked pond, Jack was amazed at how many cars filled the uncut field. The spectacle reminded Jack of a tailgate party for UK football games.

After parking near the wooded entrance, Jack and Luke made their way towards the huge bonfire. Weaving through cars, Jack could see several groups of kids scattered throughout the open field with various drinks in their hands. He could hear girls giggling and lots of chattering about the football game that Jessamine County had won. It seemed everyone was in a festive spirit. Though Jack had graduated just three years ago, he felt old around these kids.

Arriving at the bonfire, Jack noticed an arc of about ten pick-up trucks loaded with kegs of beer and an assortment of hard liquor bottles. Many older kids were sitting in the back of the trucks sucking down beers and tossing the empties at high school kids. Their dark faces were lit from the red glow of a cigarette of tobacco or marijuana which was prevalent in the air.

Jack instantly recognized some familiar faces from his class and struck up the cursory "what have you been up to" conversation. Many of the "kids" from his class had already put on weight in the wrong areas. They seemed amazed at how fit Jack looked. Several made excuses for their extra pounds with the old "I just don't have time to work out" refrain. *Yeah but you have plenty of time to drink beer and smoke weed,* Jack thought. Jack enjoyed the attention he was receiving from former classmates as well as the young high school hotties that had been checking him out since he arrived wearing Luke's tight-fitting t-shirt and jeans. Pouring a Bud Light from one of the truck bed kegs, Jack felt a pair of warm, soft hands cover his eyes. The familiar voice whispered, "Guess who?"

"I have no idea. No, wait… Heather Marie Mills. Wow, long time no see, stranger!"

"Yeah, I thought you said you would never come to these things again after you graduated?"

"I thought you said you would never come to these things, ever. Remember, you're a good girl and this is a bad place. I seem to

Tim F. Miller

remember you telling me that once before."

"Well I'm not always a good girl and this doesn't have to be a bad place."

The two began walking towards the west bank of the pond behind the bonfire. Heather was leading Jack to a more secluded area where they could talk in private.

"I'm really glad you came here tonight. I had a hunch you might. I wanted to see if you were alright. I mean, this morning was kinda crazy. You come running into the library, hiding under my desk from some black dudes. The place goes crazy after the alarm was set off and then I hear that your friend Tater was killed last night. What's going on? What are you involved in? Is it connected with Tater's death?"

"Heather...it's complicated. I don't know if I should tell you anything and get you involved. It's really best if you don't know anything."

"Jack, we've known each other a long time and been through a lot. You can tell me anything." After a long pause she added, "Are you in trouble?"

Jack was staring deeply into Heather's eyes. She looked genuinely concerned about him and really good. Heather was still as beautiful as ever with long, wavy blonde hair. Her big blue eyes and round full lips created a face you wanted to look at for the rest of your life, especially in the morning, and her body was even better with long, athletic legs attached to a cute, upside down heart-shaped butt. She had been a cheerleader all through high school and was still in great shape. *Why didn't I pursue her in high school,* Jack thought before remembering her policy of dating only upperclassmen because they were more mature but that was then and now she seemed interested in him.

"Yes. I'm trouble."

"With the law?"

"No, worse...some thugs from the Zone."

"The Zone? Why would you have any trouble with them? You don't do drugs or hang out with people like that? I don't understand…what did you do?"

"I witnessed a murder. Possibly two. Heather, I saw those thugs from the library, beat Tater to death."

"What? Where did you see it?"

"At Three Goggles, behind some trash cans."

"Why would they want to kill Tater? Was Tater mixed up in drugs and part of a deal gone bad? That's what many on campus were saying this afternoon."

Jack turned his head away from Heather because he couldn't look her in the eyes for what he was about to tell her. It felt good talking to her about this crisis. He needed desperately to unload on someone and Heather was an old friend.

"No, Tater wasn't killed because of drugs or anything like that. It was an accident. He was in the wrong place at the wrong time. Those thugs thought he was me. They were chasing me because I heard a girl scream from some apartment complex in the Zone and then some black dude with blood on his hands ordered this huge black beast and some smaller, fast thugs to find me. I ran and he sent his dogs after me. I ran back to town and to Three Goggles hoping to blend in and lose them. Tater saw me and, probably wasted, thought we were playing 'beer tag'. He knocked me over into a row of trash cans. He just happened to be wearing a blue hoodie like me and the thugs caught up to him and beat him to death."

"Oh my God! That must have been horrifying. You poor thing." Heather caressed his face and gently stroked his cheek. Jack turned away ashamed.

"Yes, it was awful. I can still see his face and his eyes are haunting me. Staring at me. Pleading with me to do something. I did nothing to stop it!"

"But what could you have done? How many were there?"

"It was hard to tell in the dark but about three or four, I guess."

"There's no way you could have stop them. Listen to me; you seem to be beating yourself up over this. Do you honestly think you could have stopped them?"

"No…I don't know…maybe. I should have tried to do something. I just felt like a…"

Suddenly Jack felt a beer can land upside his head followed by an old familiar laugh. Turning quickly and with his hands balled into a fist ready to attack, he was grabbed from behind and lifted into the air paralyzed by the vise-grip like force. The laughter got louder as the powerful arms released him. Turning to face his assailant, Jack was relieved to see his old teammate and defender, Bobby Joe Bradley. *Oh thank God. Man, am I glad to you. Damn the dudes gotten huge with even bigger arms. Dude does looks like a pro wrestler!*

"Oh, my God! Bobby Joe, what the hell have you been up to?" Jack yelled enthusiastically.

"A little of this and a lot of that!" Bobby Joe smirked and then looked over at Heather. "I see you've picked up where you left off in school. Damn, Heather you still look fine!"

"Hey, Bobby Joe." Heather said flatly and slightly annoyed by the intrusion, "Jack, I'm going to get a drink but our conversation isn't over!" She turned and walked back towards the bonfire upset over Bobby Joe's appearance and interruption. She felt like she was finally making progress with Jack and getting him to open up to her, to trust her. She would have to wait yet again.

"Well, I guess some things never change. Looks like Heather still hates me."

"Oh, no. I don't think so. She was just telling me some personal stuff when you came up. That's all. Man, you look great. What are you doing?"

"Man, I'm just a squirrel looking to gather some nuts!" Bobby laughed then added, "Seriously, I own my own business. It's called Five Star Towing. We tow everything in the metro area. But the real money is in repo's."

"Repo's?"

"Repossessions. Folks who get behind in their payments on cars, trucks, boats or other luxury items must deal with their lien holder, you know, the guys who gave them their loan. If an agreement for payment isn't made, the lien holder calls me to repo or get the item back. Depending on the value of the repo item, you can get paid pretty well. Last week I made $2,000 on a Corvette repo."

"Sounds great, but what do the owners or loan borrowers think of you taking their cars or property?"

"That's just it. They don't own the car. They're often in over their head trying to buy a slice of the 'American Dream' or own 'toys' they can't afford to play with. My job is to simply take it back to the rightful, legal owner, the lien holder."

"Do you ever run into trouble on these repo's. I mean I can't imagine, folks handing over the keys to some of these 'toys'?"

"Ha, ha...oh yeah. It can get pretty dicey sometimes, but I bring some of the boys with me to get the job done. Speaking of the devils, you remember Conrad and Robbie, don't you?"

Just then two figures emerged from the woods carrying a six-pack of Bud Light and a long flashlight. It was Conrad Black and Robbie Harkness, two clowns from Jack's high school days. They were a year older than Jack and started hanging out with Bobby Joe after his senior year of basketball. In fact, they were the real reason Jack and Bobby Joe's friendship waned as they were part of a rougher, cruder crowd that fished, hunted, drank and dabbled in drugs. Showing up too often to football practice high was what got the two kicked off the team their senior year. Their bitterness at all things school related started to have an effect on Bobby Joe as he missed more school in the spring to hang out with his new crowd, the Bass, as they were called.

The Bass were in and out of trouble with both school and law enforcement officials. They were growing marijuana under the home side football bleachers. The Jessamine County Sheriff's Department got wind of the pot production, set up a night sting operation and busted the Bass. Jack wasn't even sure if Conrad and Robbie finished school and graduated.

Conrad, a short, stocky quick-tempered red-head, strolled out of the woods like a man on a mission. He hadn't changed a bit, Jack observed. *Still cocky and full of shit. Looks like he's put on a few pounds. Like he's hit the gym and pumped some iron. Great, now he's added some strength to his bullshit! He still looks like a face wanting to get punched and his eyes are as red as his hair. Still hitting that 'peace pipe' eh Connie!* Jack enjoyed calling Conrad that name as a feminine insult.

They had a history going back to elementary school. Following Conrad and awkwardly plodding into the conversation was his butt-buddy Robbie. Cursed with bad acne in high school on a pale face and long thin body, Robbie's raven black hair set him apart from most. Yet somehow, he seemed to score with the ladies because he looked so much like Ric Ocasek, lead singer of the Cars. He dressed like a rocker and yet hung out with the Bass. It was an odd coupling but a coupling none the less.

"Oh yeah. I remember you guys. What's up?" Jack gave the obligatory hand shake and bro hug.

"Damn, Miller...you look good. I see you filled out a bit. You're not the skinny little prick from high school." *Ah yes, the double-edged compliment. I remember again why I hated the little punk always looking for a fight. Don't fall for his shit Jack. Remember he's a good friend, for whatever reason, with Bobby Joe and you may need his help.*

"Yeah, I been hitting the gym and the weight room a bit and..."

"Ha, ha! I remember when you were scared shitless when Michael came to kick your ass! Bobby Joe sure saved your ass that time, didn't he?"

Jack didn't answer. He just stared intently at Robbie trying to figure out his next move when Bobby Joe jumped into fray.

"Damn, Robbie that was a long time ago and by the look of things, Jack looks like he can take care of himself now."

Boy, if you only knew how right I wish you were Jack thought as he continued to stare at Ric Ocasek's body double. *Damn, I would love more than ever to walk over there and punch a hole in that stupid acne-scarred face* Jack thought but again tried to play it cool with Bobby Joe's posse.

"Yeah right…anyway there was a call over the dispatch from a lien holder about a 2009 black limo. The lien holder said the borrower was in Lexington at the Continental dropping off a client and that now would be a good time to lift it."

"Damn, that limo will pay well. Hey Jack, looking for a little action tonight and a bit of a pay off?"

Jack's instinct was to balk at this "action" as it seemed neither fun nor profitable but he needed Bobby Joe's help for much more pressing and dangerous matters.

"Hell yeah, sounds like fun!"

"Fun? Hey pretty boy, these things can get rough. Many of these repos are violent. Guys pull guns, knives… hell, all kinds of shit can happen. Dudes don't like their toys being snatched from them," Conrad smirked.

"Yeah, I'm not sure it's a good idea taking him…" Robbie inserted.

"Fuck you two! In case you haven't noticed, I'm not that skinny guy from high school. I can handle myself!" Jack shouted trying to convince everyone around, including himself.

"Then it's settled. Conrad, you and Robbie take the wrecker. Jack will ride spotter with me."

There was a long stare off between Jack and Conrad. Both men seemed to be measuring the mettle and grit of the other. Jack could feel his heart pounding faster, pumping more blood and adrenaline through his body. He almost welcomed the opportunity to test his strength against an old schoolyard foe. Conrad could sense Jack's eagerness to pursue the fight and was not confident of the outcome, so he did what most bullies do when their bluff and bluster is called— they back down.

"Fuck this shit; I'm here to make some money. If you want to babysit, that's fine. Come on, Robbie!"

Jack continued his stare with his fists balled up ready for a Conrad bull rush at any time. He had seen Conrad do that before. It was a deceptive tactic to throw his enemy off guard by walking away and then quickly turning and rushing back like a defensive lineman assaulting the quarterback; a typical Conrad tactic that had worked in the past. Jack waited and watched as Conrad and Robbie disappeared into the woods.

"Alright, 'Rambo,' let's go make some money tonight," Bobby Joe cut in to break the tension.

Just as Jack and Conrad were engaged in a stalemate, a dark pimped-out Gran Torino rolled onto Greenwood Drive and parked across the street from the Miller's house in Nicholasville. The passenger side tinted window rolled down an inch to allow Big Jr's cigarette smoke to curl out. Inside the car were the three young thugs that had chased Jack out of the Zone last night and all over UK's campus earlier in the day.

C.J., Jumpy and Wheels were expelled from Bryan Station High School for selling drugs. They had been recruited by Big Jr from the football team as sophomores looking for fast cash and even faster women. He introduced the trio to the drug world in Lexington run by Marcus X. Big Jr flashed wads of cash, threw huge parties to "wine and dine" the trio to the surreal lifestyle. Once addicted to the drugs and lifestyle, they would peddle pot and ecstasy to students at school.

However, a random drug search by the Lexington K-9 unit sniffed out the drugs in the boy's lockers. Big Jr was pissed. The boys had been sloppy and his contacts in Lexington Five-O hadn't tipped him off. They boys were beholden to Big Jr for their livelihoods as they had no diplomas and a criminal record. After a year in Juvenile Detention, the boys were paroled but still on a five year probation. One false move and they would be heading to "big boy" prison.

The boys respected the size and strength of Big Jr but loved his bigger heart. He was the big "brother-father" figure missing in their lives. Though he had them addicted to drugs and the criminal lifestyle, he was a strong male role model that was valued in their neighborhood and culture. Big Jr was slow to anger but once he got mad it was difficult to calm him down. At the peak of his anger, he seemed to grow to the size of a Kodiak bear. They had witnessed his brutal murder of three rival gang members with his bare hands and his trademark Henry Aaron model Louisville Slugger baseball bat. Fights usually began with Big Jr throwing his prey around like a cat toying with yarn. Then he would slam his black bat into the legs or midsection to cripple them. Once paralyzed in pain, Big Jr would split their heads open with home run swings, laughing and taunting them the whole time.

As always, the boys had to clean up his mess with rubber gloves, plastic bags and duct tape. The bodies were usually wrapped tight and thrown into dumpster when they had time. They were apprentices learning the craft from their master who showed them benevolence with more drugs and tricked out prostitutes. It was the only world they knew.

Big Jr took a deep drag off his Marlboro Light looking intently at the front door of 116 Greenwood Drive. The scouting report he received, described a middle class family headed by a local Baptist minister, Rev. Matthew Miller. The report further stated that presently the family consisted of the reverend's wife, Melinda, and nineteen year old son Luke. Big Jr figured this would be where a scared white boy would return. Scanning the neatly trimmed yard, Big Jr imagined a typical white boy environment with a two parent house in a friendly neighborhood void of violence and real fear.

This "cookie-cutter" world existed only on television and in rich white neighborhoods out in the suburbs. It was a foreign world to Big Jr that he secretly longed for. Having visited the estate of Marcus X on many occasions in a posh golf course community, he envied the peace, serenity and security of that environment.

He had been raised by a strict pious grandmother in a tough neighborhood of Lexington when Marcus X first approached him in high school to be his body guard. He refused. His grandmother saw the evil and danger of drugs. She warned her only grandson of the perils of the devil's fast path to success with drugs, easy money and easier women. Big Jr developed into a D-1 college prospect in high school as an offensive lineman. He was a three year varsity letterman at Henry Clay High School but several big schools backed off his recruitment after a busted knee required season-ending surgery his senior year and low college entrance test scores. Nonetheless, UK invited him to try out and he made the practice squad as a walk on. He was on the path to earn a full scholarship when he blew out his knee yet again.

The recovery was slow and painful and a new coaching staff at UK seemed uninterested and dropped him from the active practice squad list. Depressed and angry, Big Jr stopped his therapy workouts and lost access to the pain medication. Marcus X swooped in to ease his pain with Oxycontin and other controlled prescription drugs. Once Big Jr accepted the "helping hand" of the local drug lord, he was hooked. The lifestyle of big money and power was as addicting as the pain medication and Big Jr earned his slice of the pie for doing little more than being big. Occasionally he had to get rough and use violence but he was used to that on the football field where you fought hard in five second bursts and then returned to normal. His football background and even temper served him well as body guard to Marcus X.

Big Jr enjoyed daydreaming about his past glories on the playing fields and the streets. He made sure the boys remained silent in the car when they were "on the job". No music and conversation was kept to a minimum. He hated the bluster and chit chat of teenage boys and threatened to crush skulls if they didn't obey. He taught them to be more observant and less talkative. A wise person learns more keeping his mouth closed and eyes open.

The boys quickly sat up when they noticed the outside light had been turned on at the reverend's house. An older, white man in relatively good shape stepped out onto the front porch toting a baseball bat. He quickly walked across the well-kept lawn toward their car calling out to them. Big Jr threw his cigarette out the window and ordered

102

Jumpy to hit the gas. Jumpy glared at him in shock. He had never seen Big Jr scared or run from anything.

"Damn it, Jumpy! Floor it!" Big Jr screamed. Jumpy's foot slammed the gas pedal and launched the Gran Torino forward with a loud screech. Big Jr looked back at the reverend with a sense of relief and awe. As the car pulled onto Third Street, he quietly told Jumpy to slow down.

"We don't need to draw the attention of the local police. We're a bit out of place in 'Hicksville'!" Big Jr calmly assured Jumpy.

"What the hell happened back there? I mean, damn it Big Jr!" Jumpy shouted.

"What do you mean?"

"What does he mean?" Wheels added incredulously "Damn, Big Jr we just ran from an old white dude! What the fuck?"

"That old white dude is a minister. A man of the cloth, you know, a man of God! I don't mess with them. You'd be wise to heed my words on this. There is a God and He don't like it when you fuck with his ministers. Sometimes you gotta know your limitations. You boys should remember that. Now shut the fuck up and let's get back to Lexington."

Reverend Miller walked back to the house with a sense of satisfaction and trepidation. His thoughts ran wild with various scenarios about who those men were in the car and what was their intention. *What and who were they after? Did they come to the wrong address?*

The one thought that seemed to make the most sense involved his middle son, Jack. *Are these the men that Jack witnessed killing his friend Tater last night in Lexington? It must be. Why else would a car like that be in this neighborhood?* The most troubling thought shook the reverend to his core— *they know who witnessed the murder and where he lives.* This revelation was a haunting reminder about how precious and precarious life on this earth was.

Dear Heavenly Father, Your cherished gift of life is so fragile and dear to us. I

103

pray that You give us strength to preserve and protect that beloved gift. As the reverend finished his prayer, he gripped the Ted Williams model Louisville Slugger tighter and thought about how close he came to using it. In his mind, the use of violence was only justified in the defense of home and family.

As a minister, he had seen his share of useless acts of violence that had destroyed families and ruined the lives of all those surrounded by it. He had argued the point for years in the pulpit that violence was the result of mankind's inability to resolve disputes with reason. God had created man with innate abilities such as the power to think and reason solutions to problems. It was what separated man from the animals and the beasts. Violence was a base, emotional reaction carried out by those incapable or unwilling to resolve issues peacefully. However distasteful acts of violence are to a civilized society, the reverend reasoned, there were times of "justified violence".

The Bible certainly gave numerous examples of how the patriarchs used violence to settle disputes in an effort to protect their lives, property and culture. Rev. Matthew Miller understood that the world was full of violent people who could not be reasoned with or engaged in thoughtful discourse and dialect and those people threatened the peace and order of society. There was only one way to deal with those types and often violent force was the solution.

In times of a crisis, even reasonable, thoughtful men must become unreasonable and violent to protect those most precious in their lives and for the reverend, it was his family. His son was in real danger and needed more protection than a baseball bat in the hands of a once great hitter in his day. He knew the gang of thugs he chased off would not be so easily scared away the next time. In fact, the next visit would likely be lethal.

He needed help and his thoughts ran to one of his deacons in the church, Roy Swann. Roy had served as police chief of Nicholasville for the past fifteen years as well as deacon and trustee to Nicholasville Baptist. He was also one of Matthew's most trusted advisors and friends. Often the two had worked together for years with troubled teens in the church and community to bring peace to families. They visited hospitals, nursing homes and sometimes jails in an effort to comfort their neighbors in times of great distress. Roy was also a big hitter from the left side of the plate for the church softball team that Matthew organized into a five-time county championship team.

Matthew pulled out his cell phone and hit Swann's private cell number. Chief Swann assured Matthew that a squad car would be at his house instantly and provide "around the clock" protection. Matthew's mind was temporarily eased by the police chief but quickly shifted to the present location of his two sons. *Where are they? Its after one o'clock.* The reverend sat down in his recliner still gripping the bat frustrated by the helplessness of waiting. Staring out the window in the front room, Matthew uttered a silent prayer.

A familiar set of headlights streaked across the Miller's front room and Matthew's face. He opened his eyes to the sight of Jack's car. Jumping from the recliner, Matthew raced to the front door to greet his two sons but only one emerged from the driver's side, Luke. Alarmed, Matthew pushed open the screen door running down the steps to the car.

"Where's Jack?"

"Oh, hi dad. What are you doing still up and why are holding a baseball bat?"

"We had some visitors here not long ago, probably looking for Jack and they weren't old friends of his."

"Really? Oh man, what has Jack gotten into? Damn…" Luke added looking away lost in thought.

"Hey, you still haven't told me where your brother is." Matthew inserted poking Luke with the bat.

"I'm not sure. He left Shearer's field with Bobby Joe about a half hour ago."

"Bobby Joe? Bobby Joe Bradley?"

"Yep."

"What in the world would he be doing with him? My God, he's jumping out of the frying pan and into another. That guy's shady. Always has been. What do you know about this? What do you know about Bobby Joe?"

"Not much, really. He owns a tow truck company in town but does some side business in Lexington."

"What kind of 'side business'?"

"Uh…I'm not sure, exactly"

"Luke William Miller. Look at me. Tell me what you know. Everything."

Luke had seen that look in his father's eyes only once before and it was not good. There was a combination of fear, anger and determination behind those steely hazel eyes. Trying to hide the truth from his father had never been a good idea and had usually never worked.

Luke and his father often clashed over many things, mostly Luke's indolent lifestyle and zeal for pleasures of the earth. That zeal had landed him in trouble so often that he was now living in the basement of his father's home again. This was no time to be coy or deceptive. His brother's life was in danger and they needed to work together.

"Look, most of this is really just rumor."

"That's okay. Tell me what you've heard?"

"Bobby Joe does a lot of high end repos in Lexington and they can be very dangerous."

"And?"

"And… its believed that he sells some drugs on the side. He's never been arrested or anything like that but 'word on the street' is that he has contacts in the Lexington PD that shields him."

The words "drugs" and "bad cops" hit Matthew hard. He lowered his head, biting his lower lip trying to make sense of this bizarre scenario playing in his ordered world. Shaking his head wistfully, Matthew broke the long silence.

"I don't like this. I don't like it at all. Jack's in trouble and in over his head. I felt like there was more to the story than he was telling. Tonight, a pimped-out Gran Torino graces our neighborhood loaded with no-good thugs waiting like a mountain lion to pounce on its prey. And now Jack has run off with another sketchy character connected to the very drug world he's probably running from." Just uttering those last words sent a palpable fear down Matthew's spine.

Again, he was deep in thought staring across the street. His eyes had seen the suffering of others lost in the drug world that seemed to be pulling his son into peril. *Oh, dear God, please place Your loving hand over my son. Please guide and protect him as the Good Shepard whose sheep have run astray.* Tears streaked across the Reverend's face as he looked up to see a police cruiser from the Nicholasville PD pull into their driveway.

<u>Chapter Ten</u>

"A great many men, when they smell battle afar, chafe to get in the fray. When they say so themselves they generally fail to convince their hearers that they are anxious as they would like to make believe, and as they approach danger they become more subdued. This rule is not universal for I have known a few men who were always aching for a fight when there was no enemy near, who were as good as their word when the battle did come. But the number of such men is small."

—Ulysses S Grant

There was a familiar comfort as Jack climbed into Bobby Joe's Ford 250 King Cab. Something about being around Bobby Joe made Jack feel at ease and safe. The big guy could be cruel and mean-spirited to others but not to Jack. Not since that day on the basketball court in high school during try-outs.

For reasons unbeknownst to Jack, Bobby Joe had taken over as big brother and guardian. He stood up for him in the "Michael Westbrook" affair and from that day on, no one else tried anything with Jack. In some strange way it was similar to John Steinbeck's characters of Lenny and George from *Of Mice and Men*. In this case, "Lenny" fired up his diesel-fueled truck with the sounds of Toby Keith blasting from the stereo. "George" had to find a way to tell his big guardian about the gang from the Zone that chased him earlier in the day and he needed to do it soon while driving to Lexington with the two numb nuts, Conrad and Robbie, following in the tow truck.

Jack was unsure exactly how he would broach the subject given the fact that he hadn't talked to Bobby Joe in years. The last thing he wanted was to come across as some weak, blubbering kid scared of shadows from the Zone. Jack quickly reassured himself that the gang from the Zone was a real threat and a deadly one at that and he needed his "Lenny" to help. Jack tried to concoct a way in his mind to move a small talk conversation into his death threat from the Zone but it seemed an absurd scenario. *Hey Bobby Joe, what kind of gas mileage does this huge beast get? Oh, that's not too bad...by the way there's a gang of black thugs*

108

from the Zone trying to kill me because I witnessed a murder last night. Oh wait, possibly two murders. What do you say old buddy? Think you could help me out this jam like old times? Jack frowned as he played out the ridiculous scene in his head. *Okay that obviously won't work.*

"Hey, don't let Conrad and Robbie spook you about repos. They aren't always bad. Sometimes they're real easy if you catch them off guard. Often, I can divert the owners away from their cars long enough for Conrad and Robbie to move the tow and boom up the vehicle. I'm usually the 'clown' or distraction and protection for the guys while they strap down the wheels. If the owner gets freaky, I step in and keep them away from my boys working on the car. Keeping between the owner and my boys is the primary job of the clown. You know like in a bull fight. The clown is really the bravest guy in the ring especially if the matador gets in trouble. It's the clown that saves him by getting the bull distracted and running at him. That's what I do on these repos. So really, I'm the only one that faces any danger."

"Has anyone ever pulled a knife or gun?"

"Yeah, but its rare. Don't worry about that tonight. The lien holder is Jeff Watts. Do you remember Jeff? He was in your brother, Joseph's class?"

"No, not really. I'm mean; I've heard the name but didn't really know him."

"Oh, well anyway he said the limo owner is nuts but not real violent. He used his size to scare off others trying to repo the limo. Jeff said he knows the guy pretty well and says he's full of shit. You know, all bark and no bite. He's built like a pit bull and has a nasty temper, but not likely to pull a weapon."

"What if he does?"

"Well, I'll just have to take it from him."

"You've done that before?"

"Yep. One thing I've learned in this business is that most people aren't prone to violence. They talk big, bark loud and puff up, but when actually confronted by someone not afraid…they back down. Big ole dudes that act like they could tear you apart, just crumple like little school girls. There's just no shit in their necks. You know what I mean?"

"Yeah…I guess. What about guys like you? Ever come across any of them?"

There was a dead silence in the truck for what seemed like ten minutes. Jack's mind was flooded with dread. *Oh man, did I offend him? Crap! You ask too many stupid questions. It's been a while since you've talked to him and now you've questioned his manhood and toughness. Good job, idiot. You have killer thugs chasing you from Lexington and now you've offended your only real hope of surviving this. Damn!*

"Yeah" Bobby Joe answered with a small laugh. "There was a big ass black guy once that cracked me over the head with a bat. See this scar?" Bobby Joe pointed to a large faint line that extended out of the right side of his hairline and ran another three inches into his hair. "I was repo-ing the fucker's car and he kinda freaked out. Like he was going to cry. This huge fucker was about six foot eight, weighing about three hundred and fifty pounds solid. Just standing there weeping like a little puss. Then he tells me he's got his school books in the trunk and begs me to let him get them out. Well shit, I started feeling sorry for the fucker… mostly because he's a sorry ass pussy, crying like a little girl. Its disgusting. So, like an idiot, I let him go to the trunk while I strap up the wheels. Well the big fucker cracks me over the head. I fall face down on the ground. He's cussing me up pretty good while dragging me off the road. He takes the straps off the car and about $500 cash out of my pocket. My head is pounding and I'm real dizzy. Blood spewing everywhere. Anyhow, he tells I'm lucky its daylight and he's in a hurry and doesn't have time to finish me off." Bobby goes silent for a few moments and then adds ruefully, "I was lucky that day…I swear to God, if I see that fucker again…I'll kill him."

"Oh man, you were lucky…speaking of luck, I wasn't so lucky last night." Jack paused to see Bobby Joe's reaction and whether it was okay to proceed. Bobby Joe continued a long stare down Harrodsburg Road

110

entering Lexington. Sensing it was safe, Jack added, "I witnessed a murder last night…possibly two."

"What?" Bobby Joe turned quickly towards Jack. "What the hell are you talking about? Who got murdered?"

"A good friend from UK and a girl that I had met the night before at Three Goggles."

"Damn! How did it happen? How did they get killed?"

Jack took a deep breath trying to figure out the best way to tell the story without making himself look like an ass. He respected and even valued Bobby Joe's opinion of him and wanted him to see that he wasn't that scared teenager from high school that avoided confrontations like in the Michael Westbrook affair. He carefully crafted the story.

"I met this girl, Candace, at Three Goggles and then saw her again the next day in one of my classes at UK. We sorta hit off pretty well and just started walking around campus talking. Not really paying attention to where we were going. Anyhow we drifted into the Zone."

"The Zone? Damn, man, don't you know how dangerous that place is?"

"Well, yeah…my friend, Tater, told me all about the place and to steer clear of it."

"Damn good advice. You should listen to him."

"I wish I could… he was killed last night."

"What?"

"Anyhow, Candace gets this phone call and starts running towards this run-down looking apartment complex. She bangs on the door and this huge black dude lets her in?"

"Where the hell are you? Why didn't you go in with her?"

"I was trying to catch up with her. It was dark and kinda hard to follow her. Anyhow, she's gone for a while and then I hear this God-awful scream. I'm pretty sure it was Candace. I'm horrified and stunned... I don't really know what to do and then that huge black dude opens the door again and sends out a bunch of young black fuckers to look for me. Again, I don't know exactly what to do and then I see another big dude standing at the door with a big knife and blood all over his right hand."

"Fuck me! Then what happened?" Bobby Joe stated staring intently at Jack while waiting at a red light in downtown Lexington.

"There was a big fence next to me, I hopped over it and ran down this huge hill. I could hear them behind me. They chased me back onto campus. I ran to Three Goggles trying to blend in with the crowd and lose them. Well my buddy Tater thought we were playing a game, knocks me over and the thugs follow him. They caught up to him and beat him to death."

"You watched your friend take a beating?" Bobby Joe said incredulously.

"Yeah."

Bobby Joe just shook his head trying to find the right words to comfort his friend without indicting him as a cowardly prick. "Well if they killed your friend, I assume, it was because they thought he was you, why do you think they are still after you?"

"Because a friend of Candace's, who I met that night, was with those thugs and told them they killed the wrong guy and that he knew who I was. Damn, this morning they were waiting for me at my first class on campus and chased me again. I was able to lose them but...damn, they know who I am and I'm sure it won't be long before they pick up my scent again."

Suddenly Jack felt his cell phone vibrating in his pocket. He thought he had turned it off. He dug down into his pants pocket and saw that Luke had left him a text message: "Some black dudes in pimp mobile were watching r house. Dad chased them off and cops r here now. Where r u?"

"Oh shit. Luke just texted that there were some thugs at my parent's house tonight?"

"Damn, Miller…what the hell did you step into this time?"

Jack just nodded his head slowly saying nothing and staring out the window. They were in downtown Lexington and it just dawned on him that they were not far from the Zone. He could feel an eerie foreboding encompass his body creating an uncontrollable shake. *Oh God what am I doing? Why am I back in Lexington? Please help me. Help me find the right way. I need You more than ever. Please wrap Your loving arms around me and protect me from this evil. I have acted cowardly. Give me the strength to redeem myself. I'm not the person I want to be and definitely not worthy of calling myself a Christian. Help me Lord. Calm my fears and show me the way. I'm in Your hands.*

Jack felt a strong hand grab him by the back of the neck and pat him a few times.

"Ah, don't worry Jack, old boy. Maybe they're just trying to scare you. Anyway, after the repo tonight maybe you better stay at my place. You don't want to bring any more attention to your parents." Jack nodded quietly still staring out the window lost in thought before Bobby Joe added, "Hey cheer up, man. Bobby Joe's on this. I got your back. Just like before, man! We'll figure out something and get you outta this mess, alright?" Jack turned back to his old defender with a huge sense of relief.

"Thanks, man. I knew I could count you."

The bright lights of the Continental Hotel came into view as Bobby Joe slowed his massive truck surveying the entrance for his repo job.

The Continental was an upscale hotel across the street from Rupp Arena and the Hyatt Regency. During basketball season the Hotel's bar, Dooley's, was hopping with Lexington's finest citizens rubbing elbows, among other things, with former athletic stars from UK. It was the place to be on game days. However, on this crisp fall night, the action was a bit slow with the usual downtown crowd of business types mixed with a younger college crowd. A handful of bar patrons paced the downtown streets easily moving from one bar to the other.

A dark thirty foot limousine stretched across the front entrance walkway to the Continental. On the driver's side door was the company's logo magnet, **"IT'S A STRETCH"**. Jack smiled *Wow, what a cheesy name for a limo service.*

"That's our car!" Bobby Joe cried out and then reached into his pocket pulling out his cell phone using the two-way walkie-talkie service to call Conrad. "Hey dude, circle around Algonquin Street and pullover on West Short Street. We'll map out a plan of attack."

"Copy, Big Dog! Out!" Conrad replied.

Conrad edged the Five Star tow truck off the road into an "Emergency Vehicles-Only" zone. Bobby Joe pulled up behind him and flashed his lights signaling him to come back for a pow-wow. Conrad and Robbie jumped out the tow truck and ran back to see what the boss had planned for tonight's repo.

"Alright, Conrad you think you can run point and be the clown tonight?"

"Hell yeah! It aint nothing but a thang, Bo!"

"You been drinking?"

"Hell yeah. We all have. Remember we just left a party, Bo!"

"I know numb nuts! I mean since we left the party. You hit any of that Wild Turkey you got stowed under the front seat of my tow truck?"

"Yeah he did...hell we both did. We figured you'd let us run this repo, so we hit the sauce a bit." Robbie interjected.

"Ah...a little liquid courage, eh? Damn it guys, I need you sober for this. There's likely to be an altercation and you can't be without your senses. What if the cops get called or involved? Then what? You both are fucked up in the head and will get arrested and there goes my big repo payday!"

"Bo, I'm not drunk, wasted or anything. I've got my head on. Let run clown. I'll take the two-way. Walk down West Main Street and VIN the limo. Once the VIN checks out, I'll call Robbie to bring the tow and I'll hook it up. Then Robbie and I will take off. No problem, Bo."

"Yeah…no problem. Dude, the limo owner is built like a bowling ball with the temperament of a pit bull. Jeff said his name is Billy Wilkerson, a former pro wrestler who dabbled a bit in MMA. He's small but compact weighing about 280-300 pounds and about 5'9 or 5'10. Jeff said another tow service tried but was run off by big Billy!"

"Ah shit, I'll run circles around the big bull. Keep him distracted while Robbie straps it up."

"Sure, it's just one dude. Come on Bo, Conrad and me got this" Robbie added slapping hands with Conrad and doing the 'bro hug'.

Bobby Joe had never let these two run a repo because they were simply too stupid and unreliable to do a good job. But they had been with him a long time and needed to learn the trade. Besides he was worried about Jack's predicament and didn't want get too distracted from helping his little buddy.

"Alright…I'll be watching from Triangle Park across the street. If it gets out of hand, I'll bail your asses out. But if I have to get involved then you two get nothing from the repo. You understand?"

"Sure, no problem. Just stay in the truck and watch us work our magic." Conrad stated with the satisfaction of a fox being given the key to the henhouse.

"Hey, David Blaine before you do your street magic, you'll need the work order from the lien holder."

"Right, boss"

Conrad snatched the work order from Bobby Joe's hand and the two "magicians" ran back to the tow truck. Conrad opened the driver's side door to put the work order in the visor but instead reached under the seat and pulled out the Wild Turkey. Looking back at Bobby Joe through the back window of the tow truck, Conrad uncapped the bottle and took a few quick swigs. Robbie shielded his partner from Bobby Joe's view and then jumped into the driver's seat. Conrad shoved the work order in his pants pocket and waved at Bobby Joe with a "shit-eating" grin before heading down North Broadway to West Main Street by foot.

There was a fairly large crowd walking around West Main Street as Triangle Park's colorful fountains always drew an ample audience of shoppers exiting the Shops at Lexington Center. Conrad zipped up his dark hoodie while navigating his way around business suits with clients chasing skirts. It was the oldest game in town and one that Conrad would love to join but at the moment he was concentrating on a payday in a potentially dangerous arena.

Briskly moving down West Main Street, Conrad spotted the long black limo roughly taking up three parking spaces. Conrad grimaced at the sight of a boxed in limo. Standing in front of the Continental, Conrad stared at the parking dilemma trying to decide his course of action when, fortunately, fate stepped in as the front car easily slid out and into traffic. A smile spread across his face as he ran to the driver's side of the limo to read the VIN on the dashboard.

After matching the numbers with the lien holder's work order, Conrad called Robbie to send the Five Star Towing truck but failed to notice a blue Toyota Corolla had backed into the prized parking space. Conrad quickly turned around and waved off the car but the driver ignored his pleas and continued backing into the space.

"Hey dude, you can't park here. I'm holding this spot for a tow truck." Conrad barked. He was never known for his tact or diplomacy which could explain the two scars on his forehead.

"You can't hold a spot, asshole. Get outta the way!" the driver responded with equal defiant tact.

Conrad boldly reached into the car, turned off the motor and then pulled the driver out of the car. The ease with which he was able to yank the driver out of his car emboldened Conrad. Grabbing the much younger and about thirty pounds lighter driver by his jacket with his meaty fists, Conrad let the "Wild Turkey courage" take over.

"Look assface. You either pull this car out now or I will and you won't like the way I do it!"

"O—kay." The younger driver shakily replied having quickly assessed the situation and calculated the odds of winning this confrontation was a longer shot than winning the lottery. Trying to gather his composure, the driver straightened his crumpled jacket, looked around before being roughly shoved back into the car by Conrad.

"Get the fuck in the car, dickless, before I lose my temper! And don't think about reporting this to anyone because I have your license plate number and will chase your sorry ass down!"

The engine roared to life and quickly merged into West Main Street. Another huge grin spread across Conrad's face as he had conquered yet another smaller prey and sharpened his fighting prowess on a small toothpick. He now hoped that the former pro wrestler would try to stop the repo. In fact, he would take his time strapping the limo just to invite such a confrontation. Beating up smaller prey had lost its appeal. It was time to try bigger game and why not tonight, Conrad mused.

The flashing lights of the Five Star Towing truck pulled Conrad back to the task at hand. He waved Robbie back and guided the lowered boom up and under the limo. Robbie lifted the limo slightly aloft and then proceeded to strap it down. The two repo men worked the straps like a well-choreographed dance team.

Both men were vigorously attending to the front limo wheels completely oblivious to the lurking danger. Conrad was so accustomed to strapping the car that he forgot his role in this caper as the clown. With his back turned to the front entrance of the Continental, Conrad imperiled the operation as big Billy Wilkinson came lumbering out the bar like a mother bear protecting her young. His right shoulder plowed into Conrad's spine driving him hard into the pavement. Conrad's face kissed the asphalt and left him dazed. Big Billy then pulled Conrad's hair back and spiked his face again on the pavement opening a large gash over an old scar. Horrified, Robbie ran around the limo with a tire iron swinging wildly at Billy who simply rose up and grabbed his arm in mid-air and flung him backwards across the sidewalk and up against the front entrance of the Continental.

He moved quickly onto Robbie grabbing his neck with his big beefy left hand preparing to land his right fist into the "Ric Ocasek" face. The first punch was quickly followed by another that had opened up Robbie's lip. Terrified about where the next blow would land, Robbie closed his eyes and started to scream through his bloody lips.

Big Billy pulled back his fist for a short jab at the skinny man's neck to shut him up when his vision blurred causing him to stagger around clumsily. Unsure of what happened but feeling a sharp pain coming from the back of his head, he turned slowly and saw a Sasquatch towering over him. Bobby Joe pulled his right hand back and delivered another wrecking ball shot across Billy's left cheek. The blow opened a two inch gash as blood began streaming from down his face.

Stunned the former pro wrestler felt his cheek looking at the blood as a rage built up and exploded in a primordial scream. He launched himself into Bobby Joe's abdomen like a bowling ball on steroids and pinned him against the limo. Bobby Joe easily slipped out of the hold and put Billy in a full Nelson headlock down on the pavement.

"Whoa…easy big boy! Calm down. We have repo papers on this limo and we're taking it. It will happen with or without your cooperation."

"Fuck you! I don't owe a dime on my limo. Get the fuck off me!"

"It's not your limo, pal. You're four months behind in payments and your lien-holder at Patriot Finance wants it back. If you give me the keys, we'll drive it back without putting it on a tow. Maybe you can work something out with Jeff and there'll be no damage to the limo."

"Fuck you! You're not getting my limo!" Just as the last words left Big Billy's mouth, he felt his head lift off the pavement before slamming again into the ground. This blow popped a front tooth loose as his mouth filled with blood.

"You're not listening Billy!"

Two cops on horseback clomped up on the scene as a large crowd had gathered to watch the repo ruckus. Most were bar patrons filing out of Dooley's to become spectators of some good gladiator action on an otherwise dull quiet night. One cop hopped off his horse handing his rein to his partner and ordered Bobby Joe off the round bleeding figure lying face down. Bobby Joe released his grip and told the officer that he was carrying out a legal repo on the limo and was protecting his crew from an assault by the wounded bear holding his hand across his bloody mouth.

"I'm going to need to see those papers." the officer replied with his right hand touching his night stick.

"No problem." Bobby Joe ran over to the tow truck and opened the driver side door. He pulled the visor down and futilely looked all over the front seat. Frustrated he returned to Conrad and grabbed him up off the pavement.

"Where's the repo papers, numb nuts?" Bobby Joe firmly inquired from his broken employee. Conrad still dazed and staring out at the street slowly lowered his right to his pants. Bobby Joe quickly snatched the papers out of his pockets and returned to the officers.

Jack slammed the truck door darting across the street to catch up on the action. He had watched Bobby Joe land the first blow on Billy Wilkinson's head while safely sitting in the King Cab of the F-250 at Triangle Park. Uneasy about the outcome of the confrontation, Jack waited until Bobby Joe had the situation under control before he got out of the truck.

Walking briskly to the scene, Jack helped Conrad to his feet as Robbie pulled the first aid kit out of the tow truck and applied a gauze pad to his injured friend's head and wadded up several more pads to stop the bleeding of his own mouth.

Satisfied that the papers were in order, the cops warned Billy against any further action. However, that message didn't resonate with the former pro wrestler who watched in horror Bobby Joe re-strapping his limo. The blood raged through his body as he ignored the cops warning and his own wounded body and ran head long towards Bobby Joe. The rotund bull crashed into the side of his limo as Bobby Joe side-stepped him like a matador. The collision knocked Billy unconscious as the cop on foot placed handcuffs on him and the mounted one called in for a squad car to pick up the wounded bull.

"Damn boys, I send you on a simple repo and look at you. Beaten up and bloodied." Bobby Joe stated with a slight grin.

"The son of a bitch cheap-shoted me from behind! I was sucker punched!" Conrad shot back.

"Oh yeah…how's it feel? I've certainly seen you do worse. Besides what were you doing with your back turned, numb nuts?"

"I was helping Robbie strap up the car."

"Helping Robbie strap up the car? Who was running point and interference Conrad? Who was supposed to be the clown, Conrad? You, that's who! Damn it, Conrad you've seen me do it a thousand times. Your job as clown is to run interference and distract the owner away from the car. You're supposed to protect Robbie!"

"I know. I know. Damn it, I just lost my head a bit. I'm so used to running straps, I guess I forgot."

"Yeah, you almost lost your head alright. Dude was relocating it to the pavement."

"What the hell took you so long getting over here?"

"Well fuck, I had to cross a busy street." Bobby fired back incredulously and then added, "Besides, I thought Robbie had your back." The very thought of bean-pole Robbie coming to the rescue left Bobby Joe laughing.

"Well at least he got the big fucker off me. Where was your boy,

Jack, the whole time?"

"He was with me watching you two idiots fuck up a simple repo. He was right behind me crossing the street to save your sorry asses." Bobby Joe said matter-of-factly before adding, "He helped you up off the pavement, didn't he?"

Conrad's cold stare at Jack could have turned the light drizzle into snow. He hated Jack now more than ever. It looked as if he had been replaced as Bobby Joe's 'boy' by his former grade school nemesis. He couldn't believe that Jack was any different than the scared pussy from high school that ran from a fight with Michael Westbrook. Although his body was much bigger and developed, Conrad believed that Jack was still a pussy inside.

"Dude, I was right behind Bobby Joe. After I saw him slam the big boy to the ground, I made sure no one else jumped in from the crowd. Hell, I was doing your job." Jack added for good measure feeling his own blood pressure rise but knowing it was a lie. Bobby Joe laughed even louder.

"Bull shit! You were probably still in the truck with your thumb up your ass!" Conrad seething with fury then added, "Yeah, you helped me…after the cops got here."

"Fuck you! How the hell would you know? When I got to your sorry ass you were bleeding all over the place and couldn't see shit! Hell, you were crying!"

"Bull shit, I was crying!"

"Yeah, C.B.…..dude you were crying." Robbie interjected trying to stop the bleeding of Conrad's head with several more gauze pads.

"Shut the fuck up and let's get the limo back to the shop. You coming, Bo?"

"Nah! Jack and me got something more important we gotta take care of. Right Jack?"

"Yep!"

Chapter Eleven

"A team is where a boy can prove his courage on his own. A gang is where a coward goes to hide."

−Mickey Mantle

Getting back in the truck safely, all Jack could think about was how heroic Bobby Joe had performed in action. He marveled at the swiftness of his moves and the powerful force of punches thrown. Bobby Joe was like a tornado that came into an area quickly and selectively landing authoritative blows that left devastation in the wake. Jack couldn't help but try and make sense of what just happened. He analyzed every move and step Bobby Joe took in the beating administered to the limo driver. The limo driver was no slouch. He was a round wrecking ball professionally trained to beat the hell out of people in the ring yet he seemed overmatched by some country rube with no background in skilled combat.

Jack was even more amazed at Bobby Joe's calm demeanor during the fight. He seemed in control of his emotions while the rotund pit bull was a raging mess striking out wildly at his foe. Even Bobby Joe's punches appeared to be measured like a skill craftsman. No motion or energy seemed wasted. When he threw the first punch, his body's weight shifted perfectly forward as he dropped his knuckles across the back of the round man's head like an anchor at sea. It was a stunning blow that would have toppled an ordinary man, but just dazed the limo driver.

The second blow was both quick and heavy opening a large gash across the cheek. It was a fearless assault on a known professional fighter. Again, Jack was astonished by Bobby Joe's audacity to attack such a man. The confidence one must have in their abilities as a brawler to take on so many different types of people who are also more motivated to preserve their possessions.

Jack was even dumbfounded at how Bobby Joe seemed to anticipate the charge of the bull, deftly taking the rush into his midsection crashing into the limo and then counter maneuvering the Toro into a full-nelson headlock. It all seemed calculated, almost scripted.

Bobby Joe's efficiency of motion and use of force without emotion was impressive. He was a skilled artisan applying his craft in the gladiator's arena. *How do you do that? How can you fight and not be mad? How does a man conjure up the courage to strike another man without anger and still be in control? Is there a button or trigger that gets pulled inside that allows one to set loose a torrent of violence on another person? If so, where can one acquire that trigger mechanism because its heroic as hell!* Jack ruminated. He had to know how Bobby Joe could tap this reservoir of courage to unleash violence on others without losing his senses or control.

"How do you do it?" Jack inquired with a quivering voice mixed with awe and trepidation.

"Do what?" Bobby Joe stated matter of factly as if they were talking about building a patio deck.

"How do you find the strength...the inner courage to attack someone? I mean, you weren't even mad and that dude really hadn't done anything to you, personally, and yet you hit him like he had stolen something from you or was doing your girlfriend?"

"Ah, he was stealing from me. It was a job that paid well and he stood between me and that pay check."

"Yeah, I guess...but you didn't even know him."

"So?"

"So, how can you muster up the feelings...you know..."

"Courage?"

"Yeah." Jack was reluctant to use the word because he believed it rarely applied to him. He had heard others misuse the word about him in the sports arena for actions taken in competition. But that was a game and this was the real world of life, an uncontrolled, chaotic setting.

"I don't know. I just act. Its almost instinctual, I guess. I see a play going down and I act. I never really thought about it."

"Never thought it? My God, you rush into a dangerous, violent situation and don't think about it? How can you do that? I mean, don't you ever think or worry about the consequences or 'what ifs'? Like, what if the guy's got a gun or knife? What if there's more than one guy with the dude your repo-ing? Or even worse, what about payback or revenge? You beat up the dude and he says he'll get you back and he ambushes you somewhere when you least expect it? Do you ever think about that?"

"No. I just act and react to what I see or do. You think too much. While you're thinking about all the consequences or what might happen or could go wrong, you've talked yourself out of fighting or taking action. You can't do that."

"But how? How do you just shut off your brain to stop thinking and just act?"

"I don't know. You smart, intellectual guys never seem to figure it out. While you guys are thinking things through, opportunities to strike are being missed. You're frozen in thought. You just need to move and act on instinct."

"Maybe that's the problem. Some of us don't have the 'action' instinct. It must be innate in some while others have the coward gene."

"Damn it, Miller! You are not a coward. Don't ever say that again. I've seen you in action. Hell, that's what I admired most about you that time on the basketball court when you tried out for the varsity. You came after me, the biggest dude on the court and a varsity player."

"That was basketball. It's different."

"How? Hell man, you had that killer look in your eye when you swung at me."

"That's because you were talking trash and then threw a cheap shot at me."

"Exactly! I was trying to get you mad. Throw you off your game.

You came in all cocky and confident and I got in your head...forced you to get mad. Remember what Coach Stevens used to say about getting in your opponent's head. Once you got in there, he was finished."

"Yeah, you sure as hell did."

"Well, what were you feeling at that moment?"

"I was pissed. You were making me look bad, especially during try-outs in front of the coaches."

"That's right and what were you thinking about? Did you think about the consequences or even the fact that the guy you were swinging at could kill you?"

"No. I just reacted," Jack stated quietly coming quickly to the conclusion that Bobby Joe was pursuing.

"Exactly! You just reacted to it without thinking. That's what you do. That's the button!"

"That makes sense, but that was a personal thing. I was being challenged physically. That limo driver wasn't attacking you or doing really anything to you."

"You make it personal. He was attacking my two boys. You may not like Conrad or Robbie but they work for me and are as loyal as whipped pups. I feel responsible for them. When that fat bull had his beefy hand around my boy's throat and pinned against the wall, it was personal!"

That last statement left Jack in silent thought. He tried desperately to connect what Bobby Joe was saying to his own convictions. *Was it possible for me to go into "Bobby Joe" mode? Was there a trigger or mechanism I could activate? How does this form of courage relate to the quote in Dr. Daniel's class about the ability to love others? Was it possible that Bobby Joe loved others, especially Connie and Robbie? Must be a different kind of altruistic love because no one could really love those two idiots. Bobby Joe was right about my basketball rage. In sports, when someone challenged me, especially physically, I fought back with force. Pushed or shoved to the floor, I would jump back up in their face and shove them back. It always happened in the paint in basketball when a big dude would tell me not to come in there. Of course, I had to. No fear, just a rush of adrenalin and competitive juices.*

"Look at how you responded to Conrad when he talked shit about you at Shearer's and then again when he said you hadn't left the truck. He basically called you chicken shit."

"Yeah…that pissed me off." Jack's quiet admission led him to a memory he hadn't thought about in a long time.

He didn't like Conrad. Never really did. They had known each other since elementary school. Conrad had always been a small, scrappy little guy with a chip on his shoulder. He and Jack had crossed paths several times on the playground in games such as kick ball, four square and dodgeball. There was more than just a competitive uneasiness between them that dated back to first grade.

Jack and Conrad had the same first grade teacher, Mrs. Mathis, but they also shared their first crush, Melanie Davis. Jack was seated across from her while Conrad sat several seats away in the front. They both loved her long, brown shiny hair and dark sun-kissed skin. Jack had known her since kindergarten was held at his father's church and had gotten in trouble for pulling her hair. He had to visit the church's principal, his father, to explain his unorthodox approach to flirting with the prettiest girl in the school. The explanation fell flat but his rear end was lit up by his father's paddle— the "board of education."

Conrad hated Jack from the start because of his previous year acquaintance with Melanie and how they talked all the time. Most of the kids just assumed they were "going together" but they weren't. Jack was too shy and unsure of himself to write the elementary school dating "will you go with me?" note. Conrad seethed with anger every time he looked back and saw the two talking or passing notes.

He believed Jack's proximity to Melanie was his only advantage so he thought up ways to offset the unfair seating assignment with embarrassing attacks on Jack. If Jack answered a question wrong in class, Conrad made some noise or laughed out loud, though he rarely knew any of the answers himself. He tried several times to trip Jack walking to the front of the class to turn in a paper or sharpen his pencil. None of these tactics seemed to work as Jack would simply step over his foot and give him a mean look.

One day, Conrad decided to step up his efforts against Jack with a direct assault. He planned his attack for the bathroom, the elementary school arena for gladiatorial contests. While waiting in line along the wall in the first grade hallway to get a drink of water before using the bathroom, Conrad jumped ahead in line to stand directly behind Jack. As Jack was drinking from the fountain, Conrad shoved his face into the water and laughed at him. Jack was mad but didn't want to get in trouble at school mostly because worse trouble would be waiting for him when he got home from his father. He knew his parent's rules about fighting in school which weren't much different from fighting at home: a spanking and loss of play time after school, the latter being more severe to active boys than the former.

Instead of an overt physical confrontation, Jack opted for the standard name-calling rebuttal— he called Conrad a booger-eater. The kids in the hallway immediately roared out loud with laughter to Jack's response which further infuriated Conrad. It was bad enough that Melanie seemed to like Jack, but he also seemed to be a popular kid in class. Conrad speculated that Jack's popularity was due entirely to the fact that he had an older brother that was even more popular in school.

Conrad was determined to make Jack look stupid in front of everyone and prove to Melanie that he was the best man for her. He followed Jack into the bathroom and started pushing him several times saying, "What did you call me?" By this time several boys gathered around to watch what was sure to be a good fight. They formed the standard "fight circle" as no one wanted to miss the action or let the combatants walk away.

Jack felt pressure from all sides to respond to Conrad's challenge. Once again, fearing his father's wrath and his mother's disappointment, Jack simply washed his hands hoping to ignore his way out of trouble. Conrad seized on the apparent weakness and continued the verbal assault calling Jack several names such as "scaredy-cat", "wussy-boy" and "butt-face". He could hear a chorus of other voices join in on the verbal assault, especially a high-pitched screed from a long neck kid named Robbie.

As Jack turned to dry his hands under the automatic hand dryer mounted on the wall, Conrad ran up behind him and pushed his head up against it. He instantly saw stars and felt dizzy as the room seemed to swirl around a din of laughter. He stumbled around trying to get his bearings as he felt a large knot rise up on his head. Looking down at his hand, Jack could see driblets of blood. The sight made him cry and the laughter got even louder. Now everyone seemed to chime in calling him a cry baby over and over again.

The loud commotion with mixed laughter caused Mrs. Mathis to storm into the boy's bathroom. It got real quiet really quick. It also didn't take long for her to figure out what had just happened. Jack looked hurt and was quietly sobbing near the sink. While the other boys were shifting about nervously looking down at the floor, Mrs. Mathis ran over to Jack and wrapped her arms around him. After briefly consoling him, she stood up and demanded indignantly what had happened. The room remained quiet with no volunteers stepping forward to account for the raucous activity that had just taken place.

Mrs. Mathis stared at the tops of the boy's heads for several minutes before returning to Jack and in a low voice repeated the question. Jack opened his teary eyes and scanned the room before locking onto Conrad. He wanted desperately to tell Mrs. Mathis everything that Conrad had done to him so that the school's principal, Mr. Hall, would paddle his little scrawny butt. However, Jack was well versed in the "guy code" and the First Commandment: **Thou Shall Not Tell on Others**, especially in a fight. Pushing the tears away with his shirt sleeve, Jack told Mrs. Mathis that he tripped and hit his head against the sink. When asked repeatedly if he was pushed, Jack simply said, "No. It was no one's fault. Just a clumsy accident." The confession and omission of blame sent a huge sense of relief to the spectators as they were ordered immediately back to class. Mrs. Mathis held Jack back.

"Look, I think I know what happened and you don't want to tell on one of the boys…If someone is bothering you or bullying you, you should tell me." After a long moment of silence, Jack looked up and replied, "No one's bothering or being a bully to me…I just tripped."

"Okay…you're a brave little boy to take this on yourself and again I want you to know that I'm here to help you if you 'trip' again, okay?"

"Yes, ma'am."

"Okay, now clean up a bit and come back to class."

When Jack returned he could see the smirks on the faces of the boys and the rest of the day Melanie seemed to ignore him. The "Conrad Black" fight was the talk of the first grade hallway for several weeks. Jack knew he had to do something to change his image and the mindset of his fickle peers if he was going to survive elementary school. He was not afraid of fighting, per say, as he did that on a daily basis with his brothers. He was afraid of losing a fight, especially in school, and Conrad, though smaller, was an aggressive bully that seemed confident of the outcome of the potential fight.

One night after dinner, Jack's father told him of a similar situation when he was a young kid in school. The bully he faced was equally loud and obnoxious. He had pushed, shoved and punched young Matthew once too often and fighting back was his only way to stop the incessant bullying. Matthew noticed how much his tormentor enjoyed swinging really high on the school swing set. The little punk would loudly boast how high he could swing and jump out further than any other mortal at the school and deliver the perfect landing.

Jack's father further explained how when he watched the bully swing, he seemed to close his eyes on the descent. That observation sparked an idea for the perfect payback plan. Without hesitation, young Matthew stealthily walked over to the swings and waited for his bully to hit his highest ascent and then quickly moved into action. As the bully started down, young Matthew stuck out his fist and drilled the closed eyed boy flush on the nose. The impact of the blow shot the bully out of the swing and splayed him out on his backside. All the kids laughed as the bloodied bully ran away holding his nose.

Matthew told his son this story because Mrs. Mathis told him what had happened at school and how Jack hadn't seemed himself since the bathroom "incident". She believed that Jack had been attacked and was too afraid of what his peers would think of him if he squealed on them.

Rubbing his son's head, Matthew explained that sometimes in life you have no choice but to fight. He knew that the bullying would continue unless you stood up for yourself. "Sometimes, the only way to get rid of a bully" Matthew reasoned, "was to fight them. Even if you lost, it showed the bully you weren't a patsy who could be picked on all the time. If a bully knows you won't fight back, then they own you."

"What does that mean?" Jack asked.

"It means, they'll never stop attacking or hurting you and you'll always be afraid of, not just your bully but, others who see you as a weakling. Son, that's no way live. Best to confront fear than live under its awful spell."

"Did you get in trouble?"

"Nope."

Jack felt a sense of relief after hearing his father's story. His father had essentially given him permission to get in a fight at school. Jack loved and adored his father. He was never wrong about anything. He was a pillar of the community as a minister whom others sought for advice and counsel but what most impressed the Miller boys was his athletic prowess. He seemed to excel at every sport he played and when the "World's Greatest Dad" tells you its okay to fight back at school, then it's on.

Jack's plan of attack was simple; just follow your Dad's tactics and apply them to Conrad who also loved the swings and boasting how far he could jump from them. One afternoon during recess, Jack watched anxiously as Conrad ran immediately to the swing set and actually pushed a girl out of "his swing". She ran off screaming and crying but, as usual, no one paid her any attention. Standing by a large oak tree, Jack waited for his moment when Conrad reached the apex of his ascent. Up and down. Up and down. Conrad pushed and pulled the swing chains to drive him higher in the sky while taunting kids below that he was going to land on them if they didn't move.

Suddenly his eyes spotted Jack moving toward the swings. He was determined to jump on Jack with his next high arching swing. Just as he peaked about twelve feet in the air, he screamed in horror as Jack had run up to his swing and held out his fist waiting to land it on his face.

Jack's fist crumpled on impact across Conrad's face knocking him instantly out the swing and onto the ground. Stunned and hurt from the blow and backside landing, Conrad slowly lifted his head and felt blood rushing from his mouth. He could feel one of his baby teeth swimming free in his mouth. He spit it from his mouth. The sight of his own blood and the pain from the punch and fall caused Conrad to cry loudly and obnoxiously. The wailing of the bully was instantly heard by all kids on the playground who quickly dropped what they were doing to see what had happened.

The spectacle of Conrad bleeding and sobbing caused a roar of laughter from the schoolyard. Jack stood his ground waiting for Conrad's bull rush. Sensing no imminent attack, Jack released a torrent of insults at Conrad as each taunt ended with "Connie". Conrad quickly surveyed the playground atmosphere and determined they were solidly on Jack's side and he could count on no help from anyone. Even his neighborhood ally, Robbie, seemed daunted by the event and stood silent.

Conrad ran passed Jack screaming for a teacher to tell on him. Several teachers ran over to admonish Jack. Two older ladies grabbed him by the arm to march him immediately to the principal's office. Just as they reached the school's entrance, Mrs. Mathis intercepted them. She told them that Jack was her student and her responsibility. After a few angry words were exchanged, mostly at Jack, the teachers reluctantly handed him over to her. Mrs. Mathis, his kind grandmotherly figure at the school, took Jack by the hand and walked to her classroom.

"Alright, Jack. I have a feeling I know what this is about. I'm not going to ask you to tattle or tell on anyone. You don't ever have to tell me what this about. But I want your word as a gentleman that this thing is over. No more fights. Do you hear me?"

"Yes, ma'am."

"I'm serious Jack. Don't try to take advantage of this situation and become a bully yourself. You understand young man?"

"Yes ma'am. I promise."

"Alright, now start writing 'Fighting at school is unacceptable' a hundred times on the board and we'll be done with it."

Jack felt a tidal wave of relief wash over his body as he relived the fight in his mind while inking his punishment sentences on the dry erase board. Jack believed the days of Conrad's bullying ways were over as everyone witnessed him breaking the 1st Commandment of the "guy code".

Reliving that memory from the distant past brought a smile across Jack's face. Bobby Joe's comment about Conrad had jolted a recessed memory and reminded him that he had shown courage before and won a fight outside of his family. Fighting your brothers everyday didn't exactly count as courageous— just a point of survival in the Miller house.

Scrapping and spilling blood of others in a heated atmosphere was different. It was sign of strength and show of force to others that you were no patsy or wimp. Jack smiled again reveling in the thought of his own courage in battle. But nagging thoughts of doubt crept back in. *That was years ago when I was a child. The worst that could happen to you in a school fight was a busted nose, lip or eye. Now, as an adult, people get beaten to death, shot or killed over a dispute or misunderstanding. No one seems to fight with just fists anymore. People seem to take losing a fight to the extremes by pulling a knife or gun to save face. The stakes seem much higher and more permanent in fights today.*

Jack tried his best to silence these doubts and fears with little reminders of past acts of courage especially in the sports arena. He also drew solace in the fact that he was no longer a tall, thin drink of water. As Bobby Joe had observed, he had built up his body so physically he was more than capable of defending himself but his greatest obstacle and hurdle was his mentality and Jack was determined to steel his nerves and fight the good fight.

Jack broke the long silence of the drive through Lexington, looking back at Bobby Joe for a few more seconds and then inquired, "Make it personal, huh?"

"Yep. That will fire you up and let you go to town on someone. Hell, turn loose on them like they stole your girlfriend or beat your momma."

"Sounds about right. That might just be the trick. By the way, where the hell are we going?"

Chapter 12

"He who has conquered his own coward spirit has conquered the whole outward world."

—Thomas Hughes, **Tom Brown's Schooldays**

Lost in a web of self-doubt, loathing and fear, Jack's hyperactive mind rendered him temporarily disoriented. Trekking through Lexington for seemingly an eternity, time and distance got away from him. Waking from the fog of the distant past combined with recent horrors of violence and cowardice acts of betrayal, Jack refocused his attention to the ominous present. Since leaving the Continental, Jack assumed his night was over and that Bobby Joe was providing him safe passage to his home on the northern edge of Nicholasville. They had started out heading south along Richmond Road towards Jessamine County, but instead of turning right onto the bypass, Man O War Boulevard, Bobby Joe veered left heading back into an unfamiliar area of Lexington.

Though Jack had never ventured into the eastside of Lexington, he had certainly heard stories of nefarious characters living in the notorious seedy side of Lexington. Bobby Joe made several more deliberate turns into areas that seemed to get darker. Jack could feel an uneasiness welling up from his stomach and encompassing his whole body. He also felt himself physically shaking. He wasn't sure if it was nerves, the cold night air or both, but he needed to know where they were going.

The greatest fear was the unknown and the inability to control the events in your environment. Bobby Joe was obviously in control of Jack's environment while driving to an unknown location. After posing the simple question about their destination, Jack felt even more uneasy about the duration of time for the response from Bobby Joe. He sensed that Bobby Joe was debating how much he should reveal of his immediate plans given Jack's proclivity to fear. After what was really about twenty seconds, Bobby Joe quietly announced, "I gotta make a pick up."

"A pick up? What kind of pick up?" Jack stated looking down at his watch, "Its after one in the morning."

"The kind of pick up that happens after one in the morning."

"Come on smart-ass, what's going on?"

Bobby Joe wheeled the big diesel-powered king cab into a dimly lit laundromat. Backing the truck deftly into a nearly faded out parking slot, Bobby Joe shifted the behemoth into park while leaving the engine running and dimming his headlights.

"Look, I've got to pick up some medicine."

"Medicine? At a laundromat…at one in the morning? Seriously, what's going on? Are you buying drugs?"

"Alright preacher's kid, yes, I'm buying drugs."

"What the hell. I thought you were clean…that you had turned your life around…you know, gone legit with your own business. But you're still doing drugs…a junky?"

"Fuck no! I'm no damn junky! Do I look like junky? Did I look like a junky tonight busting that bulldog's head? Did I look like a junky showing the repo papers to the cops at Triangle Park? Hell no! I just need something a little stronger than the over the counter drugs to ease the pain in my knees."

"Like what? Cocaine, heroin…weed?" Jack inquired a little embarrassed about his lack of knowledge about the illegal pharmaceutical business. Bobby Joe sat transfixed on the front door of the laundromat pondering how or if should answer the question. He was unaccustomed to people challenging him or demanding anything from him. But Jack was different. He was a good friend that Bobby Joe felt a kinship to and who relied on him for protection. It was difficult to explain to others or really even to himself, but for some odd reason he really liked playing the role of guardian to Jack.

At a deeper level, it could go back to Jack's brother, Joseph, backing and supporting him during their high school playing days when

Coach Stevens planned to kick him off the team for constant team rules violations, including possible possession of pot. However, Joseph intervened on his behalf saving him from being dismissed from the team and high school ignominy.

After Joseph graduated and moved on to college, Bobby Joe extended his gratitude to the next Miller male, Jack. The Michael Westbrook affair had sealed his fate as Jack's guardian in Bobby Joe's mind. Though they had drifted apart for a few years, seeing Jack at Shearer's Field rekindled his old affection. Knowing Jack's timid spirit, Bobby Joe was hesitant to tell him too much too soon but knew he had to come clean about where they were and what he was about to do.

"Cocaine. But its alright. I just do a little to numb everything, especially my aching knees. It also helps to calm and steady my nerves. For some reason, it brings things back into focus."

"Does this go back to your days at St. Catharine's? There were rumors that you were doing drugs, got caught by the coach and was kicked off the team."

"Yeah, well that's bullshit. That's the lie Coach Williams told the media and school administrators but it wasn't true. The truth is more complicated. We had been butting heads since I arrived on campus. He had a real bug up his ass about me and encouraged the upper-class bigs to get real physical with me in practice. You know to teach me a lesson or send a tough message. I don't know what else you would call it other than horse shit harassment of a newbie. Coach Williams sure as hell wasn't like that when he recruited me the previous spring. Anyway, some of the varsity guys told me they had never seen the coach go after a freshman like he went after me. I don't know if they were trying to scare me or what but it pissed me off. I fought back in the practices and coach screamed at me, not the fuckers that started it. He told me this was 'big boy' ball not high school and everyone at this level was bigger and stronger and that I had to adjust or go home. I knew what he was trying to do. Since I was a big freshman, he thought he would get the other freshmen in line by attacking me. Twisted psychology but I guess it had worked in the past as he had successful teams. Anyway, that asshole's philosophical style cost me my scholarship and career when one of the big fuckers got up under me on a jump shot and I tore ligaments in my ankle. The injury set me back six weeks, but Coach Williams wanted to get me back sooner. He accused me of all sorts of crazy shit, like being too lazy and not working hard in therapy. One day I simply skipped therapy just to spite the coach. He called me into his office and we got into a little altercation. Things got heated, words were exchanged and then I lost my cool and punched the fucker in the face. Damn, I aint goin lie. That shit felt good. Watching that little fucker fall to floor and cry like a little bitch. Damn, I didn't even care. I knew he wouldn't call the cops or anything. He was too embarrassed about getting his ass kicked. So, he came up with this bullshit story knowing I wouldn't challenge it for fear of having charges pressed against me. I walked away with no regrets except that my ankle never really healed properly thanks to that maniac's quick therapy program and losing my scholarship also meant losing health care benefits and proper therapy."

"Damn…I can't believe he didn't press charges. What did he tell your parents?"

"Same thing he told the school administrators…that I was doing drugs. He told them that he had been told by 'unnamed players' that I was doing drugs and that when he confronted me, I attacked him."

"Were you doing drugs? I don't mean to get into your business, but there were rumors in high school that when you started hanging out with Conrad and Robbie after basketball, you guys smoked alot of pot on your fishing trips."

"Yeah, I smoked a little weed in high school but not at St. Catharine's. They had a strict drug policy with random urine tests. So I was clean until I lost my scholarship and my medical coverage. Trying to get back too soon, I re-injured the ankle and again it pushed recovery time back and the pain returned big time! I was depressed and shit and found it wasn't too hard to find more potent drugs to help my pain. I'm not trying to justify my actions or the drugs. Just trying to explain how the drugs helped me cope with my situation."

"Damn, Bobby Joe. I'm sorry about that. I didn't know any of that shit. We obviously just heard one side of the story and assumed it was true. Look, I'm not judging you or anything but it's just that this stuff worries me. This place where we're at is too close to the Zone and the shit I witnessed."

"I know, I know. Don't worry. I got things under control here."

"So, what happens? You meet a drug dealer here and buy a shit load of coke and sell the rest on the side?"

. "Hell no! I'm no drug dealer. I just buy enough for myself. You know, to ease the pain in my ankle. Fuck, Miller I can't believe you would even think that. I would never sell that shit. I'm only here because its actually cheaper and more effective than prescription drugs. The stronger drugs, like Oxycontin, are too much of a hassle to get from a doctor. So, I go to a 'pharmacist' with odd hours and locations."

It grew quiet in the king cab as Jack had to appraise the new revelations from Bobby Joe. Just an hour ago, he saw Bobby Joe as a hero who saved the guys from a repo gone badly. Now he was a confessed drug addict. Though Bobby Joe didn't say he was a "drug addict", in Jack's world anyone who had done illegal drugs was a "druggy" or "junky" and had him concerned about his reliability. *Damn, is this where Bobby Joe's strength and courage emanate? Do the drugs coat his brain, calm his nerves and give him the euphoric high and strength to attack others without hesitation?*

Jack acknowledged that he didn't know much about drugs or its effects. He was raised to fear them as they were the "Devil's medicine". Rev. Miller would never tolerate any of his boys trying drugs or infecting God's temples with Satan's elixirs. It was a deep-seated fear planted by the reverend in the boys at an early age.

He preached against its harmful effects in the church sanctuary and society seemed to agree. In schools, children were taught as early as middle school about the dangerous effects and impact drugs wreaked. For Jack, these lessons were reinforced in college as he watched many kids do drugs and then lose control making fools of themselves.

Usually the kids that smoked pot or pushed harder drugs didn't last long in school as they became campus "burn-outs". They stopped going

138

to classes and used the free time to escape all their stresses and worries. Before you knew it they were hooked and simply sought new ways to get different highs. Jack had seen no positive outcome from doing drugs and generally steered clear of those who did. His friend's hardest drugs were Jack Daniel's and even that was diluted with lots of soda.

He found himself in yet another debate about Bobby Joe's own drug revelation. *Is it possible to snort a little coke once in a while and still lead a productive life?* None of Jack's limited life experiences or knowledge seemed to have an answer for that question but one thing he did know: Bobby Joe seemed strong, confident and courageous but more importantly, in control.

The lights of a large car streamed across their faces in the parking lot of the poorly lit laundromat and then proceeded to the back of the flat one story concrete building.

"Alright, I'll be back in a second." Bobby Joe stated flatly reaching into the back seat and retrieving a long heavy duffel bag.

"What's in the bag?"

"My laundry."

"You're going to push a load of laundry while buying some drugs?" Jack added incredulously.

"Sure. It's gotta look legit. There's narcs all over these places looking to make a score for their department or simply shake down a business owner for a cut. The owner of this fine establishment is very careful with strict rules. He wants to run a clean business front."

"Nice play on words there Bobby Joe. So, he's clean on the surface or front but dirty in the back?"

"Actually, that's exactly right. His laundromat is a legitimate, clean front to cover his shit in the back room. Plus, I think he has some cops on the take covering his ass. Hand me that box of detergent under your seat."

Sure enough, Jack ran his fingers under the passenger side seat and found a small box of laundry soap. The whole scene seemed absurd to Jack as he handed Bobby Joe the small box. A box of laundry soap was the last thing Jack expected to discover in Bobby Joe's truck much less what you would take with you on a drug deal. Jack felt uneasy about staying in the truck alone while his guardian went into a dangerous drug haven.

"Hey, let me go with you."

"I don't know Jack…you sure? Its kinda nasty in there. Not exactly the country club, friendly types waiting to greet in you there, you know?"

"It can't be worse than sitting out here in the dark not knowing what's going on."

"Alright. Here, you can run my laundry. Hey, keep the whites and darks separate…oh yeah and wash my whites in hot water."

Jack couldn't believe the absurdity of what he was hearing coming from this huge beastly man who earlier had pounded a man's head into the pavement and was presently going into a drug deal. This same dude brought his laundry and gave specific instructions about the cleaning care of his clothes. The whole scene seemed surreal. On any other day, this setting would be funny watching a large man separate his whites and colors and carefully measure his detergent in a laundromat. But approaching the front entrance of the dark small business, Jack was not in a humorous mood but instead felt another cold wave of fear and trepidation crawl over him.

Chapter 13

"Cowards die many times before their deaths; the valiant never taste of death but once."

—Shakespeare

The sign simply read "LAUNDROMAT". It was a white painted board with black letters sitting atop a wide cinder block base with large windows. The bright interior lights made its customers visible from the street. There appeared to be a few people milling around though a quick scan of the parking revealed no cars save the large Cadillac that just arrived and parked around the back. *Must be locals who walked over to run their laundry*, Jack surmised. *But why would they be doing their laundry so late at night?* The further Jack dug into this line of thinking, the more he worried. A cold gust of wind rapped against his body taking his breath away. Sensing Jack's reluctance and slowed pace, Bobby Joe grabbed his elbow pulling him forward with a reassuring nod.

Opening the door, Jack's apprehension heightened as he spotted several dark figures scattered about in the corners of the large one room laundry center and others propped up against the walls that did not appear to be patrons. In fact, Jack concluded the place looked more like a homeless shelter though a few machines were in operation. There was a distinct smell of mold on green painted cinder blocks. The concrete floor held sixty year old stains whose origin one could only imagine judging by the present company. There were long wooden benches against the front wall with two long metal tables directly facing the benches for sorting laundry or holding baskets. Along the side walls were extensive rows of Dexter coin-operated dryers. Above the dryers were signs warning patrons not to sit on the washing machines. The slot fed washing machines were directly across from the dryers and cost just $1.50. The newest machine in the laundromat was the bill changer on the left back wall.

Jack reached into Bobby Joe's duffel bag and pulled out four dollars. As he fed the bills into the change machine he watched Bobby

Joe walk to the back door of the building. It was a large heavy metal door marked "private". Just above the door handle there appeared to be a two-way mirror. Looking up at the ceiling, Jack spotted a half dozen security cameras scanning the main laundry room. No one seemed to pay any attention to the newest arrivals which eased Jack's mind as he pulled out Bobby Joe's dark clothes and emptied them into the antiquated Whirlpool washing machine. He pushed through six quarters, added the detergent and closed the machine lid. Everything seemed normal, so Jack grabbed a seat on the wooden bench waiting for Bobby Joe to complete his pharmaceutical transaction and his darks to finish its washing cycle.

The extra time gave Jack's mind a chance to run free trying to make sense of what had happened as well as what Bobby Joe was doing behind the large metal door. While only a few minutes had elapsed in real time, Jack felt otherwise. His thoughts ran the spectrum of absurdity, yet logical in the paranoid mind. *What was taking so long? Wasn't this supposed to be a simple purchase and pick-up? My God, this place is a dump with even worse lighting. Maybe it's supposed to have bad lighting so law enforcement or the neighborhood can't really tell what's happening in here.*

Oh my God, what's happening in the corner, over there? Damn, is that…oh that's disgusting! God can't they find a better place to do that sorta shit? I guess all kinds of "transactions" go on here at night. I wonder if the proprietor knows this kind of shit is going on in his establishment? I wonder if he's getting a cut? Damn, why did Bobby Joe have to get his drugs tonight, of all nights? Well, he probably didn't count on babysitting a scared little shit, but damn this place is too similar to the Zone. It has the same type of mindless, faceless shadowy figures.

After a few more minutes of stewing and wallowing over the dire conditions of the present, Jack's imagination took him to a horrific conclusion. *Oh my God, is it possible that Bobby Joe was somehow connected to the same underworld as that big black fucker and his Denzel Washington-looking boss? Tater said that some big black fucker ran the whole Zone and I'll bet that was him at apartment 121. Oh shit, what if Bobby Joe works for him? I mean, Bobby Joe seems comfortable in this seedy environment and probably gets hired to run a few repos for the 'Boss' of the Zone. Shit, its all adding up. Bobby Joe gets a call about a white boy that ran away to his 'neck of the woods' and if you find him and return him, there's a big bonus in it for you. Probably a lifetime supply of coke or Oxycontin.*

Was it just a coincidence that I ran into Bobby Joe at Shearer's field or did he get tipped off? But who knew I was in town that could have tipped him off? Luke, that's who! After a few seconds Jack shook his head and laughed a bit at that last idiotic thought. *Okay that was stupid. There's no way Luke would do that, though Lord knows he should after all the shit me and Joseph did to him as a kid.*

Still Jack couldn't shake the thought that maybe Bobby Joe was somehow involved and had simply netted "Denzel's prized fish" and returned it to his nasty swamp, the Zone. Anxiously, Jack surveyed the laundromat again, looking for another exit for his escape. *Damn, looks like there's just one way in and out. Shit Jack, you're such a dumbass. You walked right into a trap and now you've got a chance to get out and you can't seem to move. You've been screwed here and have finally caught on to the situation and are still paralyzed in fear to move. Fuck you Jack! Get up and get the hell out of here while you've still got a chance. But where would I go? You go running out in Eastside and then what? You don't know this side of town at all? Damn, stop thinking so much, you've still got your phone. You can call Luke. Shit, I have my phone.* Jack quickly pulled out his phone to send Luke a text— Luke, I need u...

Suddenly, the big metal door opened and Bobby Joe appeared with a big goofy grin. He subtly motioned for Jack to come over. Instinctively and obediently, Jack jumped to his feet and furtively slid his cell phone into his front pocket while hitting send with his thumb.

"Hey, come on in."

"Really? Why?"

"Dude, its cool. I want you to meet somebody. Hey, grab my clothes first. Did you start with the darks or the whites?"

"Darks," Jack mumbled and then opened the machine still in wash cycle. "They're still wet."

"That's okay. We don't have time to finish them. Just shove them back in the bag on the bottom." Jack emptied the whites on the floor and shoved the wet clothes in first. *Why the hell am I doing this shit? God this is embarrassing and why the hell does he wear these skimpy, bikini underwear? Gross!* Jack finished shoving the whites in the top of the bag and slung it over his shoulder. *Damn this bag has a nice weighted end with these wet clothes.*

Might come in handy in a pinch.

Jack saw Bobby Joe's "shit eating" grin holding the large metal door open and for some reason felt an easiness return. The whole scene seemed too inane to be dangerous if Bobby Joe was so concerned about his laundry, Jack reasoned.

Walking past the big goof ball, Jack had trouble seeing in the darkened room. A sole green banker's lamp sitting atop a large mahogany desk lit the room as Jack's eyes adjusted. He promptly scanned the room and discovered it was ornately and eloquently decorated with dark cherry book shelves and exquisite, thick leather chairs. If you didn't know better, Jack supposed, you would think you were in a college professor or lawyer's office. The beautifully accented paintings framed in gold gave one a sense of a fine, legitimate establishment or business and for some reason gave Jack a sense of relief.

Behind the banker's lamp and mahogany desk was a dark figure with his back turned in his leather chair engaged in a deep and seemingly important conversation. Bobby Joe looked down at Jack and quietly nodded that everything was okay. Jack smiled and shoved the laundry bag into Bobby Joe's abdomen. The big man playfully whacked Jack in the crotch with the heavy wet bag. The force of the blow pushed Jack up against a tall slender figure standing behind him. Looking up, Jack could make out that it was a long black man with his arms folded wearing huge mirrored sunglasses. He seemed to be staring down at Jack with the frown of a man trying to look tough. For some reason, it didn't work. He was older and paunchy and Jack quickly surmised that he could easily take him down in a fight.

Looking back, Jack saw Bobby Joe quietly trying to suppress his laughter at Jack's reaction to the tall "scarecrow". Jack silently nodded his head at the absurdity of the situation and then instantly froze in terror as the man behind the desk wheeled around. *Holy shit! It's the fucking Denzel Washington dude.* Jack's mind raced to the last time he saw the drug lord in the Zone outside apartment 121 with a blood covered arm dripping from a large knife. He stood there before the killer, again, too scared to move.

The Coward

What the fuck is going on? Did Bobby Joe really betray me? Oh my God…okay calm down. Don't give anything away. Let them talk first so you can find out what they know and what's going down. Jack could feel that his mouth was wide open as he turned back to Bobby Joe trying to read the big man's facial expression. He was still cracking up at how quick Jack's reactions had changed within seconds of spotting the "scarecrow".

Marcus X stood up from behind the desk and smiled. His pearly white teeth sent a cold chill down Jack's spine.

"Hey Jack…relax. I want you to meet an acquaintance of mine…Marcus X."

Marcus Xavier Williams was his full name listed on the birth certificate issued in 1967 at St. Joseph's hospital in Lexington. He grew up in a tough neighborhood near Bryan Station High School. His only memory of his mother was of her crying from a fight with his father in which he never saw her again. His father, James, told him she ran out on them because "that's what a no good bitch does". Under the rough, no-nonsense single parent, Marcus learned the manly game of football and how to pass drugs to customers. Late one night, James was murdered in a drug deal gone badly not long after Marcus had turned seventeen. A once promising middle linebacker with college scouts at every game, Marcus was kicked out of school for trying to unload some of his father's drugs to pay off a debt to the local drug lord, Earl Carruthers, aka "Easy E".

Easy E warned Marcus that he would kill him if the $5,000 debt wasn't paid within six months. Marcus was caught on campus security cameras trying to sell crack cocaine, a schedule II drug, and faced an even tougher judge who sentenced him to five years in a state penitentiary.

The big kid listed at six foot two inches tall and approximately two hundred and twenty pounds entered the prison an angry man looking to take down the first guy that messed with him. He didn't have to wait long as "fresh meat" always attracted the attention of the prison kingpin, Juan Salazar. He sent two Hispanic toughs to test the young Marcus's mettle. The seventeen year old easily dispensed of his attackers with powerful body blows that couldn't be detected by the guards just as his father had taught him.

He showed courage by going to the much older prison kingpin and telling him where he could find his boys. Salazar was impressed by the young man's gall, power, intelligence and his remarkable ability to control his acts of violence. He knew Marcus was a "short timer" with great potential to be a drug operator. He took him under his protective wing and made sure he was clean in prison while teaching him the drug trade. Marcus learned how to buy and sell drugs, recruit distributors, run a payroll and most importantly, how to stay out of trouble with the local law enforcement. Salazar taught him which cops to seek out and how to approach them. He also educated his young apprentice on how to launder or clean your "dirty money" with legitimate businesses.

Juan Salazar was so impressed with Marcus's quick aptitude for numbers and fearless approach to others that he made sure his prison stint was easy. Once on the outside, Marcus would use Salazar's contacts but he had to have a base of operations— one in a city large enough to hide in the shadows but not too big to step on big toes. Marcus wanted to be a big fish in a medium sized pond. This pond also needed a healthy market looking to score his product. Lexington fit the bill. It was his hometown with many high schools and a big college campus nearby. The market in Lexington had been virtually untapped and was ripe for an intelligent, bold, entrepreneur who didn't mind getting his hands dirty with controlled violence assuring his success.

As soon as Marcus left prison, he knew he would have to deal with Easy E immediately as the local drug lord never forgave or forgot a debt. Salazar helped fuel Marcus's fire by telling him that Easy E killed his father because he planned on getting out of the business.

According to Salazar's sources, James was trying to go legit because his son was nearing college recruitment and he didn't want to inhibit his son's chances of big time college football. Salazar had gleaned this information from the plethora of inmates who had been in and out of the state penitentiary from Lexington and worked intimately with Easy E. Those same informants apparently held no love for Easy E who had turned them over to the cops. Marcus X took the news without any emotion as the two devised a plan that served two purposes: revenge and business opportunity.

Upon returning to Lexington, Marcus quickly recruited a small cadre to carry out his business plans. Instead of waiting for Easy E to strike, Marcus launched his own attack on the unsuspecting drug lord.

The murder of Easy E Carruthers shocked no one and really didn't create much news. Many in law enforcement, as well as the criminal world, welcomed the news of his death. The police did their cursory investigation and simply ruled it a drug hit. No one mourned the demise of Easy E and Marcus immediately took over his drug operation. He showed amazing business savvy buying legitimate businesses with money fronted by Salazar and discovered a clientele of law enforcement officers from Lexington's finest. The scary figure facing Jack was a well-established figure living in two worlds: one on the surface and the other just below in the sewers.

The large, exquisitely dressed man in a custom-made three piece suit leaned across the desk to shake hands with Jack. Hesitantly Jack reached out and clasped the massive, course hand in a soft tailored French cuffed shirt with golden X cuff links.

"You look as if you've seen a ghost. Have we met before?" Marcus X inquired with a smirk.

"Oh...no. I just...*Keep it together*...was startled when you turned around."

"Well that happens. Most people are a little thrown off by the dark room but it helps me see things clearly."

"I see...I mean, I don't see...I...guess I'm just a little nervous." *Keep it together dumbass. Don't lose it now. Stop talking. Let them do all the talking* Jack glanced over at Bobby Joe who was still smirking.

"Jack...what do you think is going here?"

"Um...I'm not sure." Looking straight into the cold killer's eyes Jack saw nothing but felt a cold chill run down his spine. The silence in the room was maddening as they awaited a better response from Jack. "Um…I mean, Bobby Joe said he had to pick up some medicine for his bad knees."

The room erupted in laughter. Marcus X's bright pearly white teeth glowed in the dark and Bobby Joe's face was equally ebullient. However, turning back, Jack noticed the scarecrow hadn't changed his expression.

"Oh, don't worry about him, Jack. He's an idiot. He can't hear anything." Marcus X added still laughing about the pharmaceutical reference. "Look, you have no reason to be afraid. Its really no big deal. As Bobby Joe said…I'm a pharmacist just helping him fill a prescription for his pain. He has no medical insurance and doctors won't treat him without it and certainly won't give him the medication he needs for that kind of injury. As a former big-time athlete, I understand what he's going through. You could say, 'I feel his pain'" Marcus added with a sardonic laugh. "So, I reach out to those in the community who are left behind by the medical establishment and the legal system. Is that wrong? I guess it depends on your perspective and where you've been raised. I've simply found a niche that has been ignored and untreated and helped ease their pain."

Oh yeah, whose pain were you easing when you killed Candace with a chef's knife? Or sent your attack dogs to brutally beat Tater? Yeah, you're just a modern day Robin "Fucking" Hood reaching out to the poor wretches society has left behind. I wonder how much your benevolence costs. Damn, you are one slick talking operator. I'll give that. You can turn the shit smell of a turd into the scent of a rose. You missed your calling as a politician. Jack simply nodded his head in agreement trying not to betray his thoughts.

Marcus X's calm, controlled demeanor fed Jack's internal terror. Again, the ensuing awkward silence filled Jack with angst. He looked to Bobby Joe for any kind of signal. Jack saw that Bobby Joe's smirk had left only to be replaced with a look of genuine concern. Jack felt his chest thumping like a wrecking ball and beads of sweat formed across his forehead. An eerie sense of fore-boding made him light-headed and he could feel himself drifting out of consciousness.

Suddenly, the uncomfortable silence was broken by a familiar beeping sound. Marcus X peered down at his pager and in a low mumbled voice told his guests to make themselves at home then nodded to the scarecrow to follow him to another back door not easily discerned from the wall. Jack's eyes followed Marcus X to the door.

The dark silence was interrupted as the scarecrow stumbled into a coffee table and fell awkwardly on the floor. He scrambled to pick up his sunglasses and what was left of his dignity. Marcus X quietly scolded him and snatched away his sunglasses muttering "Give those stupid ass glasses, you stupid old fuck" as he shoved him into another room. Under any other circumstance, the scene would have been hilarious. In fact, Jack could hear Bobby Joe snickering behind him.

"Damn Miller that was funny as hell. What the hell's wrong with you? You look scared shitless. Man, I told you this aint a big deal."

"Why did he want to meet me?"

"The dude is a pretty big man about town and he needs to know everything about everyone who enters his little world. I know it sounds a bit paranoid, but hell in his line of work, its called precaution."

"What did you tell him about me? Did you tell him my name?" Jack added with a sense of dread about the possible answer.

"Hell yeah, Michael Jackson." Bobby Joe flippantly quipped. Jack sensed Bobby Joe's ease and relaxed nature in this foreign environment but still couldn't ascertain which side Bobby Joe was on.

"Seriously Bobby Joe...what did you tell him?"

"Damn, you really are scared. Look, I just told him you worked for me on repos and we were just coming back from a job downtown and that I brought you in because he hates guys sitting in the parking lot. He didn't even ask about a name or anything. Just sorta shrugged and said he wanted to see you. Hell, he's met Conrad and Robbie. You're the first dude I've brought in that he even talked to. I guess he likes you."

"Great, a drug lord is enamored with me." Jack stated silently. He felt Bobby Joe was being truthful and that eased him immensely. Bobby

Joe had never lied to him before and always had his back. With this renewed sense of trust, not that he really had a choice; Jack moved closer to Bobby Joe and whispered the startling revelation about Marcus X.

"No fucking way!"

"It's true. He's the big guy I saw standing in the doorway of apartment 121 in the Zone with blood all over him. Most likely from Candace."

"Mother fucker! Are you sure? Damn, Jack you said it was dark and you were crouching down pretty far away."

"Yeah, but the porch light was on and I clearly saw that fucker standing there with Candace's blood all over his arm. I'm telling you the truth Bobby Joe. It was him. I will never forget that face or that scene for the rest of my life."

Bobby Joe lowered his head and started pacing about the room in deep thought. Jack had never seen this side of Bobby Joe before. He was always spontaneous and reactive, never ponderous.

"Alright, I believe you. Damn, it kinda makes sense. Dude was a bit uneasy when I came by tonight. He seemed preoccupied with something else. I guess I know now what it was. Shit...we are in a bit of a mess. Don't worry though. I'll get us outta here."

Jack looked over at the hidden back door where Marcus X and the scarecrow had exited. He noticed it hadn't closed shut. Quietly he walked over to the cracked doorway outlined by a soft light. He felt that whatever was going on in that hidden room was somehow about him and he had to know.

As he lightly leaned against the door, he could hear the smacking and popping sounds like a child chewing bubble gum but the rhythm of the pops sounded strangely familiar. The voices in the darkened room were muffled. He leaned a bit harder against the door to get a view of the occupants but the door seemed stuck against something. Looking down to see what was obstructing the door; Jack saw the heel of scarecrow's shoe. *Damn that black bean pole is blocking the door.*

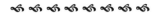

Normally, Marcus X hated to be disturbed during a business transaction and rarely bothered to take the call or respond to his pager, but tonight was different and the caller was of paramount importance. There was a potential witness to some murders running loose and scared and this required a deft touch.

For years, Marcus had been extremely careful in avoiding connection to violent crimes. He had carefully crafted and weaved a web of petty thugs to cover his criminal activity. If law enforcement sniffed around too close, he simply gave them one of his boys to convict and clean his hands of the crime. In the eyes of the law, he ran several legitimate businesses in rough areas because he knew how to handle the environment that others couldn't. He also had several aces in the hole, so to speak, in the offices of law enforcement.

A handful of Lexington's finest cops were on his "cash only" payroll. Municipal funds for the city's protectors had always been too meager and many law enforcement officers were forced to supplement their income with odd jobs such as night security for private firms or bouncers at clubs. Tragically a few turned to an easy, cash only, source of income on the very streets they patrolled.

The lure of big money, fast women and power of the badge caused some cops to turn an eye away from certain crimes, especially drugs. Many tried to justify their actions with the false rationalization that drugs were a "victimless crime" and that the only people harmed by the drugs were the users themselves. The dirty cops further reasoned that it was the user's choice to abuse drugs and that they were simply the guardians of the transactions overseeing the territory, ensuring that nothing violent occurred that would require real law enforcement.

Ironically, they were compensated better to supervise the crime than to stop it. As long as the users and abusers stay in their sphere of influence and don't enter into the respectable, law-abiding community, no harm is done, they rationalized. However, there are times when the two communities came into contact and created problems.

The Zone is a little too close to the college campus community and there have been a few incidents when they collided. Thursday night was an example of an inevitable clash and the dirty cop entrusted with enforcing the law in this area of Lexington was now sitting in a run-down laundromat at two o'clock in the morning conversing with the local drug lord.

The name on his badge was Detective Jeff Stephens. Having tracked the witness to Nicholasville and interviewed him personally, Det. Stephens alerted Marcus X to his location. However, Marcus's quarry once again lost the scent of the prey. The news rattled and disturbed the dirty cop as he feared the witness could now link him to the intricate criminal operation in the Zone. It was time to concentrate their forces and devise a plan to nab this dangerous witness, he reasoned.

"Well… you got anymore news about our problem?" Marcus inquired clearly annoyed by Stephens' presence.

"I was unaware that 'we' had a problem. If you mean, YOUR problem, then no. As I told you before, I went to his home in Nicholasville with Detective Burris. We talked to him and his family for a while. He seemed like a scared little shit. Look, I called you and told where he was. You said you had it under control. What happened?"

"I sent Big Jr and his crew to deal with it. Apparently, they got there too late. Big Jr wasn't real specific about what happened at the reverend's house but said he was still trying to track Jack's whereabouts in Nicholasville."

"What the fucks wrong with your crew lately. Seems like they can't do anything right." Stephens added with a high degree of annoyance. "Damn it, I went back down there and scratched around town and most of his known friends and associates hadn't seen him since high school. Apparently, he didn't go home much."

"That dude's hiding down there. I just know it. His whole background points to Nicholasville. White kid born and raised in a small suburban setting to a two parent home with brothers. Father is a minister and pillar in the community. That's his support team." Marcus stated pausing briefly to reflect on his own words before adding quietly, "Hell that's where I'd go if I were him."

"Well, he must be a fucking Bin Laden relative because he seems to have disappeared in a very short time."

"Did you bring his picture?"

"Yeah."

"Well, let's fucking see it!" Marcus blurted out trying to control his rising anger.

"Let's talk about my rate increase."

"Rate increase? You trying to play me you little fucking prick?"

"Easy boy."

"Boy? Look here you little white fuck!"

"Hey, shut the fuck up and calm down. You need this little white boy pretty bad and I'm holding a few aces in my hand." Stephens patted his top left coat pocket indicating where the photo was and then opened the tweed sports coat revealing his Glock G22 hand gun holstered to his belt.

Chapter 14

"Great occasions do not make heroes or cowards; they simply unveil them to the eyes of men. Silently and perceptibly, as we wake or sleep, we grow strong or weak; and last some crisis shows what we have become."

—Brooke Foss Westcott

Much can be gleaned from a person in a crisis. Some lose their senses and panic while others can calm their nerves and focus on the problem. How one reacts and handles difficult situations is often an accurate character trait. Its easy to put on a smile and brave face when things go well but the true test of one's mettle is how one reacts and behaves in an emergency.

For some reason, Bobby Joe could concentrate and see the problems clearly in a crisis. He had that unique ability to hone in on obstacles and quickly formulate solutions without real fear of consequences. In fact, his daring was often his panacea. He would boldly attempt what few had the courage to try. As a result, he rarely failed in an emergency.

The present situation in the laundromat constituted a crisis and Bobby Joe knew he had to act decisively. He sensed that Marcus X was most likely plotting their demise in the back hidden room with the person on the pager. He darted across the room to try and open the big metal door with the two-way mirror. He jerked at the handle several times but it was locked.

Uh oh, this could be a problem Bobby Joe surmised. *Alright this is the only way out unless we try to go through the hidden exit. That's a no go because Marcus X and his crew are probably armed getting ready to hit us. We need to get the metal door opened, but how?* Bobby Joe hurriedly hit upon an idea. It wasn't the best idea or one with any guarantee of success but nonetheless it was a plan for getting the big metal door opened.

Grabbing Jack by the elbow, he whispered, "Hey, the door's locked. Get the scarecrow to come in here. I'm sure he has a key. When he comes through, I'll grab him, get the key and we'll bust outta here."

"What if he doesn't have the key?"

"Then we're fucked."

"This is your plan?"

"It's the best I've got under the circumstances. You got a better idea?"

Jack pondered for a moment before Bobby Joe grabbed him tightly with his fists balled up in his shirt. "We aint got time for this shit. While you're thinking, their loading guns, boy. This is go time. Now get that fucker out here."

"How?"

"Damn it Jack, you're a smart boy. Think of something."

Jack didn't like the look in Bobby Joe's eyes. He seemed scared and that added to Jack's anxiety but he knew this was a crisis they shared and they had to work together. There was no time for devising, planning or scheming a plan of action with the least possible bad outcomes. Now was a time for action. Jack gave a quick push with the back door nudging the scarecrow. The tall thin man swung around peering into the darkened room and then down at Jack with an angry sneer.

"What the hell are you doing?" the scarecrow protested.

"I need to go to the bathroom" Jack hesitantly responded hoping it was a convincing enough request.

"Fuck, this aint no kindergarten, boy. Just go!"

"I can't. The door's locked."

Marcus X could hear the disturbance while he was in the midst of an employee shake-down. His stress level was reaching a boiling point which meant he often made quick decisions with little thought. He prioritized problems assigning time to the biggest and most urgent ones. At the moment, finding Jack Miller and killing him was priority one.

Dealing with greedy cops overstepping their boundaries was number two. Now an old, worn out employee interrupting a delicate confrontation requiring his immediate attention wasn't even on the radar of priorities.

"Leroy, what the fuck is going on?"

"White boy wants to go to the bathroom."

"Then take him to the fucking bathroom. Damn, do I have to make every little decision Leroy? God man, I wonder how you survived for sixty years without me? Go… and take those stupid-ass glasses off!"

Leroy was hurt, yet again, by the admonishment from Marcus X. He felt the younger, tough-acting little punks had no respect for their elders. In his mind, he helped Marcus X transition Easy E's operation smoothly by talking former employees and clients into staying with the new boss in town. Without his help, Marcus X would have never successfully taken over the Zone and made it prosper as it had the past ten years. At least that's how Leroy told the story to those who would listen. *Damn, these kids today just don't listen to their elders and show them proper respect like we did in the day* Leroy rued shaking his head as he pulled open the door.

He stuffed his prized sunglasses in his shirt pocket and followed the white boy across the room to the metal door. Suddenly, Leroy felt the right side of his face explode in pain. The old scarecrow crumbled to the floor like Ray Bolger's Scarecrow in the Wizard of Oz. Bobby Joe swiftly closed the back door and deftly searched his body for the keys. After finding them in the old man's pants pocket, he then lifted him into a sitting position on a large leather chair and propped it against the back hidden door while using the unconscious old man's hand to jam up the door handle. Bobby Joe's efficient moves were like a skilled craftsman plying his trade.

Running back across the room, he jammed several keys into the metal door before finally connecting with the right one and throwing it open. Bobby Joe reached back and retrieved his laundry bag from the floor before shoving Jack through the door. Jack gave a quizzical look at

Bobby Joe.

"I need these clothes. You have no idea how difficult it is to find good clothes that fit someone my size. Now come on!"

The two white figures pushed forward through the bright laundry room. The buzzing of dryers and the soapy, sudsy slosh of the washing machines filled the air. Jack felt light-headed and dizzy as he opened the glass entrance door. The rush of fresh cold air hit his face. He turned back to see Bobby Joe pushing the change machine up against the large metal door. *Damn, he thinks of everything* Jack thought as he spun back around towards the cold air.

Just as he started to run out, his face slammed flush into a large man's chest. Jack stepped back and looked up at a horrifying image. It was Big Jr wearing a huge grin. He easily lifted Jack up off his feet with his large beefy hands like a pair of eagle's talons clutching its prey.

"Well, well. Look at what we have here. The scared little white rabbit just fell into my hands. I've been looking all over Hell's creation for you and you're right here in my own backyard. Hey boys," Big Jr shouted back at his crew in his Gran Torino, "looky here at what Big Jr. found."

Just as Big Jr. uttered that last word, he felt a powerful blow to his body from the glass door entrance. Bobby Joe had rammed his body against the glass entrance like a raging bull shattering the door and driving Big Jr. to the ground. Shards of glass cut up both men pretty good but Bobby Joe scrambled to his feet first and threw a heavy punch to the large man's stunned face. He followed that blow with yet another and then stood up over the pummeled body.

"Holy shit Jack! Look at this son of a bitch. It's the black fucker that beat me with a baseball bat." Bobby Joe proceeded to kick the large man a couple of times before adding, "Hey, where's your bat, boy?"

Jack couldn't believe how easily Bobby Joe had taken out the large Yeti. Instinctively he ran to the truck and opened the passenger side door. Looking back at the laundromat he shouted "Come on, damn it. We gotta get outta here!"

Bobby Joe looked back down at his wounded prey and calmly said, "Damn boy, its your lucky day. I oughta finish your ass off but I'm in a hurry." He noticed several young punks filtering out of a car. He seized a large glass shard and held it against Big Jr.'s throat. "You little turds better get back in that car or I'll slit his throat right now!"

The ploy seemed to work as the three toughs stood paralyzed in indecision before following the taller boy back into the car as instructed. They didn't know what to do. Thinking was never required or even encouraged in this gang. Big Jr had always handled that and now he was splayed out on the sidewalk bloodied and beaten like a dying Toro in a bull fight. The very sight stunned and frightened them. They never thought it possible to see Big Jr. beaten by anyone, especially a white dude.

"What the fuck? CJ, what should we do, man?" Wheels implored.

"I'm not sure…but we can't go out there. That white dude will kill him for sure." CJ answered shaking his head in awe, "Damn…"

"We can't just sit here like scared little pussies while our boy's bleeding to death. We gotta do something!" Jumpy shouted without thinking.

"Alright, Jumpy. You go out there big boy and take out that big red-neck!" CJ retorted with equally ferocity. After a few silent seconds, "That's what I thought. Stop acting like your tough. We all know you're full of shit!"

"You, shut the fuck up, dark chocolate. You aint the fucking boss!" Jumpy knew that name would rile his crony as the car grew silent. CJ just shook his head and held his temper. He knew Jumpy was a hot-headed reactionary and fighting with him in the car wouldn't solve their problem. So, as he often did, he let Jumpy's insult pass.

Meanwhile, Bobby Joe delivered a final shot to Big Jr's testicles with his heavy wet laundry bag and then raced across the parking lot to his truck. Bleeding profusely on his right side from a large gash on his forearm and smaller one over his eye, Bobby Joe slammed his door shut, jammed his key into the ignition and fired up the truck. Jack stared at him in awe. Bobby Joe seemed to be an invincible force of nature that fearlessly tore through opponents and obstacles like paper bags. Shaking his head in amazement, Jack noticed his courageous protector was bleeding everywhere and seemed unfazed by the whole event. His nonchalant manner was as if he had just changed the oil in the car or taken out the trash. Bobby Joe glanced back over at Jack.

"What's the matter?"

"Damn, Hulk! You just dropped two huge dudes, cut up your body slamming through a glass door and act like it's no big deal."

"Hey, what can I say? Just another night in the repo business!" Bobby Joe stated matter-of-factly with a wink and a smile.

❧ ❧ ❧ ❧ ❧ ❧ ❧ ❧

Marcus X never enjoyed confrontations with colleagues, enemies or employees but he didn't back down. Often, he found that if he blew up on people he could scream them down to submission. It was a bluffing technique he learned early in life and usually worked without resorting to violence but he was perfectly prepared to go that route if necessary as most of his adversaries knew.

The present situation with a Det. Stephens was wearing his patience thin. He despised shakedowns from his drug mules, operatives and distributors and he especially hated it from cops. In his mind, cops were the lowest form of animal on the planet. He saw little difference between his rival drug operators and those crooks with badges that cut into his profit margin in the ledger. Staring down at the wafer-thin charlatan with a badge, Marcus X decided it was time to roar.

"Look, that little gun doesn't scare me and no fucking cop is going to play me. Now…give me the fucking photo, Jeffy!"

"Hey, what did I tell you about calling me Jeffy? Its Jeffrey or Detective Stephens, you fat fuck."

"Oh, I'm a fat fuck? You little dick-sucking pussy. What do you think the boys in blue will think about your little queer-ass when I send them photos of you sucking little black dicks? Huh...Jeffy?"

Detective Stephen's decided it was time to settle this problem once and for all. He reached for his gun but before he could grab it, Marcus X was on him with a right forearm to the neck and penned him against the wall. He reached down and pulled the Glock out of Det. Stephens' holster. Stephens was gasping for air but unable to get out of the death grip.

"Don't ever try something like that again. You dirty cops are a dime a dozen. I can easily kill your sorry, skinny ass and dump you in a landfill and no one would miss you. Now hand over that photo."

Marcus X pulled back his forearm and released the detective. Stephens was more embarrassed than hurt by the incident. Cops were supposed to be feared and respected by the community, especially filthy drug pushers. Marcus X had also called him out on his peculiar sexual appetite and that was even more humiliating. He hated that Marcus X had something tangible that he could hold over him and hated even more than he hadn't been more careful in his degenerate activities.

It further galled him that Marcus had taken his gun. Cops were responsible for their firearms and took pride in them. *No one was supposed to take them from you, especially a stupid, fat drug pusher in a routine shakedown* Stephens' rued. Sensing no other recourse, he reached into his coat pocket and pulled out a small manila envelope. He angrily threw it down on a small table next to Marcus X.

"Can I have my gun back now?"

"Hold on. I want to see what I've been chasing down for two days" Marcus replied and pulled the photo out of the envelope. His eyes widened in shock and disbelief. "Son of a bitch!"

"What?"

Marcus ran to the side hidden door and tried to turn the jammed handle. Furiously, he banged and violently jerked the handle before throwing his body against the door. The door gave way with the scream of old Leroy writhing in pain from his hand jammed into the handle.

The force of Marcus's blow to the door snapped it like a brittle twig. Marcus ignored the Leroy's wailing and raced to the big metal door that was also obstructed. Frustrated, he ran back into the hidden room and exited out behind the laundromat muttering "what the hell's going on?"

Stephens stared at the angry drug lord in confusion but gathered himself and followed Marcus out of the back of the building. He anxiously watched his volatile drug partner race along the side of the laundromat into the cold dark night.

Marcus was screaming at a large black pick-up truck that had roared out of the front parking lot and turned left onto the street. Through a dimly lit street light, the detective could see two white males in the truck and the red flash of the brake lights. Apparently, the driver was slowing down even though there was no traffic light or stop sign near within a mile. More alarmingly, Stephens saw Marcus X pull out his Glock and take dead aim standing from the street curb. Just as he was about to pull the trigger, Stephens slammed his arm down.

"What the hell are you doing?" Stephens screamed.

"Getting rid of my problem!" Marcus retorted with equal force. He then turned toward the detective as if he intended to take care of another problem.

"Look dumbass, you're not shooting them with my gun. I can't be connected to any of this shit. Oh and don't look at me like that. I have enough shit on you too, to push your black ass back into the pen for a very long time."

"You aint got shit! Just trying to bluff your way out of a hole."

"Alright...go ahead. Pull that trigger and watch every cop in this city descend on your ass in a heartbeat. I have several certified letters sitting in my lawyer's office waiting to be sent to the police if I'm missing for more than 48 hours. You see, I carefully set up a little protection of my own when dealing with low rent scum. If that law office doesn't get a call from me with my security code, then those letters are released and they have all sorts of crimes directly linked to you; accompanied, of course, with photos and DNA samples. You dumb fucks, literally put your hands all over everything."

Marcus stared at the cop for a few seconds quickly trying to weigh the pros and cons of every conceivable scenario from pulling the trigger and ridding himself of one problem. His whole life, Marcus seemed to have a gift for making the right decision quickly in tough jams. The ability to see all sides of a problem and the results of various actions helped him come to speedy conclusions. This acute skill kept him alive in the some of the most dangerous environments. Brute strength and daring were great attributes on the street but the thinking man still ruled.

Marcus took a deep breath calming his nerves and clearing his senses. He slowly lifted the Glock and pointed it at the detective when the screeching sound of another large automobile broke the silent tension. Marcus squinted his eyes a bit to see a dark Gran Torino heading out of the parking lot. Marcus ran over to stop the car and give its passengers specific instructions for pursuit.

Initially, the car didn't slow down until Marcus fired a shot over the roof of the car. The Gran Torino abruptly stopped with the driver screaming obscenities. The drug lord proceeded to bang on the driver side window. The tinted glass window slowly lowered revealing a severely beaten driver. Marcus winced at the sight of Big Jr's red swollen face, busted lip and large open gash under his chin. The beefy driver shoved a towel under his chin to stop the bleeding but was clearly in no mood to discuss strategy. Big Jr. had just one thought in his head and that was revenge. *What the fuck does the Boss want now? Can't he see I'm fucking bleeding over the place? Damn, Marcus what now?*

"Hey, you dumb fuck. Didn't you see me waving you to stop?"

"Yeah...but damn, I got a chance to catch those little fucks. Why are you holding me up?"

"How the hell did they get by you guys? Hell, there's four of you and just two of them and I'm sure one of them didn't do anything."

"Look, the big fucker blind-sided me and these worthless shits sat in the car!"

"Hey, bullshit! We tried to..." Jumpy protested.

"Oh, shut the fuck up! I don't want to hear your cowardly excuses!" Big Jr. roared back.

"Alright, everyone shut the hell up. Look, follow his truck. He doesn't seem to be in a hurry. In fact," Marcus squinted again looking down the road, "it looks like he wants us to follow him. Well that's a big fucking mistake. Have your phone on. We'll follow close behind. We're finishing this tonight."

"Right Boss." Big Jr. obediently assented but still boiling over the whole fiasco. His heavy foot floored the gas pedal as the car accelerated into the street and within seconds turned left onto Richmond Road to catch with the large black pick-up truck.

"Alright, Detective Stephens, let's get your car and end this."

The look in Marcus X's eyes sent chills down the detective's small thin spine. He didn't like how things had transpired over the past twenty minutes. He no longer felt like the man in charge of this volatile operation. It was like the lion turning on its trainer who had overused his whip. The beast no longer feared the consequences or pain of the whip and the trainer was just a vulnerable man ripe for killing. Events were spiraling out his control and now he appeared to be nothing but a pawn being played by a chess master. Without his gun, he had no choice but to get in his unmarked squad car and obey the chess master/ lion.

Chapter 15

"He must not cling to life, for then he will be a coward, and will not escape. He must not merely wait for death, for then he will be a suicide, and will not escape. He must seek his life in a spirit of furious indifference to it."

—Brooke Foss Westcott

The black Ford 250 King Cab eased slowly to a stop on Richmond Road heading south. Bobby Joe reached down into his duffel bag and pulled out a t-shirt wrapping it tightly around his right forearm. The gash was fairly deep and needed stitches as it didn't take long for the white t-shirt to turn crimson red.

"Damn, Bobby we need to get you to an ER or something. You're bleeding like crazy."

"Nah, I'll be fine. It's just a little scratch." Bobby Joe added with a wink. "Look back and under the seat. You'll see a little blue medicine kit." Jack immediately did as instructed and found the blue box. Leaning back to the front seat, he opened it.

"Alright, get out the gauze pads and the little brown bottle of peroxide." Bobby instructed as he slowed to a stop light. He looked back to see if he was being followed. It was difficult to tell just yet as several cars had pulled up behind him.

The sight of a few cars this late at night on Richmond Road didn't surprise him. He periodically looked into his rearview mirror for anything looking suspicious as Jack poured the peroxide all over his right forearm and then loaded the wound with gauze pads. Wincing, Bobby Joe carefully and tightly wrapped the wound with white medical tape. He then added an elastic brown Ace wrap. Satisfied with his amateur medical prep work, Bobby Joe pulled down his sun visor and flipped open the mirror. He blanched slightly at the sight of a small gash above his right eye and daubed it with a wad of gauze pads. He then pulled out his cell phone and punched a preset number.

"Who are you calling?"

"Conrad. But his line is busy." *Fuck what is that bastard doing? He knows better. When he sees my number show up, he's supposed to answer, damn it.*

"Really? Why?" Jack asked in obvious irritation.

"Setting a little trap for some coons."

"Oh really… coons, Bobby?" Jack muttered with disgust. He hated that expression and many other derogatory names about a person's race or ethnicity. He was raised by a man of the cloth who taught him to love and treasure all God's creatures and besides, a person can't help what race they're born into.

Jack hated how, too often, he let other's hateful names pass without a rebuke or protest. *Damn it Bobby! You're better than that. You have a kind and generous spirit. Why resort to this demeaning level when talking about others? I can't continue to let this pass. He needs to know better.*

"What's wrong with coons? It's not like I called them nigg-"

"Damn it Bobby, that's not cool. Its crass and crude. You're better than that. 'Coons' and the 'n-word' are just unnecessarily harmful."

"Ah come on, preacher boy. I don't mean anything by it. What should I call them? Negroes…blacks…African-Americans?"

"Yeah, you can call them black guys or African-Americans."

"Look, I don't go for that political correct shit. Besides, I think of the "n-word", if that makes you happy, as a type of person, not necessarily a color or race."

"Oh really? I gotta hear this logic."

"Sure. A 'n-word' is a punk. Like some jerk that steals from you or acts all tough and bullies people or talks a lot of shit. Yeah, it's a dude that runs his mouth, like they own the place. They're constantly talking and running others down."

"Like Conrad."

"Well... yeah I guess. I don't really see him that way. But I guess others could."

"So white dudes can be the n-word?"

"Damn Miller, you can't even say the word. It's just me sitting in here. You don't have to worry about others hearing you."

"I honestly dislike the word so much I cringe hearing it and wouldn't let it enter my vocabulary."

"Your vocabulary, huh?" Bobby Joe paused for a few seconds to ponder his next defensive statement. He hated verbal sparring with guys he thought were smarter and especially with those he liked and respected. "Well I didn't invent the word."

"I know. I'm not trying to be a little prick and I hate political correctness as much anyone else but the history behind that word is awful. When you study history and you see how damaging the word was used to demean and demoralize a group of people simply for the color of their skin and how it came to symbolize the inferiority of a race...well its just disgusting. Besides you know a lot of black dudes that are cool and that you respect."

"Yeah, I know... Derrick Sanders, Enoch Taylor and Larry Higgins are some cool dudes. In fact, I helped Larry get a job last month and Enoch's helped me a few times on repos. Dude, I'm not a racist."

"I don't think you are either. Not in your soul. You're a generous dude who would help anyone but when you use that offensive language, man, no one sees your spirit, they just hear your hateful words."

"Yeah, I guess I see your point." Bobby Joe relented and stared out the window and then back again at the rear view mirror. "Well, let's say I have set a trap for some bad dudes that just so happen to be black."

"I guess that's better but I would have just said 'some bad fuckers' but that's just me." Jack laughed trying to break the awkward tension in the king cab.

"Oh, 'fuckers' is better than nigg...black guys?"

"Yeah, because 'fuckers' don't belong to any one race. Every race has a few of them. Anyway, what's your plan and does it have anything to do with why you are driving so slowly?"

"Yep. I don't want to lose them. We need to start playing on our home court. Take them out of the city and into unfamiliar turf. They won't be as sure-footed or confident in our neck of the woods. We need to finish this shit tonight."

"Sounds good to me. These past two days have been hell. What sort of trap did you have in mind?"

"The best kind of trap. One where the prey thinks they're the predator and chases you right into your own briar patch, so to speak."

✧ ✧ ✧ ✧ ✧ ✧ ✧ ✧

Big Jr was so angry that he paid no attention to the gashes about his body or the searing pain in his face. He stared out the window trying to follow the movements of the target of his animus. He couldn't remember the last time anyone got the best of him especially in a physical confrontation. Rarely did anyone dare to challenge him and those few who tried, paid a heavy price.

The beating took an even heavier toll as it was in front of his crew, his boys. They revered, respected and feared him. To take a thrashing like that without the ability to respond looked bad. Big Jr was so focused on the road that he zoned out the din of chatter in the car. Normally, he scolded the boys for their nonsensical blather but he couldn't hear them through his focused hate.

Jumpy and Wheels were doing all the talking. Most of their babbling centered on what they had just witnessed and no one's version blamed Big Jr for what had happened or questioned his toughness. They were too scared to challenge his physical prowess especially in his present state of anger. This was a side of him they had never seen and it frightened them even more. He had always been one in control and knew how to harness his emotions.

He taught them that that was the key to fighting. Let your enemy swing wildly at you in a fit of rage while you use your head, conserve your energy and then unleash a torrent of violence when you sense a vulnerable opportunity. The secondary discussion focused on what to do next.

"Look Big Jr, I think we oughta speed up! Get right next to the white fuckers and gun them down. You know, make it look like a drug deal gone bad." Jumpy argued.

"Damn, you watch too many movies, Jumpy! Shit those crazy white boys probably have several shot guns and shit in their truck just waiting for some stupid-ass brothas to ride up on them." Wheels countered.

As the conversation continued to spiral downward with one ridiculous solution after another, the boys noticed Big Jr's temperament became more agitated. He gripped the steering wheel as if he was trying to choke the life out of someone and he was bleeding more. Wheels decided it was time to clue his boss in on his present declining health.

"Big Jr, you're bleeding all over the place. You need wrap that shit up or something. Hell, its starting to get all over you damn car."

Somehow that reference to his car broke Big Jr from his trance. He looked down at the pain in his arm and felt the blood soaking through his shirt.

"Gimme me your shirt." Big Jr growled.

"What do you mean? I aint giving you my shirt. Hell, you're going get it all bloody and shit."

Big Jr. slowly turned toward the small obnoxious figure sitting next to him in the passenger seat with a menacing look of evil. It instantly sent chills through the car as Jumpy slapped Wheels on the head from the back seat and insisted he comply immediately.

"Yeah, yeah Big Jr. Whatever you want, man. My bad. I just wasn't thinking right. Damn, these crazy rednecks have me fucked up." Wheels pleaded as he quickly yanked off his prized long sleeve Polo and offered it up. Big Jr snatched it away.

"Now hold the wheel steady while I wrap my left arm." The behemoth carefully and skillfully wrapped his arm snugly with the shirt using the sleeves to tightly tie a type of tourniquet. He knew he had to get stitches soon or he would weaken from loss of blood. But he was more concerned about payback than his own mortality.

"Alright, you guys need to shut up and keep your eyes glued to that big black truck." Big Jr. barked with authority.

"Hell, it aint hard. He aint driving like he's trying to lose us." Wheels added.

"Yeah, that's kinda creepy. You think he knows someone's chasing him?" Jumpy interjected.

"Oh, he knows, dumbass. He knows. The fuckers slowing down…he wants us to follow. Probably taking us somewhere. Some place he feels safe. Well I got news you, fuck face, that place don't exist on Earth. Big Jr.'s coming for your ass and this shit ends tonight!" Big Jr. stated with rising intensity.

๛ ๛ ๛ ๛ ๛ ๛ ๛ ๛

Bobby Joe wheeled his truck right off Nicholasville Road and onto Brannon Road. Brannon Road used to be rural, dotted with a handful of small farms with large barns to house tobacco. Now it was covered with elegant subdivisions that afforded the Lexington worker the ability to live comfortably in a neighboring county with a smaller tax bill. It was hardly the idyllic setting of Bobby Joe's youth as many farmers sold out to developers well above the fair market value. However, his parents were the exception, holding out for the rustic, country living they had always known and treasured.

Looking anxiously into his rearview mirror, Bobby Joe punched the keys on his cell phone hoping to connect with Conrad. He could hear the phone ringing and it instantly put him at ease as Conrad's voice answered.

"Hey, I need you guys to get down to my parent's house immediately. Drive the tow truck and use the old service road behind their farm coming in through the south entrance."

"What the hell's going on Bo?"

"I aint got time to explain right now. Just get your asses up there. I have a little repo job for you guys and it pays really well. Is Robbie with you?"

"Yeah, he's right here, Bo. Alright, that pay thing sounds really good. We're in the tow now. See ya soon."

"Look, when you come up the old service road, shut your lights off and wait back in the woods. You'll see my truck off the road in an embankment. There'll be a classic 1970 Gran Torino parked near it. Tow it back to the station, understand?"

"Gotcha, Bo. Tow Gran Torino back to station…out."

Bobby Joe slid his cell phone back into his pants pocket and winced a bit from his shoulder and injured forearm. Every body movement seemed to trigger the pain on his right side. He glanced back into his rearview and saw that the Gran Torino had slowed but was still following.

"Hey, you sure you want to bring all this shit to your parents?"

"They're in Florida. Dad got tired of trying to run a tobacco farm by himself and mom convinced him to buy a condo on the beach in Panama City."

"Well, who lives there now?"

"I do. I bought it from my father and made some alterations to the barn. It's used mostly to store a lot of my hunting gear and ATV toys."

After driving about ten minutes on Brannon Road, Bobby Joe sped into a hard left turn leaving a large set of tire tracks before he entered an unmarked dirt road. The deeper they drove in, the more wooded and darker it became. It was an eerie, unsettling road that even in the daylight would give one pause.

Jack couldn't remember if he had been back here before scanning the roadside for some familiar clues. *Nope this doesn't look familiar at all. Oh dear God, please wrap your loving arms around me and give me the strength and courage to face this. I am a stranger in a strange land,* Jack prayed. The truck had been traveling slowly for about five minutes and then abruptly accelerated as Bobby Joe warned Jack to grab the "oh shit" handle above his head.

"What the hell are you doing?"

"We're about to have a nasty little accident. After the truck hits the embankment, you'll need to grab a flashlight from the back seat and follow me into the woods."

"What?"

"We've got to make it look as if we panicked when we saw that we were being followed. Had an accident and are now running desperately into the woods to get away."

"Yeah…okay, but isn't that what we're doing?"

"Yeah, but we won't be lost. We'll be running to my barn where I have a shotgun waiting for them."

"Don't you think they're carrying guns?"

"Nope. At least not the big guy. He's not the type. Besides, when I crashed into him earlier, I didn't feel any hardware…just a lot of 'software'… if you know what I mean." Bobby Joe added with a wink.

"What about Conrad and Robbie. What will they be doing? Won't they run into our Zone trouble?"

"Nope. By the time they get here, those black fuckers will be on foot chasing us through the woods. Conrad and Robbie will hook up their ride and tow them back to the shop. Our Zone fuckers will be trapped on foot in my backyard. Now…hold on tight…this is gonna be rough!"

Bobby Joe yanked the steering wheel hard to the right and swerved off the dirt path into a small ditch. The big truck bounced out with a hard thud that side-swiped several rows of tree branches streaking across the passenger side. Bobby Joe floored the gas pedal accelerating the truck towards a bigger embankment for a few seconds before slamming down the brakes and crashing into an old tree stump.

The force of the abrupt stop and contact with the stump creased the front bumper of the truck and deployed the air bags. Jack's face hurt from the explosion of the air bag but adeptly pushed it out of his way as he watched Bobby Joe scramble out of the truck. Craning his head back to his left, Jack saw Bobby Joe digging through his truck box in the payload. He retrieved two flashlights and ran around to Jack's side of the truck. The passenger side door was jammed as both Jack and Bobby Joe yanked on it and pounded it for a few minutes before it gave way and opened. Bobby Joe reached into the glove compartment and pulled out a revolver hand gun.

"Here, take this gun and flashlight…just in case we get separated. You okay?"

"Yeah…damn man, when you set a trap…you set a trap." Jack said shaking his head in both pain and wonderment. The cold night air stung Jack's lungs as he emptied out into the culvert. The landing was painful as Jack's sprained ankle had stiffened. He ably limped over to the steep incline using the side of the truck for balance.

"Yeah, well its gotta look real. Now come on, old man. Why are you limping so badly? Did you bust your ankle in the crash?" Bobby Joe instructed.

"Nah. This ankle is injured from last night's run through the Zone. I busted it going down a hill like this one."

"Think you'll be able to climb this one?"

"I have no choice."

The two men started up the steep embankment grabbing stray vines and clumps of jutting rocks to gain balance. Each step was cautious and slow. Searching for a solid foot hold and reaching for the next rock above was painfully slow.

Jack worried that the plan was doomed to fail as they would be caught by the Zone gang slipping and sliding down the embankment. Every tug and pull up the hill reminding him of how badly his ankle was sprained. *Damn, this ankle might have stretched or torn ligaments. Its similar to the pain I felt after that pick-up game last year at the Seaton Center when I really fucked it up. Stupid jack-ass getting up under me on my jump shot causing me to land awkwardly on his dumb foot. God that hurt, but… I couldn't put any weight on the foot after that fall. So, it must be a bad sprain. I can work through that. Hell, I've got to or else….*

In daylight, the fifteen foot vertical cliff would have been difficult to climb much less in the dark with several cuts, sprains and bruises from the crash, but the two persevered. Somehow, Jack was able to ignore the pain and pull himself up to the top first. He flipped on his flashlight and scanned the approaching woods trying to find the barn.

The light revealed nothing but a dense series of trees before him. He felt a sense of dread over the daunting task of maneuvering through the impenetrable mass of woods with a busted ankle. Looking back down the cliff he noticed his big buddy was struggling to scale the cliff.

Jack's pain was miniscule compared to what Bobby Joe was experiencing. His arm started bleeding again through the wrappings and his shoulder ached with each tug on a vine or pull up on an exposed rock. Reaching down, Jack grabbed Bobby Joe's arm and yanked up. Bobby Joe screamed in anguish and jerked back his arm.

"Fuck, Miller what are trying to do…tear my arm off?"

"Sorry, sorry…I forgot about the arm. Damn man, its bleeding again."

"Thanks Dr. Miller for your keen observation! Just stand back, I'll get up there." Bobby Joe grimaced as he lunged upward at an old exposed root and clambered to the top. He slowly rose to his feet and stood erect stretching out his wounded arm and shoulder to ease the pain.

Peering into the woods and down at the road, he directed Jack to follow him. Walking back towards the road and away from the crashed truck, Bobby Joe perched himself on a large boulder.

"Why are we stopping? Shouldn't we be heading towards your barn?" Jack asked.

"Do you still have the gun I gave you?"

Reaching back and feeling for the small weapon, Jack affirmed that the gun was still in the back of his waistband though not as secure as he wanted. He pulled it out and tried to put it in his front pocket but it felt awkward and he was afraid it might go off. So he adjusted it several times and concluded it would have to stay in his back waistband. Bobby Joe watched his buddy with slight amusement and annoyance.

"Do you even know how to fire that thing?"

"Yeah, I guess. You just point and pull the trigger, right?"

"Yeah…just make the sure the safety's off. Here, I'll show you." Bobby Joe insisted. Jack handed him the revolver and watched him expertly slide the safety to the off position.

"There you go. Now be careful. Its ready to rock and fire."

"Okay, but seriously, shouldn't we be heading to your barn?"

"Not just yet. We're waiting for the prey to catch up." Bobby Joe mumbled as his eyes searched down the road for signs of the Gran Torino. A smile came across his face as he spotted a flicker of light sprinkle through the tree-lined old service road.

"Speak of the devils…here they come."

Jack squinted and watched in horror as the large dark vehicle from the laundromat slowly crept along the dirt path. Instinctively he turned toward the woods to run, but Bobby Joe grabbed his arm.

"Not yet, Jack. We've got to wait until they find the truck."

<u>Chapter 16</u>

"That which in mean men we entitle patience is pale cold cowardice in noble breasts."

—Shakespeare

There was a stillness in the cold night air along the countryside just on the outskirts of Lexington on the Fayette-Jessamine County border. Massive oak trees hung over several roads littered across the rural expanse with its overreaching branches gently swaying, trying to block passage to the rich lush plains that once produced a vast quantity of tobacco. Prized for its beauty, fertility and distance from the city, the farmland was an ideal possession for the local gentry. However, it's not too distant past also held the secrets of a shameful owner who regularly watched strange fruit swing from the venerable hardwoods reminding visitors of the silent code of servility and order in the era of southern Redemption.

Creeping slowly down one of these troubled roads, the gang members from the Zone unwittingly entered a world from the past that had never treated their people kindly. Big Jr.'s vision of the road was partially blinded by the rage in his soul. He couldn't remember the last time anyone had gotten the best of him or when he had felt such an intense hate. *How in the world did I allow that white fucker to beat me like that? I've been hit before, but damn, not like that. I was so damn numb from the initial hit. Like I couldn't move. Just paralyzed as that fucker punched the hell out of me!*

Each second, he relived the event he gripped the steering wheel even harder. His rage blinded him to the pursuit of the truck owner that had caused the anger. Several times members of his posse screamed at him to turn left or right as he lost sight of the truck's red lights. Each time he scolded his crew to silence because he "knew what the fuck he was doing".

In reality, Big Jr was experiencing a rare emotion— fear. Just acknowledging its existence, in himself, was unthinkable and inconceivable, or so he thought, and yet here he was trembling in pain, anger, self-doubt and fear. *What the hell is going on? Damn, big boy, get it together. If you're going to catch that ole redneck, you need your head on straight. Stop losing focus on the road. Think things through. Get control!*

"Alright, damn it, I saw him turn left. Just calm down. I can turn around. Just shut the fuck up!"

"Hey Big Jr, what did the Boss say back at the laundromat?" Jumpy inquired breaking the momentary silence.

"He said he wanted us to follow but don't do anything until he gets there" Big Jr muttered as he spun his classic muscle car into a hard left turn and then quickly jerked the wheel back to the right and onto an old dirt path.

"Fuck that shit! They might get away. Besides I don't even see another car following us. How's the Boss gonna even find us if he aint even near us?" Wheels implored.

"I've got my cell phone, idiot. Now stop asking stupid-ass questions. I'm trying to concentrate on what to do."

"Shouldn't we do as the Boss said?" C.J. calmly offered from the back seat.

"Hell no! We need to take care of this shit ourselves. This is our problem. Besides, the Boss will be happy to see that we can handle this kind of problem and, hell, gives us more shit to do. And more shit, means more money!" Jumpy smugly grinned exposing a set of fake golden caps on his front two teeth.

"Shut up, Jumpy. That aint the way it works with the Boss." Big Jr ordered and then stared into the rearview mirror for several seconds. "What do you think we should do then, C.J.?"

The car got eerily quiet as the stunned boys turned toward their taller and quieter comrade. The very fact that their boss and mentor had asked advice from anyone, much less one of them, left the obnoxiously loud boys quiet in anticipation of an answer.

176

"Well...since you're asking. I think we should definitely wait. First of all, its dark as hell out in this country. I mean shit, there aint no street lights of any kind out here. Secondly, none of us know where the hell we are. Its obvious these white boys are leading us somewhere that they are extremely familiar with. They're taking us out of our comfort zone to God knows where. Thirdly, and this is the most important point, the Boss said to wait. You guys know how he gets when we don't do exactly what he says. He fucking blows up. You know that Big Jr."

Again, silence ensued as the car moved slowly down the darkened, tree-lined path. The gang was trying to make sense of what C.J. had offered. They knew he was right but instinctively the three wanted to a lash out at their prey without hesitation. All eyes returned to Big Jr in anticipation of his response.

"Look around you, Big Jr. The big white dude has led us to hillbilly land. I've heard all kinds of crazy shit happens to black folks out here. This place gives me the creeps."

"Man, skip that! You're afraid of your own damn shadow, dark chocolate! I aint afraid of no crazy white boys!" Jumpy added.

"Fuck you Jumpy! I'm tired of that 'dark chocolate' shit. It aint funny!" C.J. insisted with an intensity rarely seen by the boys. The two stared at each other waiting for a false move to start a fist fight stemming from a quarrel that occurred several months ago in apartment 121 over a girl. Big Jr glared at the rearview mirror waiting for something to go down.

"Damn boys! There aint no need to fight each other. The fight is out there with the white boys. I aint afraid cause I got my piece right here and aint nobody messing with my ass!" Wheels declared flashing his small .38 revolver.

"Where the hell did you get that piece of shit?" Big Jr snapped.

"Hell, it aint no piece of shit, Big Jr. I got it from Geoffrey. He said its called a 'Saturday Night Special' and I got it for a good price."

"It's a piece of shit and its called a 'Saturday Night Special' because most people are fucked up on Saturday night and would never buy that shit on any other night, dumbass." Big Jr's insulting declaration eased the tension in the car as everyone except Wheels started laughing.

"Hey, why the hell didn't you pull that piece of shit out when that white fucker was on top of me?"

The car returned to silence as all eyes focused on Wheels in the front seat. He seemed to cower next to the girth of Big Jr and the last question ate away at his manhood. For a moment the loud, big mouth seemed unable to speak. He weakly offered, "I forgot that I had it. Its so small that I keep it in my front pocket."

Big Jr. simply shook his head in anger and frustration at this latest revelation. *Are you fucking kidding me? I took that beating for nothing? You could have pulled that shitty revolver out and finished this whole thing thirty minutes ago* Big Jr mulled over before angrily shouting, "Damn it Wheels! What the hell's wrong with you? You see some white fucker beating on me and you sit with a fucking gun and do nothing?"

"I swear, Big Jr. I had no idea I had the gun on me. I just noticed it a few minutes ago" Wheels pleaded.

"I believe it. Hell, Wheels is stupid as shit!"

"Shut up, Jumpy!"

"Alright both of you, shut the hell up." Big Jr insisted as his eyes focused on a large truck jammed into a ditch off the road about two hundred yards away. "Well, looky what we have here. Looks like our little white boys panicked and had a little accident."

The Gran Torino slowed to a crawl as Big Jr glared at the big black truck resting awkwardly down in the gully. The back end of the truck was poking out towards the road. Big Jr. shifted the car into park.

Looking back into the car he barked, "Everybody stay put. I'm going to check out what happened here. Wheels, get that the piece of shit out and shoot at anything that looks white. The rest of you, be ready to attack when or if you see anything that looks suspicious. For God's sake Wheels, hold that gun steady. Stop playing with it like a toy. You're going to shoot one of us."

"Sorry, Big Jr."

The massive driver and once skilled lineman languidly eased out of the front seat with several momentum building thrusts towards the door. The boys learned to suppress the comical sight of their large boss's exit out of any tight fit, especially the driver's side with the wheel jammed into his oversized abdomen. They knew the pain of Big Jr's sensitivity. It simply wasn't worth the laughter of the amusing sight. It was just one of many reasons Big Jr. didn't drive. But tonight was different and his mind was set on revenge.

Standing erect and stretching his sore back and shoulders, Big Jr winced as he adjusted the makeshift t-shirt bandage around his arm. The gash seemed to stop bleeding but it was still painful. Peering out into the blackness of the surrounding trees mounted on a steep cliff, Big Jr. leaned his large bald head back into the car, "Gimme my bat C.J." Dutifully, the tall slender youth handed him the black 44 ounce Henry Aaron model bat.

Looking back at the crashed truck, Big Jr proceeded cautiously tapping the bat on the pavement in a nervous manner. There was something about the way the truck was positioned off the road and wedged into the deep gully that gave him pause.

Approaching the truck's front door, he could see that the air bags had deployed. His car's headlights provided just enough light to also see that there was a slight indentation in the front bumper resting snuggly into an old tree stump, but not too severe. *That shit could easily be banged out*, Big Jr surmised. *This shit seems too clean*, he mumbled while nodding his head.

He ran his hand across the side and back of the truck and peered back down the road at the skid marks. *Damn, what the hell caused them to suddenly jerk off the road and crash head long into a tree?* That question kept gnawing at him like an ensnared animal working away at his bindings but unaware of where the real trap lay. *Maybe a deer ran across the road and forced them to swerve? Ah, shit that's not likely Big Jr. These country rednecks in a big truck wouldn't budge if they saw an animal cross the road. Hell, that's their dinner for the night,* Big Jr. smiled at the funny generalization of rural white folks. *Damn, I could use a flashlight right now. Wonder if the redneck has one in his truck box?*

Returning to the back of the wrecked truck, he banged and prodded at the tool box in the payload but couldn't get it open. *Well fuck, now what?* Confused and bewildered he rose his head and scanned the dense dark cluttered woods hanging over the road. *Where the hell did they go?*

Tapping his bat against the back gate, he dipped down into the gully gingerly holding onto the passenger side of the truck. He noticed the door was left ajar. Pulling it open further he observed traces of blood on the front seat on the driver's side. *Well, well looks like the big boy's hurt. Must've been from the scuffle earlier because there's no broken glass. However, our little white boy doesn't seem hurt from looks of things on his side.*

Big Jr.'s eyes returned to the headlights of his car. He could make out that his boys were getting antsy. Suddenly his eyes shot up to the side of the cliff. He saw a flicker of light coming from the top of the embankment. *Well, our stupid white boys aren't too far away. Dumbasses have flashlights but those assets have turned against them. Its now my guiding light,* he mused and jogged tepidly back to his car. Leaning into the driver's side window he ordered his posse to get out quietly.

"Don't slam the door. Hell, don't even close the door. We don't want to scare away the little white rabbits."

"What the hell's he talking about? We aint looking for rabbits are we C.J.?"

"Oh damn it, Wheels. No. He means the white guys." C.J. replied sharply.

"Oh…yeah…right."

"Shut the fuck up. No more talking. Just listen and use your fucking eyes. See that small light? We need to follow it." Big Jr snapped.

180

"Damn Big Jr., that's at the top of a big fucking hill." Jumpy inserted quietly.

"More like a mountain. Damn, that shits bigger than the one near our apartment." C.J. added.

"Hey, what did I say about talking? Come on. Let's get up that hill. It looks like the light is moving."

The climb to the top was relatively easy for his posse. They crawled up the incline like hiking experts adeptly grabbing rocks above and securing footholds from which they propelled upward. Their powerful athletic legs helped them adjust to the uneven juts in the earth as they scrambled to the top.

However, the trek was not easy for their obese boss. On a good day in the afternoon light, he would have struggled to get up the cliff, but at night with body injuries, he was severely handicapped. Each stretch and tug brought pain anew. He winced and grimaced silently trying to move his large mass upward but rarely advanced as each foothold gave way. He seemed to be slipping and sliding more than climbing. Looking up at the boys on top, Big Jr. said, "Do you still see the light?"

"Yeah, but its moving Big Jr. You need to hurry up or we'll lose them." Jumpy cried.

"Fuck, you think I'm playing around down here. It aint easy pushing this powerful frame up this damn hill. Look, take off your belts and link them."

"What the hell's he talking about?" Wheels inquired of C.J.

"Damn boy, he wants us to make a rope to lower down so we can pull him up." C.J. answered with annoyance.

"We aint never gonna be able to pull his fat ass up." Jumpy declared flatly.

"Oh, I bet you won't say that to his face!" Wheels challenged.

"Damn it you two stop eyeing each other like that. Let's do what he said. Do you guys want to chase those white boys without Big Jr?" C.J. countered.

Looking at each other while thinking about the laundromat scene and what that huge mountain man did to Big Jr, the boys quickly took off their belts and linked them together by the buckles. C.J. lowered the makeshift rescue rope down to his boss. Big Jr wrapped the leather strap around his right hand and pulled. At first the powerful tug gave way as the boys at the top weren't prepared for the sheer size and weight below. They quickly reassembled their formation based on their own weight distribution as Jumpy positioned himself behind a small tree and pulled at Wheels' waist. Somehow the trio managed to create a fulcrum on the side of the hill and pulled Big Jr to the top.

Once atop the steep craggy-faced embankment, Big Jr rubbed his aching shoulder and stared into the dense woods searching for the light trail of the frightened prey.

"Damn, boys I don't see it. Where did you guys last see it heading?"

"Big Jr. it was moving that way." Wheels answered pointing leftward trying to convince the others of his fealty to his boss.

"Look…there it is. Its moving again." Jumpy shouted with joy at his ability to spot and track the treasured prey.

"Okay, good Jumpy. Now let's spread out a bit and chase that light. Boys, if you have to run to keep up, then do it. Don't wait on me. Wheels, you still got that gun?"

"Yeah boss, right here."

"Good, if you have to use it, use it. But try not to kill them. I want my payback, especially on the big fucker." Big Jr. ordered. The very thought of catching up to the mountain man brought a rare smile across his face. *I'm gonna really enjoy hurting that fucker before he dies.*

❧ ❧ ❧ ❧ ❧ ❧ ❧ ❧

Jack's ankle was throbbing in pain as he reached down several times to rub it. He knew he had no time to spare but what good was running through the dense woods and uneven ground if your foot's busted. He looked over at Bobby Joe who seemed to be worse off. He looked ashen and worn. This trek through the woods was zapping him of his strength and energy. The two stopped for a moment to catch their breath and rest their injuries.

"Shut off your light." Bobby Joe puffed through a pained gasp of air. "This will confuse them for a while. Look back and listen carefully. You'll hear them arguing with each other over which way to go. It'll buy us some time to rest up."

"I still don't think it's a good idea using these flashlights. Damn, it's a huge risk having them follow us."

"That's exactly what we need them to do. Otherwise they'll get lost. We need them to follow us into the briar patch, Br'er Rabbit."

"You mean the barn. Damn, Bobby Joe you don't look so good. You sure you'll be okay? How far away is your barn?"

"Not too far…and don't worry about me. I'll be fine when the heats on and the shit goes down."

That last phrase was reassuring as Jack began rubbing his ankle again. He looked back and heard the snapping of twigs and branches from many different directions. The predators seemed to be heading in the wrong direction.

"Geesh, those fuckers are stupid as hell. They couldn't track a fresh turd on a hot Louisiana morning" Bobby Joe sneered. Pulling himself back to a standing position and rotating his right arm around slowly, Bobby Joe attentively adjusted the wrap on his wounded right forearm. It was still bleeding but not as profusely. The tight bandage apparently slowed the flow and closed the gash enough that he wasn't as light-headed as before in Lexington.

"I guess we're going to help them out by turning our flashlights on again, right?"

"Yep."

"Look, Bobby what's the big plan. How does this thing end? I need to know what you're thinking. You're pretty fucked up right now and hell, we both know we can't rely on me to do anything heroic."

"That's bull shit Jack! I told you, don't talk like that. You have plenty of guts. Hell, if I didn't think so I wouldn't have come out here with you. I believe in you, man. I know there's an angry dude down in there that's ready to explode on someone and hell, I want to see that shit." Bobby Joe added reassuringly.

The little pep talk did wonders for Jack's confidence. Bobby Joe noticed a perceptible change in Jack's mien. He stood upright and shook out the stiffness in his legs as if he were preparing for a jaunt. Bobby Joe smiled with confidence at how his words had affected his buddy's attitude and demeanor. He now seemed poised for what lay ahead.

Wincing in pain, Bobby Joe wasn't so sure about his own ability to be a hundred percent when everything went down in a certain bloody confrontation but felt easier about Jack. When pushed into a desperate corner, he felt certain Jack would have his back though there was no basis for this line of thinking since Jack had shown no inclination towards violence, especially as of late, but for some reason Bobby Joe believed.

The power of friendship and bonds of brotherhood were strong. He felt it and was sure Jack did too. *Jack's smart and braver than he knows. He's not a boastful idiot like Conrad who really only attacks the weak. I've never felt he would back me in a tough situation. More likely to run. Robbie might try but he's too damn weak and small to help. He doesn't lack guts, just strength. But Jack... has both. He just doesn't know it.*

"Look, my barn's through that patch of trees. There's a clearing beyond the trees. We'll go into my barn and get my shotgun."

"Then what? We shoot it out?"

"Well, only if they have guns. But I don't think that's likely. The big one definitely isn't packing. I didn't feel one on him when we tangled earlier at the laundromat. Besides, like I said before, he's not the type. He wants to beat the hell out of you with his hands or that fucking baseball bat we saw him playing with at the bottom of the hill. A little gun is not his style."

"What about the others?"

"Well, you tell me. Did they use a gun on your friend Tater behind Three Goggles?"

"No."

"Okay then…look, once we get them to follow us to the clearing, they'll see the barn. Its lit up by a big fucking utility light next to the barn. Once inside, we'll set a trap."

"What kind of trap."

"The kind where the fucking rats don't come out."

"We're killing them?" Jack asked with dread and hesitation fearing the answer he was certain to hear.

"Hell, Jack we aren't bringing them into the barn for a debate about their immoral ways. These boys followed us to kill us and they will. You know that. Damn, you saw it with your own eyes. Don't you want to get pay back for that girl, what's her name?"

"Candace."

"Yeah, Candace and your boy, Tater. Damn, Jack that oughta fire yer ass up just thinking about what they did."

No sooner did those words come out of Bobby Joe's mouth than the haunting scream of Candace came crashing down like cymbals in his head. He could see her beautiful innocent face laughing playfully in class. Her long red auburn hair splashed about the autumn leaves lying on her back seductively drawing him towards her. The soft supple feel of her skin awakened his senses. Alas, the image of his buddy being beaten to a pulp by those worthless deadbeats caused him to ache inside thinking about Tater's lifeless eyes staring at him. Jack could feel a surge of anger and adrenaline course through his veins.

"Yeah it does, damn it. It does. There's no way those fuckers don't die tonight. Its payback time." Jack murmured.

"That's my boy! Alright, you ready to rock and roll?"

"Yep."

"Okay, let's hit those flashlights and help lure them to the barn."

The pair flashed their lights back toward the sounds of their pursuers and began walking cautiously through the clumps of trees. Not being able to use his light for guidance, Jack stumbled several times a like a drunken old sot on the uneven ground littered with several dead branches. Bobby Joe was slightly ahead of him because he knew the way out, but Jack was falling further behind. His ankle was getting worse with each jagged step, stumble and slip. *This shits impossible to run through in daylight. How in the hell is Bobby Joe getting through so fast? Oh Shit…it sounds like they're getting closer. Real fucking close.*

The fast snapping twigs sent shivers down Jack's spine. *Fuck, what if I don't make it to the barn. That traps no good to me. Hell, I'll be dead. Screw this, its time to start running.* Jack turned the flashlight forward to see what was ahead instead of leading the quarry to him.

As he started to run, his stiffened ankle, again, burned with pain. *Can't think about that right now. Have to ignore it.* Jack's ability to disregard pain and agony served him well as he scampered through the obstacle course of downed trees and low branches. Several smaller vines and thickets scratched and tore across his body slightly slowing him. Ably clawing back, he freed himself from one obstruction and hindrance to another.

He trailed Bobby Joe as best he could watching the light dart about the woods. The big guy was fairly nimble bouncing about in the darkened woods. Jack could see that he was gaining until his foot

186

jammed into a dead tree causing him to land awkwardly in a sunken foot hole.

The fall was hard and left Jack slightly woozy and confused. The sound of his pursuers brought him out of his foggy state. Looking up, he could see the clearing and a large light pole illuminating the barn. He could also see Bobby Joe waving at him to hurry. Pulling himself to his feet, he instinctively reached for his gun in his waistband. *Oh shit! Shit! Shit! Shit! Where the fuck is my gun?* Panicking, Jack flashed his light across the ground in a vain search for his gun. All he could see was dirt, branches, billions of leaves scattered about and some type of thick shrubbery

"Come on, Jack. Hurry. I can hear them coming on quickly behind you." Bobby Joe called out.

Jack could also hear what sounded like an angry cluster-fuck behind him. His Zone pursuers were struggling as well weaving through the morass of tangled vines and thorny thickets reaching out to scratch someone. He could hear their angry voices cussing at "mother-fucking nature" and blaming stupid white people for living out in this "stupid shit hole".

Jack understood their frustration but his was greater as he couldn't locate his "mother-fucking gun". *Damn, I wonder if I dropped it further back where we rested above the road. Yeah, I'm sure that's where it is because I remember adjusting it before we headed into the woods. It must be near that big rock Bobby Joe was sitting on. Oh shit, I can't go back there.*

Turning back towards the barn, Jack pulled himself out of a crouched position and started jogging into the clearing about a hundred yards away. He couldn't help feeling naked and vulnerable without his gun. Though big Bobby Joe was waiting for him at the barn entrance, it wasn't the same as the cold metal piece of "life insurance".

Spinning the combination lock attached to the large barn door, Bobby Joe frustratingly yanked down trying to pop off the lock. He couldn't see the numbers very well and ordered Jack to hold his light on it. The sounds from the woods were getting louder as Bobby Joe's hands spun the lock dial several times before finally hitting on the right sequence. He popped the lock and angrily threw it down. Pulling the wooden door open, Jack was instantly hit with the scent of freshly cut hay. He could feel his chest tighten as his breathing became difficult. He had asthma and all kinds of grasses forced his respiratory tubes to contract. Stress made it even worse.

"Damn, Bobby Joe. I didn't think you'd actually have hay in here."

"What the hell, Miller. It's a barn with a hay loft. What'd you expect was gonna be in here?"

"Yeah…I guess… but damn…" Jack tugged at his neck. He could feel his lungs tighten already and his skin itch.

"Oh that's right…you have asthma. I forgot. I remember, you ditched out of that hay ride in high school after Senior Night. Fuck me. Oh well, we aint got time to go anywhere else."

"I know. I'll be alright. What's the plan?"

"Alright, you'll need to climb up to the hay loft and hide behind that stack of hay." Bobby Joe pointed to his right facing the darkened barn. Jack's eyes followed Bobby Joe's finger to the top of the old two story hay loft. He scanned the top level. There was a makeshift ladder propped up to the second tier where several neatly stacked hay bales were littered against the walls with a wide loading door at the back center. His eyes returned to the floor covered with loose straw and several stalls; one had an old John Deere tractor parked in it.

There were hundreds of tools hung about the far wall to the left of the entrance. Jack's eyes returned to Bobby Joe who was pulling open a wide door on a tool shed. He pulled out a double barreled shot gun and began loading it with shells. *Oh, thank God, Bobby Joe has that shotgun. I wonder if now's a good time to tell him about my missing gun? Shit that'll only piss him off and he'll lose confidence in me. I can't keep letting him down with my ineptitude. Best to say nothing.*

"Alright Jack, climb up that ladder to the top and hide behind that stack of hay. I know its shit for your lungs but we really don't have a lot
188

of other options."

"Why do I need to be up there?"

"You're the bait. Sorry pal. Once they enter, the outside light will show them there's a loft and you'll need to move about a bit to draw them up. It'll be pretty dark down here at floor level. I'll be here behind the door with my shot gun. Once you go up the ladder, I'll shut the door. You beam your flashlight on them and I'll do the rest."

"What do you mean…the rest?"

"Look Jack, as I told you, this shit ends tonight."

"I don't know Bobby Joe…shouldn't we call the cops or something? I'm not sure we should just kill them this way. It seems like murder. I mean… I know they're chasing us and all but damn…" Jack implored rubbing his neck and chest trying to inhale through his tightening lungs.

"Call the cops? Like the one you said was talking to Marcus X? We call the cops and we're more likely to die tonight than these shits chasing us" Bobby Joe added with growing agitation.

"What about the Nicholasville police? They're not in on this shit?"

"Are you sure? Can you be one hundred percent sure that Marcus X and that other dirty cop don't have contacts down here? They found your parent's house pretty damn quick, didn't they?"

"Yeah" Jack mumbled trying to make sense of Bobby Joe's line of thinking.

"Look, I know for a fact there are good guys in the NPD and a few dirty ones. You call them and you're rolling the dice on which one you get" Bobby Joe stated flatly. "I'm not willing to risk my life on that call." He could see that his reasoning hadn't quite convinced Jack. "Look, let's say we call the 'good cops'. They come down here and arrest these thugs. They'll be out in less than 24 hours and hunt your ass down again."

"Not if they're arrested for first degree murder. I'm gonna tell them everything about the murder in the Zone and at Three Goggles."

"You're willing to go to court and testify against these thugs? How cute. You don't understand son, Marcus X is too powerful and well connected to city leaders. If he goes on trial, he could spill the beans on a lot of powerful people in Lexington. That aint gonna happen. They'll never convict him. The prosecution will find some legal loophole and drop all charges or reduce them to misdemeanors. I don't know a lot about the law but I do know this— Marcus won't be convicted on a capital offense. More like something minor and his ass will be back on the street and you'll forever be watching your back... oh and mine as well, cause Marcus don't forget nobody."

"I know...but it just seems like murder and I don't know if I could live with that stain on my soul. I've done nothing wrong except desert two people who thought they could count on me."

"Jack...I'm counting on you as well. I know this isn't an ideal situation but we've got to make chicken salad out of chicken shit. Chicken shit is we die. Chicken salad is we live. Those are really our only options, as I see it. These are killers we're dealing with and there's only one way to deal with them."

"I don't know..."

"Look, Jack. You're a thinker and I understand your hesitancy but what has your way gotten you? Two dead friends and you're running for your life. You got me involved. I didn't seek this out. But I didn't run from it or you. I need you buddy. Can I count on you?"

"Absolutely. You can and I'm really sorry I got you into this shit. I knew I could count on you and I guess in the back of my mind I knew it had to come down to something like this. There's really no other good outcome for us" Jack added looking down at the floor.

Bobby Joe could see that his little buddy was really struggling over the moral implications. He, however, had no qualms about doing what had to be done. He was raised differently than Jack.

Jack was brought up under the Bible with its moral compass and had an education that trained his mind to assess and analyze problems. Bobby Joe was a street fighter that survived in this environment with guile and daring. Careful thought and analysis would get you killed in this jungle. They were simply two different animals existing in vastly different worlds and Jack was now in Bobby Joe's arena. He knew Jack needed to trust his street brawler's instincts though apparently, he hadn't fully convinced him. Bobby Joe could see Jack's reluctance. *What the hell's going to convince this guy? I guess I have no choice but to lie to him.*

"Look Jack, if it makes you feel better. I won't shoot them. Once we have them at gunpoint we'll call the cops. Hell, I'll even let you do it. Is that better?"

"Yes…yes, it is! Thanks, big guy. Wow, that's amazing how much better I feel about this now."

"Alright, now get your ass up that ladder and be a quiet until they come in."

Jack flashed a big toothy grin as he painfully pulled himself up to the loft and moved behind the hay bales. Bobby Joe sensed an instant change in his buddy's body language. No more hesitancy or reluctance. *Man, I hate lying to him but he's not ready for what has to be done. I guess it's just not in him* Bobby Joe wistfully shook his head and crouched down behind the tool shed.

ఆ ఆ ఆ ఆ ఆ ఆ ఆ ఆ

C.J. didn't like the woods, especially in the dark. He had seen too many slasher movies to know that nothing good happened in the woods. He was convinced that crazy rednecks lived here to get away from black folks who lived in the city. There were cops to enforce laws in the city but out here in the wilderness, the natives meted out their own brand of justice, he reasoned.

C.J. saw the woods as a racial barrier between two distinct lifestyles. He was raised in the city and felt safe amongst the skyscrapers and bustling traffic. The ebb and flow of the city soothed his spirit;

whereas the quiet, serene outdoors and clustered woods spooked him. Behind every crackle of a branch or moan of the wind through the trees lurked an evil white presence.

C.J. was far different than his cronies, Wheels and Jumpy. He was quiet and introspective. Though he, too, was a high school dropout; the circumstances were different. His grandmother, who raised him, was sick and needed constant care. He dropped out of school to work more hours delivering pizza. However, the small increase in pay was not enough to keep up with the pace of his grandmother's healthcare. He needed a lot more money and quickly.

He had seen Big Jr. driving his pricey muscle car through his neighborhood flashing wads of cash to local idiots to make simple deliveries. C.J. had no moral qualms about making the easy transition of delivering drugs instead of pizzas, especially with the greater pay off. In his mind, the ends justified the means as he started out to save his grandmother. However, once entrapped in the fast and dangerous world of drugs, C.J.'s moral justification blurred. He witnessed the horrors and insanity of the drug world and vowed to one day get out once he had earned enough. But when and if that day ever came, was becoming more and more of an uncertainty for him.

The lifestyle of the Zone was very expensive with Marcus X deducting a great deal from his pay for rent, food and various other fees not fully explained. The eerie reality became apparent to C.J. that this "lifestyle" in the Zone was for life. There was no getting out. Still, C.J. held out hope that he could save on a big payday and exit this evil but necessary world.

Big Jr instantly took to the bright and quiet teen. His six foot three frame was barely covered with flesh as he only weighed one sixty soaking wet. To conceal his small physique, C.J. wore huge baggy clothes; it gave one the impression that he was much bigger. For some reason, his size and quiet demeanor seemed to intimidate Jumpy and Wheels; mostly because he seemed to be Big Jr's favorite.

Often, Big Jr. would ask C.J. important, introspective questions that baffled the boys. Their conversations, the boys reasoned, were nonsensical: too many "what ifs" and abstract questions about the meaning of human existence on Earth. To the uneducated minions without a curious mind, these mental exercises that C.J. and Big Jr practiced seemed ridiculous. Yet they kept quiet for fear of invoking the invective of Big Jr.

Often they would tease and taunt C.J. outside of Big Jr.'s presence but never physically challenged him due to his size and prominence to their boss. Jumpy and Wheels sensed that C.J. deplored violence and was never fully committed to their jobs as henchmen. They watched him meekly assault several victims and even back away until Big Jr arrived on the scene. C.J. knew the boys hated his reluctance to join in on attacks and also felt they believed he was weak and cowardly. The very idea of being a coward never really bothered him though he didn't believe it to be true.

The boys constantly tried to goad him into a fight, but C.J. always talked his way out of a confrontation. C.J. had a gifted intellect and ability to reason and talk his way out of a physical encounter. Though he grew up in a hostile, violent environment it didn't emanate through him. He denounced the senseless acts of assault on fellow human beings as the desperate means of the unenlightened; besides the sight of blood made him sick.

C.J. eagerly joined the gang for altruistic reasons but reluctantly participated in the assaults. He felt compelled to attack drug dealers and other "ne'er do wells" that had cheated the Boss in some way or another. But the brutal attack and beating of a potential witness to a murder seemed unjust and turned his stomach. The attack of the white dude at Three Goggles deeply troubled him and he only participated lightly when Big Jr arrived. Though he understood the importance of tracking down and killing these white guys who could put them away for a long time in prison, he wasn't fully committed to the cause.

Now he found himself running blindly into an unfamiliar and dangerous wooded jungle where the prey are quickly becoming the predator. Sadly, only C.J. recognized this drastic turn of events. His cronies were cussing and clawing at the multitude of natural obstacles in the woods while desperately trying to keep up with the bobbing light ahead.

C.J. cautiously followed the verbal outbursts of his associates and tried to make sense of where they were going and what was going to happen. He could also hear Big Jr behind him let loose a few choice words about the "fucking hillbilly land" they were trouncing through.

Damn, Big Jr's falling further behind. I can barely hear him. I hate chasing after these white dudes with just those idiots in the lead. We don't need to catch up to them without Big Jr. But he ordered us to catch up to them and he'll never make it in time… damn, I hate the idea of catching up without the boss. Listen to those idiots arguing about which way the lights are moving. I can't believe I'm following them…the old expression 'the blind leading the blind'. Oh great, now they're screaming at me to hurry because they see a clearing ahead with a big ass barn. I don't like the sound of that.

"Come on C.J., hurry your skinny-ass up!" Jumpy cried.

"Damn, what's taking him so long? I thought he was right behind us?" Wheels implored.

"He was, but you know C.J. The skinny fucker's scared of his own shadow."

"I know but I wouldn't say that with Big Jr around."

"Yeah…for some reason the boss likes that skinny fuck."

"I guess it's because he's a thinker like Big Jr." Wheels reasoned.

"Yeah well, being a 'thinker' is a convenient excuse for cowardice. That fucker is useless in a fight. He never hits anyone. Just pretends… that shit pisses me off!"

"Yeah, I know. Shh…here he comes. I'm sure Big Jr's right behind him."

"Hey, where the fuck is Big Jr? I thought he was with you?" Jumpy defiantly asserted.

"Calm down Jumpy. Damn, you guys certainly made enough noise in the woods to wake every fucking redneck in the area."

"Hey, bring their ass on. I aint afraid." Jumpy declared.

C.J. just stared at the two incredulously. He couldn't believe he was stuck in the middle of nowhere with these two guys as guides and protectors. He hunched his shoulders forward to keep his big heavy coat on correctly and stared intently at the lighted barn ahead in the clearing. It looked like a trap and he wanted no part of it without Big Jr.

"Look guys…this shit looks like a trap. Those two white dudes are probably hiding in there waiting to kill us." C.J. stated flatly.

"Bullshit! They think they're safe but they aren't. Wheels' has a gun and they weren't counting on that. I say we run in and shoot their asses now. You know that's what Big Jr and Marcus X want anyway. Hell, we'll be heroes and rewarded nicely for taking care of this huge problem."

"Yeah…that sounds good to me. Let's get this shit over with. We'll pop open those doors and shoot up the place. I got plenty of bullets in my pocket. The gun fire will scare the shit out of them and reveal wherever they are hiding."

"You start shooting that gun and every fucking redneck hiding under rocks and trees will be down on us like stink on shit. Use your head for once. These guys led us down here through the woods for a reason. They're hiding in that barn waiting to ambush us. I just feel it. Besides we need to wait for Big Jr. He'll tell us what to do."

"Fuck that, dark chocolate. I aint waiting for that fat ass to wattle through the woods when the white fuckers are scared shitless hiding in that barn. Now, are you coming with us are not? If not, I swear to God, I'll come back and shoot your ass." Jumpy added with menacing authority that scared C.J. into compliance.

He knew it was the wrong thing to do but Big Jr was nowhere near and this situation was imminently more dangerous. He knew that Jumpy hated him but never thought it had gone this far and he knew in his soul that Jumpy was more than capable of killing him.

"Alright…damn it." C.J. mumbled and reluctantly followed his two antagonists across the clearing.

<u>Chapter 17</u>

"Any coward can fight a battle when he's sure of winning, but give me the man who has pluck to fight when he's sure of losing. That's my way, sir and there are many victories worse than a defeat."

—George Eliot

Bobby Joe was crouched down along the side of the barn to the left of the entrance squeezing the steel barrel of his shotgun when he heard the Zone posse arguing loudly near the clearing. He couldn't quite make out what they were saying but they seemed overconfident. Though he had quickly crafted this trap and felt it was the best plan under the circumstances, he also knew, most well laid plans rarely worked as designed. Something unforeseen usually popped up and changed everything. He knew he would have to react quickly to the unknown variable and hoped for the best possible outcome— he and Jack alive.

The trap was set to where he wouldn't have to count on Jack to do anything other than play the bait. He just didn't think Jack was ready for any physical confrontation yet and he wanted to prevent any such scenario from happening. He also knew he was weaker from loss of blood in the laundromat scrap and would have to use the shotgun. He hated the idea but really felt he had no choice in this life and death struggle. The hunted had to be willing to be as violent as the hunter if they were going to survive this horrible ordeal. *Sadly,* Bobby Joe mused *I don't think Jack really understands this. He's seen violent acts but he's never inflicted it. He's certainly capable, as most people are, I guess, but I don't think I can rely on it and definitely not risk my life on it. I'm just gonna have to handle this shit myself and my way.*

Bobby Joe was accustomed to handling things his way nearly his entire adult life as his parents rarely gave him much guidance. They were much older than typical parents and simply had a difficult time relating to children. Though they lived on a working farm, Bobby Joe's father, Big Jim as he was called, did most of the farming with the help of a few hired migrant workers. His mother, Big Judy, also had trouble raising a rebellious son who hated everything about their rural lifestyle. Though Bobby Joe's material needs were always met, he lacked the comfort and assurance of an emotional connection to his parents. They were distant and aloof. He learned to cope and guided himself to adulthood with numerous mistakes along the way but ultimately became a productive, self-reliant man though flawed with a few weaknesses for painkillers.

His childhood was void of a caring, nurturing parent which stunted his ability to trust others. He was lonely growing up on a big farm with no one around to talk to. He actually enjoyed going to school for the kinship with others his age. He really hit it off with Joseph and his family. The Millers were everything his own family was not; loving and engaged. They may have seemed loud and obnoxiously combative to their neighbors but Bobby Joe saw a family that cared about each other and brothers that were secure in their parent's love. Bobby Joe envied that parental bond and craved the affection of brotherhood. He fantasized often of being one of the Miller boys and hoped one day to prove worthy of being included. *Today very well could be that day* he surmised rising to his feet watching Jack clumsily stack a few bales as a breastwork of defense.

He was about to call out to his little buddy that his work was pointless when he heard the rapid sound of running feet approach the barn door. The door rattled a bit as the intruders tried to figure out how to open the door without making a lot of noise. They were not successful as Bobby Joe waved for Jack to stop moving and hide behind his sloppy stack of hay bales. Jack slid back behind the stacks obediently and nervously watching the door. It wasn't lost on him that once again he was reduced to observing an event from a distance hidden from danger. He hated this role he seemed to be uniquely qualified for and vowed it would be the last time. *I tired of this shit. Stop being a fucking coward who always hides and runs from danger. Damn it, stand up to your fear. Stop being a pussy! Man, I wish I had that gun. It would totally change everything* Jack assured himself. From his perch, he could see the door open slightly as a stream of light streaked across the barn floor. *Oh shit... here they come.*

Jumpy and Wheels were too eager to wait for C.J. once they reached the barn entrance and decided on their course of action. From this point on, they would rely on their daring to resolve this conflict.

Fortified with Wheel's gun, Jumpy pulled open the door and peered into the expansive hay-cluttered barn.

The outside utility light streamed in revealing very little until the boys cracked the door wider. Convinced that their prey was unarmed and hiding in fear, they confidently strolled in. Peering into a few stalls and poking cautiously into some bales of hay, they felt lost and unsure of their surroundings. There was just enough light to make out several objects once they got up close. But they didn't like poking around in the dark searching for a dangerous prey, especially the bigger one they witnessed beat up their boss. The blind inspection frustrated the Zone duo.

"Look at this country shit. Damn, this place stinks" Wheels complained in a low whisper.

"Yeah, those fucking rednecks live like pigs. Probably sleep and shit out here. Keep your eyes on anything that mov…oh shit…look up there. I just saw some hay and shit moving. I'll bet our little rabbits are hiding behind that stack of hay" Jumpy quietly observed.

Bobby Joe watched his boy perform his task on cue while crouched down against the wall behind the tool shed. *Good job, Jack. They're taking the bait. I wonder where the big fucker is? Probably didn't make it up the hill* Bobby Joe added with a chuckle.

Gripping the shotgun tighter, he pushed himself up using his legs while leaning against the wall. He anxiously watched the two dark figures grab the make-shift ladder and move it in position to scale. The first figure moved slowly up the ladder and held an object out to the side with his left hand. *Uh oh! Looks like a gun. Damn, I didn't figure on that. Best laid plans…* Bobby Joe's last thought was broken by the sight of a third figure entering the barn. He was much bigger and taller as Bobby Joe slowed his advance. *Oh damn, here's the big fucker from the laundromat. Time to end this shit!*

Bobby Joe instinctively reached into the tool shed and pulled out an old crow bar while shifting the shotgun up under his left arm. *I'm not wasting a good shell on this fucker* he decided and lifted the old heavy tool high in the air.

"Hey, where are you guys going?" C.J. asked in a low voice hoping not to wake the crazy white spirits that inhabited this God-forsaken land.

Jumpy quickly turned back towards the entrance angrily pointing his index finger to his lips and began his slow ascent up the ladder. *Oh great, the two mighty hunters...* were the last thoughts than ran through C.J.'s head before Bobby Joe landed a bone-crushing blow with the crow bar firmly embedded into the skull. The tall lanky figure slumped down to his knees and collapsed to the floor with blood gushing from the back of his head. C.J.'s worst fears of this environment were confirmed in one deadly blow. Bobby Joe adeptly pulled the crow bar out of C.J.'s head and threw it down while raising his shotgun in the next motion.

"Alright, dumb and dumber, get down! Now!" Bobby Joe ordered.

Jumpy reluctantly and slowly moved down to the barn floor as Wheels obediently descended from the top.

"And toss over that little gun you shoved into your pants. Its probably only thing down there that works" Bobby Joe added with a smile.

"Fuck you, redneck!" Wheels retorted with little conviction. In fact, it sounded more like a frightened school girl. Jumpy angrily nodded his head.

"Fuck man, don't just hand over your gun, dumbass. He's gonna kill us!"

"Shut the fuck up. I'll blow yer ass away right now, if he don't throw over that piece." Bobby Joe stated while pointing his shotgun directly at Jumpy.

"Ah shit, Wheels he aint gonna shoot!"

"Try me! Please...just try me."

Wheels dejectedly looked over at his partner and could see real fear in his eyes. With a slow sigh, he pulled the gun out of his pants and tossed it across to the feet of his assailant.

"Damn, nigga! You just got us killed!" Jumpy screamed while angrily shaking his head.

"I don't think so…" Wheels added with a huge grin.

"What the fuck are you so happy about, nigg--" was Bobby Joe's last utterance before feeling a terrible pain in his arm as he instantly dropped the shotgun. The pain was intense as he fell to his knees trying to grab back the shotgun. He saw the blood reemerge from his bandage. He couldn't feel his hand or get it to make a fist. He turned to look up at the source of the pain and saw a huge black fist smash down on his face.

The blunt force stunned him and forced him down to the floor as his right eye was stinging and his lips tasted the fresh hay on the floor. He could hear girlish laughter running towards him as the Zone boys fell upon him like hyenas. Bobby Joe grunted and absorbed several swift kicks to his abdomen. He lifted his head to the hay loft and caught eyes with Jack. *What the fuck are you waiting on Jack…pull that gun out and shoot these fuckers* Bobby Joe pleaded with his eyes.

Jack sat frozen in terror. He couldn't believe what he was witnessing. He had never seen anyone get the best of his larger-than-life protector. He wanted nothing more than to jump to the defense of his friend but again, he was unable to move. *Fuck, fuck, fuck. Do something, damn it* was the refrain that ran through Jack's brain. But his mind kept answering "what?"—*You have no gun or weapon! How can you save him? You dropped your gun like a dumbass somewhere in the woods. Fuck, he was relying on you.*

Jack began to move and stir about in the loft. He concluded that their only chance for survival was for him to find and retrieve that gun. He peered over at the hay loft door and quietly slid over and pushed it open. The creaking hinge on the door signaled the attention of the assailants below.

"Hey Big Jr, there's someone up." Wheels blurted out.

"No shit! Well, don't just stand there looking. Go up there and get him. Its our prized rabbit trying to run again" Big Jr. commanded.

The boys ran over to the ladder and quickly scaled it to the top. They watched in disbelief the sight of a white guy blindly jumping out of the barn. They raced over to the loft door and looked down to the ground outside. It was too dark to see much but they could hear some painful moans and groans.

"Shit man. That crazy white dude had to break his leg on that fucking jump. You can't see shit!" Jumpy concluded shaking his head.

"Well...where is he?" Big Jr called out.

"Fuck Big Jr, that dumbass white boy jumped out!" Wheels responded.

"Damn it that boy's always getting away. Well, get your ass down here and chase his ass. He can't get far. He's hurt and running on a busted leg!"

The boys scrambled back down the ladder and sprinted across the barn to the door and past Big Jr, who was standing over an ailing white whale of a man. Wheels paused briefly to look down at C.J. *Damn brother, that big fucker really fucked you up.* Wheels turned his head away in disgust and anger as Jumpy was calling out to him. *Don't worry C.J. we'll get these fuckers for ya.*

The landing was excruciating as Jack rolled several times on the ground before coming to a stop. He grabbed his ankle which was throbbing but he knew he had no time to rest it. As he stood he could feel a sharp pain shoot up his leg. Wincing, he limped hurriedly across the back field and into the dark woods.

He stumbled several times and nearly fell colliding clumsily against dead branches, shrubs and prickly thickets. *Damn it, this shit is everywhere. Is there no clearing at all in these fucking woods? I can't see shit. Wait...dumbass, you have a flashlight.* Jack reached back into his waistband and retrieved the flashlight. *Oh, that's much better. Okay I need to circle around to the right and retrace my steps to the road where Bobby Joe's truck is. Oh shit...those fags are chasing me again.* Jack quickly shut off his flashlight as he decided those guys would have to find him on their own without his assistance. He cursed the idea of running through the tangled morass as apparently his pursuers did as well.

"Oh shit, man. He's running into the woods again." Wheels complained.

"Come on. He can't outrun us now. He's got a busted leg and he aint using that flashlight."

Jack's mind was racing much faster than his sprained ankle. He was devising a plan that would lead the Zone boys back to the dirt road where their car was being towed by Conrad. Jack hoped that the tow truck was still there and might divert the thugs onto them and away from him. However, if the tow truck was gone then so would their ride. That revelation might cause them to give up the chase or think that their prey had followed the dirt road back to town.

It was a risky plan full of uncertainty and unpredictable behaviors but Jack felt it was a strategy. He knew he had to lose these guys and get back to save Bobby Joe. *Finding the gun was a "shot in the dark"—bad time for a pun. But maybe I can find it or something else in Bobby Joe's truck. First, I need to get them to follow me* Jack frowned as he turned the flashlight on. *Alright ankle, you've got to cooperate if I'm to stay ahead of these guys.*

"Hey look...the dumbass is using his flashlight. Ha! Hurry he's moving pretty fast to your right!" Jumpy screamed with excitement.

"Yeah, I see it but I can't see shit through these woods and these fucking thorny bushes are eating my ass up! He can see where he's going but I can't see two feet in front of me!" Wheels barked pulling several thorny limbs off of his legs and arms.

Jack had a good pace going. Bobbing and weaving through the wooded obstacle course. But he could hear that his pursuers were not faring as well. Through the curses he could tell that they were not closing in on him. In fact, they seemed to be falling further behind. Jack stopped and rested his swollen ankle. He gently stroked the side and could barely feel any bone. It had puffed up quickly but through the run and excitement of the chase, his adrenalin was pumping rapidly and masking the pain of the severe sprain. As he flashed the light back into the woods to help his quarry regain the scent, he heard one of them calling out to him by his name.

"Hey Jack! Jack! Stop this stupid ass running and let's talk. Come on man. We aint gonna hurt ya…just talk about what you saw a few days ago. That's all. Jack…can you hear me?" Jumpy implored rubbing his own twisted ankle from a sinkhole. *Fuck this stupid woods. Damn a guy could get killed just trying to get outta here.* "What about it Jack? You ready to stop running around. I know you fucked up your leg. Just stop this crazy ass running through the woods and let's talk like grown men. What do you say? It'll be just between us…no one else has to know. Just stop and we'll talk about what you saw or what you think you know. Okay?!"

Jack smiled. He knew these boys were in trouble and desperate if they were talking about offers. He stood up and applied a little weight back onto his ankle and limped awkwardly back toward the road. He could see he was getting close as the woods were thinning. His eyes also spied a set of lights not too far away. He picked up his pace when he heard his quarry screaming for him to stop. They were getting much closer and shriller.

To Jack's astonishment, he found the large boulder that he and Bobby Joe had rested on earlier at the top of the embankment. Desperately he searched in vain for the lost gun. His disappointment was quickly erased by the flicking headlights coming out of the south end of the dirt road. Squinting his eyes, he could see the top emergency lights of a large diesel tow truck that read "5 Star" along the side. *Oh, thank God. Its Conrad and Robbie. I never thought I would utter that phrase!* Jack allowed as a sense of relief coursed through his veins.

Jack braced for the awkward descent down the steep embankment, carefully easing down on his butt and using his hands as brakes. The trip down was far easier as he called out to his high school classmates.

"Hey guys! Hey guys! I need your help" he cried out in pain and exhaustion limping out of the culvert and onto the road.

"What the fuck happened to you? Where's Bobby Joe?" Conrad demanded standing upright while Robbie continued strapping up the Gran Torino.

"He's back in the barn and ..." Jack's words were interrupted by the cracking sounds of gunfire from above.

"What the fuck have you gotten us into Jack? Damn it, I knew you were trouble" Conrad screamed at Jack while crouching down behind the tow truck boom. "Who the hell's shooting at us?"

"Some guys from the Zone" Jack answered ducking behind the hooked up Gran Torino. "Look, Bobby Joe's in trouble back at his barn."

"Then why is your ass out here running away?" Robbie asked from the passenger side door of the 5 Star tow truck.

"I ran out to draw them away and find the gun I dropped back in the woods somewhere."

"You lost a gun? Fuck Miller, that's just perfect! Now you've led them toward us. That's bull-shit!" Conrad growled turning and crawling back towards Robbie. "Let's get the fuck outta here."

"Sounds good!"

"Wait...what do you mean 'lets' get outta here'? Aren't you going back to help Bobby Joe?"

"Fuck him! I told him you were trouble and now he's paying for it. I aint getting my ass shot for some dumbass like you, Jack!"

"Come on Conrad...you can't leave!"

"Watch me!" Conrad replied as he climbed into the passenger side and slid over to shift the truck into drive. Robbie slammed the door and looked back at Jack lying on his stomach behind the Gran Torino, "Sorry Jack. You're on your own!"

Jack watched helplessly as the tow truck revved its engines and sped off in a cloud of dust. He could barely make out the sight of two figures tumbling awkwardly down the steep incline. Their eyes and attention were focused on the exiting lights of the tow truck.

Jack took advantage of the darkness and truck distraction to soldier crawl across the road and hide under Bobby Joe's wrecked truck. Again, he could feel his ankle throbbing while he rested beneath the mammoth truck. He had an excellent view of the thugs walking back and forth down the road about seventy-five yards away.

The good news was that the truck set off the ground high enough for him to easily crawl under and yet the angle it was tilted allowed him to hide up against the culvert. In the silent darkness, he could make out his pursuers conversation.

"What the fuck now, Jumpy?"

"I don't know...damn it, I can't believe we lost that fucking white boy again!"

"Hey, that fucker can run. I gotta give him that. That chase the other night and earlier this morning through the campus...whoa!"

"Man, he was running for his life. Of course, he's gonna run like a mother fucker. He aint got no choice. Son of bitch developed some jets and shit."

"Man, you're crazy" Wheels laughed nodding his head. "You can't just sprout damn jets on your feet. Fuck man, what are we gonna do?"

"I don't know but Big Jr's gonna be pissed and there aint no telling what the big Boss, Marcus, is gonna do to us?"

"Fuck...I didn't even think about that...damn" Jumpy lowered his head and peered back down the road. He scrunched up his eyes staring back towards Bobby Joe's wrecked truck. "Hey, that big white dude's truck is still down there. I can barely make it out. But I think I see it over in the ditch."

"Oh shit...no way. Damn, I wonder if it's able to run?"

206

The two hustled back down the road as Jack watched anxiously crawling back behind the front driver's side tire. He could see that one of them still had a gun in his hand. *Alright, if they spot me…damn I'm going down fighting! I'll jump the boy with the gun. They're both smaller than me and I think I can take them…what do you mean 'you think you can take them?'…you've never been in a fight with anyone but your brothers. Damn it, shut up! I have no choice!* Jack allowed knowing he had to win over his own mind before he could attempt anything desperate like a full assault on two killers from the Zone.

I have the advantage of surprise and I'm much bigger and stronger… Yeah and they've killed before, what have you done? Shut up…I can do this. Jack talked himself into attack mode. *Alright, the line of demarcation or Rubicon will be when they duck under the truck and look for me or something. I'll crawl out and jump the gunman from behind get his gun and run them off…yeah and then I'll go back and get Bobby Joe. Yes…I like this!* The last thought excited him as he now had a doable plan…at least in theory. Now he had to execute it.

The Zone thugs cautiously approached the truck and walked around with their hand touching the sides. Their vision was extremely limited so they felt their way to the driver's side.

"Hey, can you open the door?" Wheels inquired.

"Yep" Jumpy replied pulling the large door open. The cab light helped illuminate the road and part of the slope.

"Are the keys in the ignition?"

"Nope. Fuck and there's not much else in here but this big bag and its wet. Fuck…it's the dude's laundry. Oh, damn and a bit of coke."

"Well bring that shit over here. I could sure use a snort right now. Hey, Jumpy your face is scratched up and shit."

"No fucking kidding. I just ran through the mother fucking woods in the dark! Hell, you're scratched up pretty good too!" Jumpy asserted trying in vain to find a good surface to draw the coke lines with. "Fuck, this aint gonna work. I can't really see what I'm doing and I aint wasting good coke on the ground" Jumpy declared shoving the vial in his pants.

"Yeah I figured. That's a shame. I could really use that hit right about now and I'm itching like a mother fucker. Probably hit about twenty damn poison ivy plants in there…hey…do you hear something?"

"What are you talking about?"

"Shhh…I think I heard some moving or something?"

"Probably some damn deers and shit. Hell, it is the fucking wildlife out here. You got a whole God damn zoo around your ass!"

"No… it sounded like it came from nearby…like from under the truck."

"Well shit, put your fucking head under the truck and look around because I can't see shit out here."

Jack had crawled away from the driver's side wheel around to the back of the truck. He could see the gunman lower his head and peer under the door. Jack was now crouched down behind the tailgate watching and waiting for his opportunity to attack. *This is it. It's now or never. Dear Heavenly Father, I pray that you give me the strength and conviction to carry out what has to be done here* Jack prayed and suddenly felt a surge of energy run through his body. It was exhilarating as he watched both guys duck under the truck on all fours.

He quickly scrambled up and launched himself into action. He rammed the gunmen's body against his partner in a full body tackle that flattened them. The stunned gunman dropped his weapon and gasped audibly in pain. Before hitting the ground, the second man slammed his head into the opened door knocking him unconscious.

Jack stood up and kicked the first man several times in the abdomen. The powerful jolts forced the man to double over in pain. Jack felt a rage and anger run through him as he grabbed the man by the chest pulling him up slightly and then landing several punches to his face. All he could think about was Candace and Tater. The images of Tater's lifeless body and Candace's lively emerald green eyes flashed over and over in his mind as he continued thrashing the man about.

He finally threw him to the ground and stared down at the destruction his hands had wrought. He could feel his body shaking uncontrollably.

It was a surreal moment that seemed as if he had been on the outside watching Bobby Joe or someone else carrying out the assault. He loosened his fists and shook his head a bit trying to get back control over his body and emotions. He could see the second man starting to wake like an old drunken sot who had staggered to the floor. Using the light from the driver's side door, Jack looked about the ground for the gun. He got down on his hands and knees in a desperate search for the only way he could save Bobby Joe.

In the corner of his eye he could see the second man start to get up just as he felt the anger return. He jumped to his feet and kicked the man in the face. He could feel it was a solid connection and knew it might even be fatal. The man's head flipped back like a rag doll as his body slumped to the ground. He moaned for several seconds before Jack grabbed him up off the ground and drove a solid punch to his midsection.

"Is that what you guys came out here for! Huh? You came out here to get your asses kicked? What's the matter…I don't hear you talking shit anymore… what's that? I can't quite make out what you're trying to say. You having trouble forming the words, you dumb shit?" Jack shouted down at his pursuers.

It felt good to release a torrent of verbal trash on these guys who had been chasing him for two days. He felt strong and in control and that felt good. He dragged the two away from the truck and searched again for the gun. Reaching down into the culvert, he felt the metallic piece and pulled it up. He confidently checked the safety and cocked the hammer of the revolver back.

"Alright you dumb shits, you have two choices. Get on your worthless feet and head down the road or I shoot your sorry asses right now."

"Damn man, do you know who you're messing with?" Wheels

implored.

"Yeah…two pieces of shit murderers who killed a beautiful girl and beat the hell out of an innocent dude last night. I oughta shoot your asses now!" Jack added with rising anger.

"Look we didn't do shit to the girl. That was Marcus!" Wheels pled.

"Shut the fuck up! Man, he's gonna kill your ass for saying that. What are you thinking? You never squeal on a brother, especially the Boss!" Jumpy snapped back.

"Both of you shut-up. You got three seconds to make up your mind. One… two.." Jack fired the revolver at their feet. The loud crack of the gun and sound of the bullet landing near them forced both to their feet instantly as they ran aimlessly down the dark road. He could hear them arguing again about which way to go: "Hell just stay on the road" one of them called out while the other screamed "that fucker can't count!"

Jack shoved the gun into his front waist and sprinted over to the embankment. He turned on his flashlight and found an easier path to the top. With his new found confidence and energy, he rapidly scaled the incline and raced over to the big rock overlooking the road. Peering back down the road, he could still hear the Zone gangsters complaining about the "mother-fucking white-ass backwoods country".

๑ ๑ ๑ ๑ ๑ ๑ ๑ ๑

Detective Stephens could hear Marcus X talking to Big Jr on the phone getting directions to where the witnesses were heading. The men were driving into a familiar territory for the Lexington detective. He had grown up near the Fayette-Jessamine county border in an older suburb. Though he attended school in Fayette County, he knew tons kids in Jessamine and often played on many of the nearby farms. He also knew just about every back road and dirt path along the border. He felt more confident in this area than around any street in Lexington, however, he also sensed he was in trouble with the local drug lord holding his gun.

He believed that he was just as dead as the two witnesses they were pursuing and even figured out what scenario Marcus X had in mind: He would kill the two witnesses with his gun and then have Big Jr beat him to death with his baseball bat. It would look as if a great fight had occurred and both parties had died from the brutal confrontation. *It's just clean enough to work. There might be some cursory background check by Internal Affairs that will probably reveal my dirty hands in the Zone. The other dirty cops will cover their asses and make me out to be the one and only bad cop. Case closed. "Dirty Cop Kills Witnesses to Drug Deal Gone Wrong on College Campus" will be the headline. Neat and clean. I've got to find a way to get my gun away from this psycho next to me!*

"Alright, turn right onto Brannon Road." Marcus X ordered.

"You know, we would have gotten here quicker, if we had left immediately. I don't trust Big Jr and his little boys to carry out this big a job. What the hell were you doing back in your office that took so long?"

"None of your fucking business! Just drive, Jeffy."

Detective Stephens didn't like the tone of his voice or the insulting name that flowed too easily off his lips. He had never talked to him like this before. *I guess this just confirms what I thought. The fucker plans on killing me tonight. He has no fear about my phone call or incriminating evidence in a safe. He must have gotten a hold of someone that assured him it was being taken care of so he could take care of me…slippery mother fucker!*

"Look, I don't like that fucking name. I told you that once before! We got a job to do. Let's just do it without all this other shit."

"Oh, don't worry! The job will get done tonight Jeffy. It'll get done…damn what the hell is coming at us?" Marcus glared out the window at a huge tow truck speeding at them. As it passed by, Marcus could make out the words "5 Star" on the driver's side door and then he saw Big Jr's Gran Torino being towed from behind.

"What the fuck? Turn this car around! Right now! They got Big Jr's car!"

Stephens' expertly spun the unmarked squad car around at a high speed as the tires squealed in agony. Instinctively he threw the red squad light on the top of his unmarked Crown Victoria and flipped the siren on. He quickly gained on the slowing tow truck and watched in relief the red brake lights flash in front of him.

"Now what? Damn it, we can't catch a break tonight" Conrad moaned.

"Hey, make sure that bottle of yours stays under the seat. They can't search the truck without a warrant or reasonable cause. So don't act stupid and argue. Just play it cool."

"Fuck you Robbie! I know what I'm doing and I know my rights. Look, here he comes now. Just stay quiet. I'll do all the talking." Conrad insisted while rolling down his window. "Yes, officer…can I help you?"

"I'm gonna need to see your license and registration, sir." Stephens' said flatly.

"Yes sir. Robbie, it's in the glove box."

"You were going pretty fast through here. Do you realize how fast you were go.."

There was an awful blast that rang through the cab. Stephens' believed it sounded like a four shot burst. Whatever the number, the two occupants were slumped over dead with their eyes wide open and mouths ajar as blood was spewing from their heads.

"Holy shit, Marcus! What the fuck?"

"These boys were witnesses and accessories to what happened tonight. They were expendable. Now get in the car and let's finish this job tonight. I'm losing a lot of quality sleep right now."

The stunned detective obeyed the directive and numbly climbed back into his car to pursue the original witnesses. Marcus got right back on the phone and dialed up Big Jr

The talk lasted a few minutes as a huge smile appeared on Marcus's face.

"What's the good news?"

"Big Jr's got the big one in the barn and the other one is hurt running scared in the woods. He said his boys are in pursuit and he even heard a few gun shots. They've probably already bagged his white ass. Turn left on this little dirt road."

"Well hell, if they've got things under control, what are we doing at 2 o'clock in the morning out here?"

"Making sure the shit's done right. These guys have fucked up before." Marcus X wistfully stated looking out the window into the darkened dirt road with large over hanging oaks. "Man, this is some creepy area you white boys hang out in."

"What do you mean 'you white boys'? I've never been back here."

"Bull shit Jeffy! You were born near here. Practically raised on these fucking farms. I know all about you, boy."

"Yeah right…what the hell now? Who's that on foot by the side of the road? Do you recognize them?"

"Fuck yeah! It's the boys who were supposed to take care of Jack Miller" Marcus barked and rolled down the window. "Where the fuck do you think you're going? Where's Jack?"

"Who?" Wheels shrugged.

"The fucking white boy you were chasing, you dumb mother fucker!" Marcus screamed.

"Well, you see…it's like this Boss. He jumped us from behind. Damn, he knows these woods like all those crazy rednecks do and got the gun from us?"

"Damn it! Why are you guys still alive?" Marcus asked in frustration.

"Well, you see boss…"

"Oh, shut up! Look, you dumbasses take a right at the end of the road here and you'll find a tow truck off the side of the road. Its got Big Jr's car on it. Drive it back to the laundromat and dispose of the bodies in the usual place… and hurry!"

"Boss…I don't have a driver's license and I …"

"Oh, shut up dumbass. Just do it or I'll shoot you myself!"

The two wounded gangsters shouted, "yes sir" and immediately ran down the road disappearing into the darkness. Detective Stephens' turned toward the drug lord waiting for his instructions.

"Damn, Jack's got a gun. He might be going back to the barn. Who knows? I can't believe the little coward fought…damn…didn't see that coming. Better warn Big Jr.. Hey, I know you know a quicker way to get to Bobby Joe's barn from here. Now wheel this thing around and let's get going."

"Sure thing." Stephens obediently replied having cooked up a little scheme of his own.

"Damn…Big Jr's phone is ringing but he's not answering! That can't be good. Step on it Jeffy!"

Chapter 18

"Covetousness like jealousy, when it has taken root, never leaves a person, but with their life. Cowardice is the dread of what will happen."

−Epictetus

The familiar became unfamiliar. The natural surrounding with ordinary, common objects became foreign and unknown to Bobby Joe as he gazed about the barn. His brain sent blurred images with mixed and confusing signals. He tried to focus on a single object that could arouse him from this groggy state but he was at a momentary loss of understanding.

Taking a few deep breaths, he closed his eyes and reopened them. He soon realized that his left eye was injured and jaw was bruised. Licking dried blood from his lips, he noticed that he was also lying face down on a floor strewn with hay and could hear a muffled voice from behind. Slowly he lifted his head and turned toward the voice. Through glazed eyes he saw a large black man sitting atop a bale of hay with a shotgun in his lap and a small phone near his face. He could also see a black baseball bat leaning against the man's right leg.

Rapidly his mind brought him back to the present state of dire affairs. He remembered the large man dropping several blows to his face that forced him to temporarily lose consciousness. As he started to lift himself from the floor he heard the large man protest.

"No, no, no little man. Stay right where you are. Flat on your belly like the fucking snake that you are" Big Jr ordered.

"Come on, man. You've got a shotgun and a bat. I don't think you have anything to worry about. Let me at least sit up."

There was a long silence as the two stared at each other with mutual hate and admiration. It had been a long time since anyone had ever gotten the better of these two gladiators in any kind of physical confrontation. Both were accustomed to whipping their opponents easily with their disproportionate size and fighting prowess. Both were daring and audacious assaulters who had the unique ability to attack with dispassion. They had acquired these skills over a period of time and in an occupation, that required them to survive. Now, one was in an advantageous position to defeat and kill a rare equal and rival in a hostile world while the other plotted to change positions.

"Go ahead. Sit up. I want to look at the son of a bitch that killed a boy."

"What boy?"

"My boy! The one with his head split open over there!" Big Jr barked pointing at C.J.'s body propped up against a stall door.

"He don't look like no boy and that boy was hunting us down to kill us. He and two other thugs were about to climb that ladder and kill MY boy!"

"Your boy wandered into a place he shouldn't have been. The Zone is no place for little white rich college boys. He should've known better."

"And that should get him killed? Come on, that's bullshit! What happened that caused you guys to hunt him down like a dog? Did he see something? Did he witness you guys doing something ILLEGAL?"

"I aint talking about that. I aint talking to no dead man about the past. What's done is done."

"I agree the past is past. Hell, we've all done some things we aint proud of but killing innocent people…damn that's just plain evil."

"What the hell do you know about it? Its evil to you country fucks who live out here in the middle of nowhere and have no idea what guys like us face every day in the city. Scratching and clawing just to survive. Fuck you, white bread and your fucked up sense of morality."

"Oh, cry me a fucking river! You're the ones making the city shit. You fucking druggies doping up kids and pushing your shit on others."

"Yeah, to dumb fucks like you!"

"I told you, man. I aint perfect but my boy Jack, he aint done shit! He doesn't deserve to be hunted down and murdered senselessly."

"And my boy C.J. does?"

"He's a fucking killer! He killed an innocent man at Three Goggles. My boy saw it."

"C.J. didn't kill shit. That boy wouldn't hurt a fly" Big Jr ran his hands across his face to hide the sadness. "This business wasn't in his nature. He was just trying to make enough money to help his family. He wasn't no killer.... I knew that early on. It just wasn't in him. He was thoughtful, you know, kinda an intellectual type and I liked him."

"Well, I'm sorry. I sure as hell didn't know. In fact, in the dark, I thought he was you. With that big baggy coat and him being so damn tall...I thought."

"Sure. I can see that. He wore big clothes to hide how thin he was. But you fucking killed him and"

"And now you're gonna kill me."

"Have to. Look, you knew how this had to end up. My Boss can't have loose ends lying around and you and your boy, Jack, are loose ends."

Bobby Joe nodded as he squeezed his right fist to test its strength. He was shocked that he felt no pain. In fact he felt a surge of adrenalin awaking his body.

"What, are you going to use my shotgun?"

"Seems the easiest solution."

"Bullshit. You're a fucking warrior. A real man doesn't need a damn gun. Toss that gun down and kill me like a real man, God damn it! Pussies use guns and you know it!" Bobby Joe added sensing he was rousing the giant into action.

The ploy seemed to work as Big Jr rose to his full six foot eight inch height and then tossed the shotgun back against the barn door. He grabbed his bat and popped it in his hands a few times trying to send shivers down Bobby Joe's spine. With each pop of the bat though, he could see no fear in his white rival.

"You're right. I have never used a gun in my life. Never needed to. Small pricks and pussies use them. But I do love to swing for the fences and I'm going to knock you're fucking head off and piss down your neck for what you did to C.J., not to mention that little shit you pulled back at the laundromat. I owe you big time!"

Big Jr hoisted the black Louisville Slugger over his head as he lumbered over to split his wounded prey's head open. Bobby Joe caught the forty-four ounce bat in descent as the two struggled for control. The bat was twisted and pulled back and forth with great force. *Damn this fucker's strong! Can't seem to get bat from him. Need to get him distracted just enough to hurt him so he'll let loose* Bobby Joe reasoned.

He pulled the bat upward as Big Jr's eyes were temporarily diverted and swiftly kicked him in the groin. Instantly the bat came free from the black titan who cried out in pain but quickly recovered to block the ensuing swing with his wounded forearm re-opening the large cut. Again, he cried out and held his throbbing arm as Bobby Joe then crashed the Henry Aaron edition against his left knee.

"Did that shit hurt? Damn, it felt like I connected good!" Bobby Joe taunted.

"Fuck you! You hit like a little girl. That last swing was a little pop up!"

"Oh, damn that was a pop up? Well shit, you're gonna love this at bat!" Bobby Joe smiled as he pulled the bat back for a full swing. Just as he turned his hips to deliver the crack, he felt a powerful fist land flush on his nose. The punch staggered the white tow truck owner backwards as his eyes instantly blurred. He never really saw the next two punches to his face. All he sensed was a burning in his face.

"I guess you didn't see that shit coming, did you big boy? Thought

218

you was just gonna wup up on some nigga, eh?"

"Hey…that word…is offensive. You shouldn't talk like that" Bobby Joe weakly offered.

"Ha…now that's funny. A white, redneck lecturing me on offensive language. I gotta hand it to ya…you're pretty clever. Trying to talk your way into buying some time. Well talking's over!"

Bobby Joe shook the cob webs out of his head and tried to stop the next shot to his chest. His injured arm nimbly deflected the powerful blow that could have stopped his heart.

Frustrated, Big Jr forcefully grabbed him by the neck. The enormity and strength of the large man's hands overwhelmed Bobby Joe who tightened his neck muscles in vain. He couldn't pull or release the vise-like grip. He wiggled and struggled mightily punching and chopping at Big Jr.'s arms but to no avail. The grip seemed to only tighten with each second. Bobby Joe knew he was in the fight of his life and had to pull out all stops to get free.

Staring into the black man's eyes he hastily hit upon an idea for his next move. Summoning all of his reserve strength, he reached out and gauged Big Jr's eyes with his thumbs. He could feel them sink into the sockets as the huge man screamed out in agony and loosened his grip. Bobby Joe continued to dig into the wailing man's orbs until he pushed himself free. Both men retreated back a few paces to catch their breath. Big Jr. gently rubbed his eyes trying to regain clarity of vision while Bobby Joe was coughing and gasping desperately for air.

Oh my God! That fucker is stronger than a bull! Damn…can't let him get in that close again or I'm dead Bobby Joe reasoned through several coughs and pants.

Mother fucker almost jabbed my damn eyes out! He's got some strong ass thumbs. Gotta find a way to bear hug his ass and keep his arms pinned Big Jr assessed.

After several minutes bent over, the two men rose and stared at each other. The long glare was one of animosity, hatred and grudging admiration. They began moving toward each other like two old professional wrestlers looking for their next opportunity to strike. The circling continued with the occasional wild jab thrown as a feeler to catch the other off guard or off balance. Neither warrior fell for the old tactic so they resorted to a few taunts.

"Boy…I've been hit by girls harder than you." Big Jr bellowed.

"I doubt that. But it doesn't surprise me that girls would hit you. I bet the little boys you fucked didn't get the same chance."

"Ha…you're a degenerate talking like that. Of the two guys in here, I guarantee you, I'm no fag. Can't say the same about your country, cow-fucking ass!"

"Ha, ha…you stupid asses think we're all alike."

"Oh, and you rednecks don't? I tell ya what, after I kill your ass, I'm gonna walk up to the house and dry fuck your mama!"

"Good luck with that, dumbass, she's in Florida."

Neither man seemed to take the bait and blindly leave their defensive positions for a wild assault on their trash talking offender.

Again, two seasoned veterans of street fighting were sizing each other up and circling, looking for an edge or weakness to attack. Bobby Joe felt the shotgun under his foot and stopped moving. Big Jr's eyes looked down at the gun with alarm. *Fuck…I've gotta get him away from the gun or I'm dead where I stand* Big Jr surmised. He watched anxiously as Bobby Joe slowly leaned down to pick it up while staring directly at him.

For his part, Bobby Joe cautiously stared at his rival knowing this was a make or break moment. *Come on big boy…look at how close I am to grabbing that shotgun. You know it's over if I grab it and…* Bobby Joe's thought was suddenly interrupted as he saw the big man's reddened eyes widen and right leg quickly advance forward to kick the gun away. Bobby Joe reacted with equal suddenness as he threw a direct shot into Big Jr's lower abdomen. The blast doubled him over as Bobby Joe rose up and delivered another flurry of shots to the head. Big Jr retreated backwards and tried to deflect and ward off the rapid fire punches but several landed flush on his face opening a huge gash.

Sensing a fatal opening, Bobby Joe shoved the big man repeatedly until he had him pinned against the back wall of the barn. He lowered his head and began working Big Jr's midsection. He could feel solid contact on each heavy blow. When Big Jr weakly tried to cover his chest, Bobby Joe simply raised his aim and smashed his face enlarging the bloody opening. However, each punch seemed to get weaker. He looked down and saw his arm covered in blood, but it wasn't Big Jr's. *Damn…I'm losing too much blood. I can't keep this shit up much longer* Bobby Joe concluded.

He backed away to assess Big Jr's condition to determine if he had time to recoup his strength for the final flourish. He was amazed to see that the big fellow was still standing. Ordinary men would have been lying face down on the ground. Catching his breath and re-wrapping his arm he saw Big Jr staggering about trying to stay upright. Bobby Joe began feeling light-headed as the room blurred and starting to spin. *Oh Shit…oh shit…I'm starting to black out* was his last thought before stumbling and falling back on his butt and against a stall gate.

Big Jr watched incredulously through his battered eyes the fall of his assailant. He couldn't understand what had happened. In fact, he was just as dizzy and light-headed as Bobby Joe. He soon realized just how unstable he was when he took a step forward. *Holy shit…I can't see straight. The room is getting real dark…oh man…*and with that final thought he slumped down against the far barn wall.

સ સ સ સ સ સ સ સ

Gently rubbing his ankle sitting atop the huge boulder overlooking the old dirt road, Jack believed he needed to rest a bit before running back through the tangled woods. Though he had his flashlight and a better sense of where he was going, Jack knew these woods were a maze where one could easily get lost and with a bum ankle and little time, the best course of action was caution. *Better to get to Bobby Joe with energy and a plan. No telling what's going on in that barn with that big black bastard. At least I don't have those little shits following* Jack allowed peering back down the road.

At once he felt his heart skip a beat seeing the flickering of car lights through the trees. Staring numbly down the path at the lights that had stopped moving, Jack tried to assess what was happening. *Who the hell could that be? They seem to have stopped near where those Zone thugs would have been…Oh damn, I wonder if its Marcus X and Det. Stephens? Oh, shit the lights are backing up…now what?* Jack thought trying desperately to make sense of what just happened. *Oh God…am I just being paranoid? Enough of this crap. Time to get moving. Bobby Joe's counting on me!* he concluded scrambling to his feet.

Flipping his flashlight on, Jack awkwardly limped back into the wooded entrance that Bobby Joe had shown him earlier. Again, his ankle alerted him to its injured status but to no avail as he plodded down and through one obstacle after another of twisted tree limbs and thick prickly vines.

The small beam of his flashlight only allowed him to see objects immediately in front of him; so he had to react quickly to the latest obstacle to avoid serious injury or anything that could slow his pursuit.

His mind left the woods to remember the triumph of his first real fight. *Oh man was I good. I knocked those dudes down. Even slugged them several times. Damn, I kicked some ass tonight! Yeah, but don't forget: only through prayer and God's hand did you do that. Never forget that big boy. You're nothing without God. Oh man…I can't let Bobby Joe down. The look in his eyes when I left him in the barn…damn! I can't let him down…gotta get there quick…that big fucker, Marcus X, is probably heading to the barn now. He's got to know the front way to Bobby Joe's place because that seemed to be the direction he was heading. Shit! I need to hurry.*

Jack's pace picked up instantly at that last thought. He couldn't allow Bobby Joe to die tonight, especially since he was responsible for this whole mess. Bobby Joe had voluntarily entered this crisis to protect his friend and thought he could rely on Jack for the same support. Each new thought propelled Jack faster through the woods which for some reason didn't seem as difficult to traverse this time. *Either I know my way better this time or I'm going the wrong way because it doesn't seem nearly as cluttered.*

Oh shit…am I getting lost? No wait…I do remember that fucking sinkhole. Oh yes…there's the big light post near the barn. The clearing's got to be close. Jack smiled at the idea of coming to Bobby Joe's rescue with his gun. Each step forward drew him closer and gladdened his heart to think about saving Bobby Joe and proving he was worth protecting.

As he came through the woods and upon the open field, he froze in his steps. He could see the headlights of a large unmarked vehicle slowly crawling past Bobby Joe's house and turning towards the barn. *Oh no…did I get here too late?*

჻ ჻ ჻ ჻ ჻ ჻ ჻ ჻

The room was hazy and blurred as Bobby Joe opened his eyes. He was still light-headed but was able to quickly pick up on his surroundings and assess what had happened. He remembered that he had been in the fight of his life with the huge bear of a man currently slumped against the wall. Looking down at his injured arm, he could see it was still bleeding but not as badly.

Gingerly using his left hand, he re-wrapped his arm and squeezed a fist to determine the damage. It hurt but surprisingly nothing fatal. Using the gate post, he pulled himself to a standing position. Again, he felt dazed and a bit woozy but gathered himself and walked over to an old barrel that had collected rain water from the leaky barn roof. He jammed his injured arm into the freezing cold water for several seconds and worked his fingers back and forth to get the numbness to go away. Opening and closing his fist, he could feel much of his strength return. He cupped some of the water and splashed it about his face to shake away the dizziness. He heard the moaning of his conquered foe nearby. *Sounds like someone's coming to. Can't allow that big fucker any chance of reviving. He's too damn strong to tangle with again, especially in my condition.*

Peering back over at the far wall of the barn, Bobby Joe could see the huge man's chest heaving and his eyes opening. Bobby Joe walked over to a hay stall and grabbed a pitchfork. He returned to find Big Jr standing and grinning like a cat toying with the mouse.

"Well, well, I see the old country boy has found him a little toy to come tickle me with. Look here, boy…that shit don't scare me and I'm going to take it from you and use it on you" Big Jr boasted feeling a renewed energy.

"Oh…you think you can take it from me? Like I took that fucking baseball bat from you?" Bobby Joe retorted thrusting the pitch fork several times at the big man's abdomen.

"Look here, boy. Put that shit down and fight me like a man! I did the same for you! I could have killed you with your own shotgun, but that aint the way a real man handles his business. Now, stop acting a pussy and put that damn thing down! Fight me honorably with your fucking hands. There's no honor in killing a man like me with tools. We both deserve to die with honor and dignity. Not like some piece of shit weak coward."

Bobby Joe was enjoying poking the big man with the business end of the farm tool but was intrigued by the "justice" of the argument. He knew there were no rules to street fighting but there was a code amongst the bigger, better fighters— call it professional courtesy and honor. For some reason that word, honor, stuck in his head. Whatever it was, Bobby Joe felt compelled to drop the pitch fork and beat the man fairly and "honorably" with just his hands.

"Alright, big boy…I done dropped your ass once before, I guess I'll have to do it again!" Bobby Joe confidently asserted and recklessly ran at Big Jr swinging wildly for the knockout blow to his head.

Big Jr nimbly ducked the roundhouse punch and countered with a devastating blast to Bobby Joe's stomach forcing him to double over gasping for air. Then he pulled Bobby Joe's hair back and dropped another heavy shot to his face. That last hit had Bobby Joe falling backwards spilling onto the floor. His face was on fire in pain as he watched in horror the big man retrieve the pitch fork from the floor.

"I told you, boy! You should have never brought this out. Now I'm going to have to use it on you!"

"What about honor and all that shit?" Bobby Joe countered still grimacing in pain.

224

"Oh, that was straight bullshit to get you drop the damn thing. Damn, I couldn't believe it worked. You are a stupid mother fucker to fall for that bullshit line."

"I should've have known you had no honor. You're just a fucking street thug. A damn monkey who takes orders! Aint got a goddamn clue or thought of his own!"

"Fuck you, redneck. You don't know shit!"

"I know you look like a goddamn gorilla holding a stupid stick. Now come on black boy! Finish this shit!"

Big Jr felt an intense anger boiling over his huge frame. No one had ever talked to him like that. Most guys he had whipped in a fight had begged and pleaded for their lives but not this guy. He was different in every way. He had never run across an opponent as strong, daring and audacious as the man he was standing over and the rage he felt earlier after the laundromat scrap had returned.

His eyes began to glaze over in anger as he hoisted the pitch fork high in the air. Just as he blindly began the descent of the farm tool, he felt an instant pain to his testicles. Looking down, he saw Bobby Joe's foot planted solidly in his groin. He sunk down to his knees in agony dropping the pitch fork to try and comfort his burning balls. Bobby Joe quickly scrambled to his feet and kicked the pitch fork away. He used his foot again only this time to deliver another painful blow to the wailing man's large abdomen. The big man cried out in pain just before Bobby Joe landed a solid punch to the top of his head. Big Jr crashed face down into the straw strewn floor writhing in pain and cursing his adversary.

"Oh…I'm a dumb white fucker, eh! Isn't that what you were saying a while ago? Huh, boy? Couldn't believe I fell for that 'honor' shit. Well I can't believe you allowed me to taunt and trash talk you into a blind shot. You fucking lost sight of what I was doing on the floor with you blind rage. Now the tables are turned, huh, big boy? Only this time, I aint playing around" Bobby Joe resolutely asserted.

He flipped the big man over and grabbed the pitch fork and then stated flatly "this shit ends tonight!"

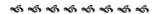

Jack crouched down behind a clump of shrubs near the edge of the woods that rose approximately ten feet above the open field below. He watched the unmarked car slow to a stop just outside of the barn. He turned off his flashlight and reached into his front waistband to make sure his gun was there. *Oh, thank God. I didn't lose it this time* Jack smiled as he pulled the gun out and checked the safety. A powerful wave of fear swept over him as he watched Marcus X get out of the car. Through the utility pole floodlight, Jack could see that Marcus X had a gun in his hand and could just make out their conversation.

"Hey, you need to get your flashlight and look up in the woods over there for our boy Jack. He may be lurking around out there with one of those idiots' gun. I don't want him crashing in on me. I'll be in the barn with Big Jr.. You stay out here." Marcus X ordered and then reached back into the car and grabbed the car keys. "I don't want you running off like the other scared white boy" Marcus X added with a brief laugh.

"Yeah sure, 'Boss', whatever you say" Stephens stated sarcastically as he retrieved a flashlight from the center console panel of the squad car. He walked around the car and beamed his light into the woods. Jack instinctively ducked down and watched helplessly as the light flashed about the trees above. Then he heard a loud "what the fuck" coming from the barn. He lifted his head to see Marcus X disappear into the barn while the detective flipped off his flashlight and followed cautiously behind. After the detective entered, he left the barn door wide open allowing anyone nearby to hear everything being said.

Oh no. Whatever's happening in that barn can't be good for Bobby Joe. I've got to get down there now. Please Heavenly Father, guide me and protect me in my hour of need. Give me the strength, conviction and courage to do what has to be done Jack prayed as he bolted down the small hill and into the clearing. It seemed like the longest run across the field as Jack felt exposed and vulnerable but there was no turning back now. He slowed his sprint to a jog as he approached the barn entrance and heard the voices getting louder.

226

He positioned himself just behind the open door and peered through the crack. He could see Det. Stephens standing directly in front of the entrance about five yards away and seemed to be intently watching the action in the barn. Jack slid over to get a better view of what Det. Stephens was seeing. *Oh damn, Bobby Joe. What the hell did they do to you?*

Tim F. Miller

Chapter 19

"It is better to be a coward for a minute than dead for the rest of your life."

—Proverb

Bobby Joe had never killed anyone in his entire life before tonight. He had been in a number of scrapes ranging from high school fights and college altercations to a handful of life-threatening confrontations in his repo business but nothing like what he had experienced on this night. Bloodied and beaten, sore and exhausted he had experienced the gamut of human emotions of fear, terror and anger. Though he had unintentionally killed one man already, he wasn't sure he could kill again. Now standing over his helpless, beaten enemy with a weapon poised to end a life, Bobby Joe hesitated. He could hear the big man groaning weakly and cursing him and Jack.

"What are you saying, you dumb fuck?"

"I said...you better finish me off now, cause I'll chase your ass down and kill you and your little boyfriend Jack!"

"Oh...I bet you'll try...well fuck you!" Bobby Joe screamed as he drove the pitch fork into the man's massive gut. He pushed down harder and harder to make the farm implement go deeper. Each thrust was followed by a low wail from the wounded giant.

"I'm not sure I can hear you too well. What were you saying about hunting me and Jack down, you fat fuck!" Bobby Joe cried out and then pulled the deeply embedded pitch fork out of Big Jr. with great force.

He stared down at the huge beast with an anger he didn't know existed. His body felt numb as he leaned against the pitch fork. Shaking his head trying to clear his thoughts and get control over his trembling

228

body, he looked up and stared blankly at the familiar figure screaming and coming up on him rapidly with a gun pointed at his head.

"What the fuck! What the fuck have done son? Put that goddamn pitch fork down or I'll blow your head off!" Marcus X shouted.

Bobby Joe unwittingly obeyed and glared at him.

"What the hell have you done in here? Damn, you've put a shit load of holes in my boy" Marcus X stated as he leaned over and examined Big Jr., who had stopped moving and wailing, with his free hand. Looking to his right side he could see C.J.'s body leaning up against a stall door with a lifeless stare. "Fuck, boy, you've done a lot damage to my crew! You know I can't let that shit go. But you got more guts and strength than I thought possible in a white boy to be able to take down my boy, Big Jr.. To be honest, I didn't think anyone could do that. Not even me" Marcus X added shaking his head in admiration. "Look, it's a damn shame things went down like this. I could use a strong fucker like you on my crew. Hell, it appears there is an opening" Marcus X offered looking down at Big Jr "but only if you tell me where Jack is. Do you understand me Bobby Joe? Where is Jack?"

Bobby Joe stared at Marcus X for several seconds with no response. The blank expression on his face led Marcus to believe he hadn't heard him so he asked again.

"Hey…can you hear me! Where is your boy Jack? Tell me where he is and I let you live. It's that simple!"

After another long pause, Bobby Joe looked squarely into Marcus' eyes and then he uttered, "Go fuck yourself!"

"Oh, go fuck myself, huh? No…fuck you!" Marcus screamed and shot Bobby Joe just above the heart. The blast drove him against the far wall as he crashed and slumped down to a sitting position. He slowly

229

reached over to ease the burning sensation in his chest with his bloody right hand.

Bobby Joe's world was spinning out of control. He tried several times to open his eyes to clear his vision, but to no avail. He knew he was losing too much blood and that it was only a matter of time before he blacked out again or simply died. He gazed past his tormentor who was still shouting at him and noticed another man standing at the entrance. He couldn't quite make out the face but he saw another figure appear to be moving from behind the barn door. He watched intently as the figure's head emerged. *Oh dear God…its Jack! He's alive! He came back. I knew he would* Bobby Joe mused just before he was slapped across the face.

Jack locked eyes with his old protector and defender and watched in horror the beating that followed. He also saw Det. Stephens lift Bobby Joe's shotgun from the floor and check to see if it was loaded. A weird smile crept across his face as he eyed with interest what his "partner" was doing on the other end of the barn.

Oh dear, looks like old Jeff has found the solution to his dire dilemma. I'll just let that sack of shit drug lord interrogate Bobby Joe. Once he gets Jack's location, I'll blow his fucking head off Det. Stephens grinned as he pulled the shotgun up and leveled it at Marcus X.

Jack was frozen in thought trying to make sense of what was happening on both ends of the barn. He knew everyone in there was looking for him but only Bobby Joe knew for certain his present location. He also knew that once his location became known he would have to fight for his life. He couldn't tell how much life was left in Bobby Joe but he held out that he could still save him. *He's still alive and hanging on. He looked right at me and still said nothing. Damn that man's brave! This shits gotta stop! Alright, here's the plan. I'm gonna pull my gun and order everyone to stop…okay that's a stupid idea. Both guys will probably turn and fire on you. Okay, okay...stupid. I know, I'll shoot the detective, take his shotgun and...damn, by that time Marcus will probably shoot Bobby Joe and come after me...oh man...what to do?*

Jack's last thought was interrupted by a gut-wrenching blare from Bobby Joe. *Oh God, he's in pain. Time to act* Jack reasoned as he stood up and pulled his gun out walking briskly from behind the door. He squeezed his revolver but nothing happened. He squeezed it again and still nothing. *Oh God the gun's empty!* Jack panicked and raced back behind the barn door.

Shocked that the detective hadn't heard the empty chamber clicks, Jack sat back in wonder and fear. Peering back through the door crack, he could see Marcus X dropping several hard punches to Bobby Joe's bloody face demanding to know where his "boy" was. He could also hear the annoying gum-popping habit of the detective and quickly assessed that that sound had saved him yet again.

Now what? Dear Lord in heaven, please help me see the right path and know what Your will is. I pray that Your will be done Jack whispered and opened his eyes. He saw an old iron crow bar gleaming from the straw just behind Det. Stephens. *Thank you, Lord,!* Jack said as he stood up again.

Crouching down and moving stealthily, Jack retrieved the crow bar from the floor, raised it up in the air and slammed it down and through the detective's skull. He could feel it sink in as the man dropped to the ground. In an eerie, surreal moment Jack darted across the room with the lever raised. He could see Marcus X start to turn with a shocked expression on his darkened face. As he wheeled around to fire on Jack, he felt a strong resistance holding back his gun. He lifted his left arm to ward off the iron object crashing down upon him.

Jack's first blow thudded painfully against the drug lord's forearm causing him to cry out. Jack wildly swung again this time connecting on his neck. Marcus X doubled over releasing the gun to grasp his ailing

231

neck. Several more powerful blows rained down upon the drug lord from the Zone knocking him to the ground as he screamed out in agony from each new swing. Jack's fury was relentless as he pummeled the body screaming out the name of Candace and Tater and how each blow was vengeance. He had never felt so dizzy and powerful in his life. He was getting tired quickly and stopped to survey the damage to the thug who had made his life a living nightmare. He tossed the crow bar to the floor and pulled Marcus X up to his face.

"Hey…big man, its Jack Miller. You know, the white dude you've been chasing for two days. The white guy who heard you kill Candace! Then you sent your dogs to kill me but killed my good friend Tater instead. Did you hear me, you fuck! You killed two people I deeply cared about and…damn it, it looks like you may have killed Bobby Joe" Jack added with sorrow staring at Bobby Joe. "Fuck you!" Jack screamed as he landed several punches across Marcus' face opening up a bloody gash.

"Hey… Jack… I knew you had it in you…" Bobby Joe weakly whispered through blood-dried lips.

"Bobby Joe…are you alright? Damn…I thought you were dead. Bobby Joe…?" Jack shook his friend several times but got no response. He cupped his face but could tell the spirit had just left his friend as a chilling wind swept across his body. Jack lowered his head in mourning. He couldn't believe his good friend and defender was gone. Anger had quickly returned as Jack reached over and pulled Marcus X up. He slapped him several times to get his attention.

"Hey, you stupid fuck. You've killed another great and dear friend of mine! That shit will never happen again and do you want to know why? Hey…listen to me when I'm talking. Do you want to know why? Because this shit ends tonight! Get it! You're going to die tonight Mr. Big Shot drug thug!" Jack shouted before walking briskly over to the pitch fork lying on the floor. He lifted it up and propped up against Marcus' chest.

"Hey big boy…wake up! I want to you to be awake and alert before I drive this thing through you! You understand?" Jack counseled before he felt his body go numb. A great force had wrapped him up tightly and pinned his arms to the side. It felt like a gigantic bear had a hold of him. Jack wiggled and thrashed about trying desperately to free himself but made no progress. In fact, the massive arms seemed to squeeze him tighter. He could feel the warm breath of his captor.

"Calm down…little white boy! Old Big Jr. has you now and there aint no way you're getting out. Stop thrashing about, boy. Its over! You're running days and being in the wrong place are over!"

Jack screamed out for the big man to release him but to no avail. His chest was burning and gasping for air as his asthma had kicked into full gear. The hay constricted his airways combined with Big Jr's clamping hold and added stress, Jack was on the verge of blacking out.

He watched in horror as Marcus X rose up from the ground. The drug kingpin used the tail of his shirt to wipe the blood from his face. His movements were brisk and agitated. He quickly advanced toward Jack and slugged him in the stomach. Jack's eyes bulged out in terror as he tried desperately to get air into his lungs. The first blow was followed by two more to the chest. Jack's head dropped as his body slumped into Big Jr.'s arms.

"Oh no…little white boy. You aint dead…not yet you aren't. Let's look at that face and see once and for all what I've been chasing for two days! Oh yeah…that's him, Big Jr! That's the stupid little white boy who doesn't know where he belongs. That's the stupid ass redneck whose made me work a bit to clean up this mess" Marcus X added looking around at his rustic setting before he spotted Det. Stephens lying face down on the floor. "Well, I give some credit, Jack old boy. You took care of one little problem for me with that worthless dirty cop. So, I tell you what…I won't prolong your death too long. Big Jr., let loose of him and back up" Marcus X ordered.

Jack could feel his lungs expand as air seeped back in allowing him temporary relief from the big bear's release. However, he was still hurt from the devastating punches and getting light-headed quickly. He lifted his head to see Marcus X pull the gun away from Bobby Joe and fire it into his leg. Jack screamed out in agony as blood gushed out of his thigh.

"I guess, you won't be doing any running anytime soon, eh Jack!" Marcus laughed looking over at Big Jr. who returned the smile. "Well, look at the time. Damn, its getting late and I've still got a lot of your shit to clean up. Well, to use your own words Jack-'this shit ends tonight'" Marcus X coldly stated as he threw the gun down and picked up the pitch fork. "I believe this was the shit that you were going to kill me with, eh Jack?"

Jack closed his eyes. He could no longer bear to see the inevitable. He could feel Big Jr. grab him by the back of his hair and kick his legs down. Exhausted, wounded and out of answers, Jack prayed *Dear Heavenly Father forgive me! Watch over me and deliver me from this evil.* He opened his eyes in horror as Marcus X raised the pitch fork above his head.

"No!!!!" Jack cried out.

Chapter 20

"The realm of dreams is a place where the subconscious mind is free and uninhibited to play out a fantasy that the conscious mind is afraid to face in reality."

—Author

Quiet filled the air with just a hint of rustled leaves breezily blowing aloft and gently settling back to the dewy grass. The sun appeared illuminating the bright orange and yellow leaves preparing for flight from majestic hardwoods across the sky whose destination was yet unknown. Many creatures awake from their slumber to begin anew their search for sustenance for survival on Earth. Playful squirrels chase each other from tree to tree and across the open friendly confines of the university campus looking for acorns to store for the oncoming winter. Birds soar high above the tree lines surveying the landscape for their next meal as the old adage, of early risers getting the worm, holds true each day.

But not all of God's creatures rise at the crack of dawn seeking life's sustenance. A few females in the human race choose to promptly arise from the comforts of their beds, gather and organize into groups for a sorority ritual that has them meet out on the front lawn for chants and songs proving their Greek spirit. It is a staging ground for the newest members to demonstrate their loyalty, fealty and enthusiasm for their sorority chapter.

One of God's fairer creatures opened her eyes in anticipation of a great and eventful day. As an upperclassman in the Beta Gamma Beta sorority and Song Chair, it was Heather Mills' job to prepare the newest members for the initiation rituals. She thoroughly enjoyed the sisterhood and camaraderie of sorority life. She fully embraced the Greek system and easily climbed into leadership roles.

Heather couldn't wait to begin life's journey into the field of numbers as a certified public accountant. Her sharp, analytical mind and thorough organizational skills made accounting a natural fit. Loading up her schedule each semester, along with her sorority responsibilities, made it difficult for her to experience the other aspects of campus life such as dating. She entered college singularly focused on attaining the tools necessary to become a financially independent woman with a social network foundation from which to draw upon. Dating and the mating game would have to wait.

Besides, she had her eye on an old high school friend who happened to live directly across Maxwell Street from her sorority house in an apartment complex with two other guys. She had quietly watched Jack Miller from afar develop into a tall handsome man though she was less than thrilled about his dating habits. She hoped it was just an immature stage that would lead him to conclude that he had yet found the right girl. Heather believed she was the right girl. Until Jack reached that development stage and realization, she would remain in the background biding her time.

Heather's alarm clock read five-thirty as she eagerly jumped out of bed in anticipation of an exciting day she had planned for the newest members of Beta Gamma Beta. Unlike her freshman experience of brushing toilets and the restrooms with their own toothbrushes, Heather was determined to end that type of hazing during initiation rites. Joyfully and fully rested, Heather joined her sisters in rousing the plebes from their sleep. Many of the girls moaned and groaned, grousing about their closets to find the appropriate clothing for the crack of the dawn scene. Chastened and hustled about, the young aspirants were herded like cattle from their upstairs bedrooms to the Grand Reception Hall on the first floor.

The Grand Reception Hall was a large, beautifully ornate room decorated in the Victorian Era. It had hosted thousands of soirees over its one hundred year existence on campus and was known as one of the finest attractions in the Greek system. Heather and her sorority sisters had spent the previous twenty four hours decorating the "Grand Ole Hall", as it was affectionately called, in an assortment of bright pinks that covered the vast, open room with pink ribbons, streamers and balloons hanging from the ceiling. Even the magnificent chandelier, center piece of the great room, had pink bulbs emitting a memorable glow with Gossamer cloth twirled of an assortment of pinks hanging loosely from above. Banners with inspirational messages were draped conspicuously about the walls. It was as if the "Pink Posse" from the Breast Cancer Awareness Society had blown up the old room in a rage of pink ecstasy. Heather was proud of what they had accomplished and the party they had planned for later that night.

Once the plebes were corralled into the Grand Reception Hall, they were entertained by a short skit about the "do's" and "don'ts" of the Beta Gamma Beta house. The senior girls then brought down several large boxes to the front of the room. Heather stood up on a chair to bark out instructions for the day to the excited, chattering recruits.

"Alright plebes, we have an exciting day planned with a few morning exercises, a light breakfast and then you're off to classes for the rest of the day. But you must be back in the house by four o'clock sharp to get ready for our spectacular dance tonight!" Heather announced before a loud chorus of screams interrupted her. "Okay, okay...calm down. I know you're excited. As you know we will serve as host to one of the fraternity houses on campus but the identity of that house won't be revealed until the dance starts tonight at nine. Now, to get the day started right all of you plebes need to strip down to your panties!"

There was an instant silence following the announcement that shocked and awed the young aspirants as they had heard that Heather was sort of a "goody-goody", no nonsense girl. However, the room quickly filled with laughter and elated shouts as they disrobed and flung their clothes to the center of the room as instructed.

"Now, our senior sisters will be giving you appropriate sorority garb for the morning exercises!" Heather declared and signaled for her fellow sisters to open the large boxes and distribute the oversized pajamas with pink hearts splashed about the tops and the bottoms. The plebes quickly draped the baggy pajamas over their bodies and they were ushered outside to the front lawn for their calisthenics.

The cold morning air hit their lungs abruptly as they stepped out into the wet grass. Shivering and clinging tightly to their big, baggy pj's for warmth, the girls were organized into neat rows of three facing Maxwell Street. Heather ran to the front to take her place as Song Chair next to Susan Phillips, Exercise Chair. Heather raised her right hand signaling silence. The morning chatter and nervous laughter came to an immediate halt as each girl froze into their ritual custom of obedience.

The morning air hung in dead silence for several seconds as the girls stared blankly at their song leader until a loud scream burst out from across the street. Soon it was followed by two shouts of "no". The primordial scream stunned the girls in baggy clothes with their mouths wide open slightly turning to look at others yet remaining obediently in formation.

Heather's eyes widen as she instinctively turned toward the sound from across the street and peered at the two story brick apartment complex in search of movement or some meaning for the wild scream that seemed to cease almost immediately after it had begun. She couldn't tell for certain whose voice it was but she knew that Jack lived over there and it was definitely a male voice. *Oh my…I hope and pray that isn't Jack. Oh no…what if it is? What could have happened to cause that kind of scream? It sounded as if someone was in great pain and hurt. I have to find out!* Heather concluded as she quickly sprinted across the street.

She wasn't sure which of the four apartments Jack lived in since she heard about it last spring from a high school friend. Frantically she grabbed the door knob but it was locked. She banged on the door and window several times but again no response. Looking at the side panel of residents she saw three slots filled: "Big Jimmy Fisher"; "The Three Amigos"; "Brandon Whitaker, Kenneth James". *It has to be The Three Amigo's. God, that's kinda cheesy* Heather surmised and punched the ringer button. She could hear it ring in one of the apartments below but there was no response after a few more tries.

Suddenly she heard a strange low voice over the intercom ask, "what?".

"Is Jack in there? I need to speak to him. Its really urgent. Can you let me in?" Heather implored. She heard the door click and she pushed it open. Running down the wide hallway past the stairwell on the left she began pounding on the door labeled "2". The door opened slightly restrained by a small chain as one eye appeared.

"Is Jack in there?"

"Who's Jack?"

"Come on, I know Jack Miller lives here. Stop playing games. I heard a horrible scream and I just wanted to check on him. You know…make sure he's okay."

"Sorry…no Jack Miller live here" the voice muttered in an odd accent.

"Okay…just let me look!"

"Okay" the strange voice muttered after a few tense seconds passed. The chain clicked and the door opened slowly. Heather ran into the dark room with the shades and curtains drawn. She detected an odd scent of some sort of Asian dish that hung in the air. Quickly scanning the room, she knew fairly certain she was in the wrong apartment.

Jack sat up immediately in his bed drenched in a cold sweat staring across the room. He couldn't quite tell where he was or what had happened as his mind was racing back and forth between two worlds: the present real world and the dream fantasy. He felt his heart pounding rapidly with his senses on full alert. He turned to his right to see a dark figure emerging toward him. Instinctively he backed away until he recognized the face of his old friend, Rick.

"Hey man…you okay?" Rick asked as Jack continued to stare at him without an answer. "Dude, seriously…you okay? You just let out the most God awful scream I'd ever heard in my life" Again no response, just a blank stare. "That must have been one helluva nightmare, Jack. But its okay…you're okay now. Whatever you just imagined or dreamed is over…its okay." Rick tried to console. "Damn, you're wet as shit. What the hell did you do in that dream that's got you so damn wet?"

Rick's calm, reassuring familiar voice helped bring Jack back to the present. His body eased and relaxed a bit as he started to believe that he was truly back from the nightmarish realm that had quickly turned fatal. *Oh dear God… thank you, thank you for delivering me from that Hell. Oh my…* Jack prayed taking deep, slower breaths. He wiped the sweat from his forehead looking down at his nearly naked body. He quickly ran his hand over his body checking for injuries. *My arms and chest seem fine and my legs…legs…my ankle…Oh dear God, thank you, thank you. The ankle's fine! Oh man that was the scariest dream…nightmare, I've ever had* he concluded.

"Dude… what the hell were you dreaming?" Rick anxiously inquired.

"Man…I don't know…I mean, damn…It was so real. So intense. Hell, I even woke up from the dream while in the dream."

"Dude, that's crazy! Sounds like some sorta drug-induced sleep or something."

"Yeah, but I don't do drugs…so I have no idea what caused this. I remember it so clear especially feeling hurt about Tater… Tater…where the hell is Tater?" Jack implored anxiously scanning back across the room towards his other roommate's bed.

Squinting their eyes in the hazy glow of the early morning, the two roomies could just make out a messy lump of blankets. Jack jumped out his bed and ran over to Tater's corner. He frantically pulled away the blankets, pillows and sheets to no avail.

"Jack, calm down dude. I'm sure he's alright. You know as well as I, he doesn't always come home. Hell, he probably found some ugly chick last night and stayed at her place." Rick offered with a laugh.

"Rick…this is what happened in my dream and Tater was dead!" Jack barked back.

"Oh, I'm sure he's not dead. You can't kill that crazy fucker. Hell, he's on too many steroids. Now, he might have.."

"Shut up Rick, this aint funny. Tater… Tater!" Jack cried out looking toward the kitchen and then back to the bathroom.

"Hey, look his shoes are over by the front door" Rick calmly asserted.

Jack scrambled out of the bathroom and into the den on the other side of the French doors of the bedroom. In the dark room, he could see a dark figure splayed out on the floor. Flicking on the light switch, Jack's eyes gleamed with joy at the familiar sight of Tater lying face down on the hardwood floor with his jeans down around his ankles and his t-shirt twisted half way off his head and swaddled under his face. He pounced on his beefy roommate and started shaking him in elation.

"Tater, Tater…you're alive. You're alive!"

Slowly lifting his head to come to his senses, Tater eased himself off the floor into a sitting position. Rubbing the sleep out of his red eyes, Tater felt a huge set of arms embrace him blabbering something about being alive.

"Damn Miller, what the fuck?" Tater mumbled.

"You big, ugly ape… you're alive. You're alive!"

"Of course, I'm alive. Damn, I just had a few extra drinks. Now get the fuck off me and stop hugging me and shit, fag!" Tater added shoving his ecstatic roommate away.

Jack smiled but obeyed knowing how cranky Tater was in the morning, especially after a full night of drinking before the start of school. Jack was still beaming in the excitement and realization that the long dark nightmare was now, truly over. He was alive and well as was his party-happy roommate, Tater.

"Now, Jack…what's all this shit about me being dead. Of course, I'm alive. I was just passed out. That's all. Hell, you've seen that before. What made you think I was dead and why the hell are we up so damn early?"

"Oh man…it's a long, long story. Let's just say I had a horrible dream and bad things happened…especially to you, big boy."

"Me? What the hell happened to me?"

"Hey big boy, what the hell are you doing lying on the floor with a perfectly good bed just a few feet away and why the hell are your pants down around your ankles?" Rick added playfully.

The question was abruptly interrupted by a pounding on the door. They could hear a girl's voice demanding they open the door immediately.

"Who the hell's that?" Rick asked staring at Tater.

"Don't ask me…I didn't meet anyone last night. At least I don't remember meeting anyone… hell I have no idea.." Tater replied rubbing his head.

Jack stood up and opened the door. He couldn't believe he was looking at Heather Marie Mills. There she was, fresh from his dream standing in front of him glaring back.

"Heather?"

"Yes, its Heather. Are you okay Jack? I heard this awful scream from across the street and thought it could be you. That maybe you were hurt or in danger?"

"Oh, no…I'm fine…I .."

"He had a nightmare, Heather! That's why he's all naked and sweaty!"

That last part hit Jack hard. He had forgotten he had just got out of bed and was in his night time attire— boxers. *Oh crap!* Jack thought as he quickly vanished behind the door.

"Oh, come on Jack. Its nothing" Heather reassured, "they're no different than your short shorts. Besides, since when did you become so modest?"

"Its true Jack. When did you develop this modesty?" Rick teased.

"I guess you're right" Jack retorted, "Anyway, Heather…I'm fine. What the hell are you doing fully dressed at this time of the morning?"

"Well, I was getting ready for our morning exercises across the street. You know, Beta Gamma Beta, when you startled everyone with that crazy loud scream. Are you sure you're okay? Did something happen?"

"Yeah, I'm fine…look Heather… there is something I would like to talk to you about if you've got time?"

"Sure, I've got a Pysch. class in an hour over at Whitehall. Care to walk me over?"

"Oh my God, really? You got a Psych class? So do I? Is it Psych. 121 at 8 o'clock?"

"Yeah" Heather smiled.

"Awesome. I'll meet you out in front of the Beta house in a few."

"Sounds good. You might want to put on some pants though or not" Heather teased as she walked away.

Jack closed the doors and was instantly heckled by his roommates. Anytime one of them had a girl over, it was standard operating procedure to harass the roommate until they left. Jack simple laughed it off and jumped into the shower. *Damn its good to see her. She looked real nice. I haven't thought about her in a while. I wonder why she was so prominent in my dream last night? Oh well, life goes on! Beautiful, beautiful life goes on.*

Sprinting across the street in cargo shorts and a hooded UK pullover with his backpack slung over one shoulder, Jack spotted Heather talking to several girls in the parking lot behind the sorority house.

'There you are. I see you've added a bit to your morning wardrobe." Heather teased.

"Yeah, about that. I'm real sorry. I totally forgot how I was dressed" Jack regretted remembering how prudish Heather was in high school.

"Oh, it's alright Jack. Don't worry about it. Trust me, the worst part of my morning was going into that Chinese apartment next door. Those guys in there are disgusting!"

"Really? Why were you in there? What happened?"

"I don't want to talk about it. Let's just say those guys are gross and leave it at that. I was at their place on accident. I thought it was your place. It said, 'Three Amigos' next to the buzzer and they buzzed me in."

"Oh, shit that's funny. Damn, Tater must have switched the name plates again. He does that from time to time. He thinks it's funny and yeah those dudes are a little different. I think they are TA's working on their masters. They don't know a whole lot of English. You probably confused them" Jacked laughed.

"Oh well, they're sick. Anyway, what was that nightmare about that spooked you so bad?"

"Oh wow…where to begin? Look I don't want to bore you with infinite details to a dream that seemed too real but let's just say I witnessed two murders and thought I woke from that dream to find that I was still dreaming with the murderers chasing me all over campus."

"Wow that is weird. Kinda scary. You still look shaken from it. Did you know the murder victims?"

"Yeah…kinda. One was Tater and the other was some mystery girl I've never seen before in my life. I don't know…its really fresh in my mind and I really don't want to talk about, you know?"

"Oh okay" Heather nodded as they crossed Avenue of Champions and walked by Stoll Field. There was an awkward silence and then Heather asked, "So Jack, who you dating these days?"

"Oh, no one. You know, just sorta looking around. You know the shy guy from high school still" Jack added sheepishly.

"That's not what I hear"

"What do you hear?"

"I hear a lot and its not about some 'shy' guy. Jack Miller has become some stud whore dog bedding girls left and right." Heather teased.

"Oh…not true. They haven't been left and right. Usually right in front of me. Besides, what do you care? You rejected me in high school, remember?"

Heather stopped walking and looked up at Jack seriously. He could sense a lecture was coming but was confused about what it could possibly be about. *Damn Heather you broke my heart in high school and now you want to lecture me about dating others. Where's that coming from?* Jack inwardly inquired. She lowered her head trying to put the words together just right.

"Jack, I know I hurt you years ago in high school but I've changed…you've changed. In high school, I was a bit superficial. I admit it. Who wasn't? Look that's not an excuse. I dated seniors because they were more mature and by the time of our senior year, I guess I liked Rick more.

He was the captain of the football and baseball team and just gorgeous. He was also really sweet and nice."

"Yeah…I get that. I was just some awkward skinny dude that fell for the best looking cheerleader. You picked Rick. Its okay…really, I'm over that."

"No, no…let me finish. Since I've started college, I've seen you a few times. You've changed a lot and not just physically. You seem way more confident and sure of yourself."

Jack nodded looking away not quite sure where this was leading.

"I don't know Jack. I just feel I was wrong to overlook you in high school. I'm a different person at a different place in life and well, I guess I want a new start with you. We've known each other since seventh grade and were practically raised together in your father's church…which, by the way, you should attend more often."

"Oh, I know. My mom sends me text messages all the time. Well, anyhow…yeah that would be nice…to start over. Why not? Hey, its getting late. Better start heading up the hill to class."

Heather agreed as they started walking again with a renewed purpose. Heather had cracked back into Jack's world. It had been stewing on her mind for some time and she was happy that it was now out in the open.

Jack was still perplexed about the conversation as well as how it connected to his thoughts of her in his dream. *I haven't seen Heather in three years and suddenly she's in my dream last night and now walking with me to class. She looks great and all, but this is just a bit weird. What does this all mean? Oh stop overanalyzing a simple coincidence and enjoy her company. She's hot! Its true…anyway looks like a packed house up at the Classroom Building* Jack smiled as he instinctively climbed the stairs two at a time.

Jack waited for Heather at the top of the stairs on the massive patio landing overlooking the south end of the campus. He opened the tall heavy door for her as they circled around looking for room 121. *Damn…121…that numbers weird for some reason. Can't quite put my finger on it. Oh well, here it is* Jack grinned as he again played the gentleman and opened the door for Heather.

The huge auditorium was filled with chatter and nervous anticipation of the new class and year. As always, Jack walked down a few steps on the center aisle and checked with Heather to see if this was a good place to sit. She nodded eagerly as they plopped down in the hard seats with a right-handed removable desk top. He pulled out his notebook and scratched out the name of the class at the top of his paper. Looking up, .he noticed a message on the board in big bold print: **COURAGE VS. COWARDICE.** *Oh my God...are you kidding me? What the...*Jack mumbled to himself and looked around the class.

"What's the matter Jack?" Heather inquired scribbling the white board message at the top of her paper.

"Oh...nothing. Just kind of a weird topic for our first class?"

"Oh, not really. Ms. Daniels is a highly reputably professor known for her edgy style of pushing students to the limit. She really delves into the psyche for answers" an overly impressed student inserted from behind nosing in on another conversation.

"That's ...great...thanks. I hope you enjoy the class." Jack stated wryly as Heather laughed and elbowed him playfully.

There was a surreal feeling about the classroom. Everything from the way Ms. Daniel entered the room and sat up on the long desk in the front to how eagerly the students responded to her probing questions. Jack couldn't help but feel he had experienced all of this before. It bothered and nagged at him.

Suddenly his eyes caught the sight of a long haired beauty walking down the far side aisle late. She stepped down several rows to a familiar face, smiled and threw her book bag down next to a hooded figure. She beamed and chit-chatted with the guy whose face and head were covered by his hoodie. *That smile...oh my God...she's gorgeous...and strangely familiar. Well, she's obviously into that dude. So might as well stop looking over there* Jack assessed as he looked back at the professor down front.

He still couldn't shake the eerie feeling that he had seen all of this before. Even some of the questions and answers Jack mouthed precisely as Heather stared at him in amazement.

"How did you know what that kid was gonna say?"

"I'm telling you Heather. There's some weird shit going on and I …what the hell? Look Heather. It's my boy, Tater, arriving late as usual."

They watched in mild amusement Tater standing at the top of the auditorium with his back pack on his left shoulder scanning the room.

"What's he doing?" Heather asked.

"He's scoping the room for hotties." Jack whispered while chuckling, "Once he locks onto a hot girl sitting alone or where there's an open seat, he'll pounce. See… look, he's spotted someone now. There he goes, swooping in for the Tater kill on some poor, unsuspecting girl…" Jack stopped in mid-sentence as he watched Tater walk down the far side wall and land right behind the beautiful long-haired girl and her hooded friend. *Oh shit…now what? No, no Tater, not her, dude. She's out of your league and besides she's obviously with the hooded boy! Okay…yeah, I see you Tater. You can stop waving and take that "shit eating" grin off your face.*

"Looks like he found someone" Heather smiled.

"Yeah" Jack nodded his head in disapproval.

"What's the matter, Jack? She looks fine…in fact she's breath-taking. Do you know her?"

"No…I don't think"

"What does that mean? You either know her or you don't."

"I don't" Jack stated flatly.

All during the class Jack's mind was running wild with an eerie sense of foreboding. He felt his heart race as he looked over several times at the girl and her hooded friend. He wanted desperately to see who was behind the hood. The girl was flirting openly with him and seemed to write on his hand which he playfully rubbed off.

By this time, Tater had moved on to different game once he realized the long-haired beauty wasn't even aware of his presence or really anyone else besides hoodie. *God, she looks so much like the girl in my dream…Carly…no…Can…Candace. Candace! Oh my God, it's her! That's where I've seen her. Its Candace. My God, it looks just like her from my dream. She's even playing and flirting with the hoodie dude like I remember.* Jack's last thought was interrupted by the sound of students packing up their bags and leaving.

"Come on Jack, class is over" Heather instructed, "What's the matter? You looked as if you've seen a ghost?"

"Oh…no…its just a weird thought I had about what Ms. Daniel said about courage and cowardice."

"Whatever…you weren't listening. You didn't take one note" Heather laughed, "I can see, I'm going to have to pull you through this class."

"Yeah…probably. What's your next class?"

"I've got an upper level business class on the other side of campus. What about you?"

"I've got nothing again until one o'clock."

"Good…you can walk me over" Heather smiled climbing the auditorium stairs leading Jack out to the spacious Classroom building patio.

Wow, Jack's very sweet and seemed genuinely interested in me before class started and then…I don't know, he sorta weirded out. Like he knew what everyone was going to say and then he got real quiet when the tall beautiful girl walked in. Well, he's a guy…that's sorta what they do I guess. Still he seems freaked out and…now where did he go? Heather panicked looking around in the mass of students moving in and about the building.

Jack had to know what was going on with this beautiful girl and why everything seemed so familiar. He watched the pair leave the auditorium but lost them in the crowd out on the patio deck. He stood over by the railing, peering down at the crowd of students walking down the big hill to the student book store.

The tree lined path had a long hand rail running down the center acting as a traffic median. *Come on Jack, get a hold of yourself. You've lost sight of the two and that's a good thing. You don't need to know what they're doing or really anything else. It's just a coincidence that she looks like the girl in your nightmare. She's obviously not, so...Oh shit. There she is! Walking down the path draped all over the hoodie dude... God...she's really something. I love how playful and full of life she seems* he pondered leaning against the patio railing.

Jack stared at the two who had stopped at the bottom of the hill near the "free speech" area of campus by the student bookstore. They were laughing and teasing each other. The hooded man turned toward the Classroom Building but kept his head down. Jack watched intently trying to see his identity. "Candace" broke from the hooded man's hold and ran to another familiar figure. It was a well-dressed light-skinned black man who smiled and hugged her as she pointed back at the hooded guy. Suddenly she darted back at him and pulled his hoodie off. Jack froze in astonishment. His eyes bulged in disbelief. *Oh no...Oh no...Dear God...no, no, no! It's Luke! My God, it's my brother Luke! I've got to stop him!* Jack muttered.

"What did you say Jack?" Heather asked catching up to him by the patio railing.

"Oh my God Heather...you're not going to believe who the guy in the hoodie is?

"Who?"

"It's Luke. My brother, Luke!"

"So. He's with a cute girl. Good for him."

"No, Heather, you don't understand. That's the girl from my nightmare and she... Oh my God...was that a dream or a premonition?"

Tim F. Miller

Coming soon… "The Courageous"

25758292R00152

Made in the USA
Columbia, SC
11 September 2018